I0593150

GOT GAME?

FOREWORD BY SHAUN SUNDAY

Copyright ©2023 Got Game?

FIRST EDITION: 2023

978-0-6456589-1-0 (pbk)
978-0-6456589-2-7 (ebk)

The moral right of the author has been asserted.
Foreword © Shaun Sunday
Trigger © Chris Radge
The Countdown © Charmaine Clancy
F2P © Gina Pinto
Syndicate Games © Pamela Jeffs
Tama-gotcha © Matilda Clancy
Final Play © Lea Scott
Delete World © Christine Betts & Kate Kelsen
Nihilistic Whispers © LR Johnson
Angel Wings Are Precious Things © Selena Jane
The Dolphin - Never *Tilt*-ing © Frank Prem
Dangerous Frontiers © Sarah Hegerty
Drift © Sarah Tegerdine
Logos © Sam Gale
Deadly Games © Debbie Kahl
Quacks Do Echo © JC Lesley
For Love of the Game © Danielle Hughes
Who Killed Francesca? © Robin Martin Thomas
The Nemesis © Robin Adolphs
The Devil's in the Detail © Michaela Sanderson
Welcome to DominionCorp © Dr Aletia Johnson
The Challenge © Robert Walmsley-Evans
The Three Lives of Mini Munchman © Emma Rennison
321 Time's Up © Jenny Woolsey
How Not to Host a Murder Party © Elizabeth Spratt
Gamer Grandma © Kellie M Cox

For information contact Info@RainforestWritingRetreat.com
Rainforest Writing Retreat is not responsible for websites (or their content) that are not owned by Rainforest Writing Retreat.

Cover layout by Charmaine Clancy
Lead editor and interior layout by Christine Titheradge
Interior edit by Gina Frisken
Interior support by Self-Publishing Lab

Other Books In This Series

CONTENTS

FOREWORD

Play is essential to life.

As adults we're encouraged to 'put away childish things' and steer away from play, but I say play and play hard!

Gaming has always been and will always be, from tabletop games and the ancient dice that are being uncovered across the world, all the way back to ancient Egypt and beyond, to the latest video games worldwide — technology for play is ever changing, but also always looking back to the ways of the past.

Some of my favourite tabletop games are Heroquest from the 1980s, 5th Edition D&D which is still being developed now, and some of my most enjoyed video games Dead Cells, Hollow Knight and Wayward Strand (the latter pair created by fellow Australians!) — There's something out there for all of us.

I had the honour and privilege of teaching newcomers to play D&D at the 2022 Rainforest Writers Retreat, and as a guest presenter introduced this throng of passionate prose writers to the concepts and mechanics of writing adventures for *Dungeons and Dragons*. The hunger for knowledge, and the excitement for new concepts and new worlds was clear and thrilling, and the enthusiasm with which they took to the idea was joyful and exhilarating.

This was a group of writers from across the country, coming together to share ideas and be introduced to new possibilities, and the concepts they developed were wonderful!

This *Got Game* anthology is something special, and you will feel the same passion radiating from these pages, that I did in that conference room, answering their questions and listening to their pitches.

Happy reading, and may the dice be ever in your favour.

—Shaun Sunday, Brainbeast Studios –
Comic writer, illustrator, and game designer

TRIGGER

chris radge

Like the long vacant stare of a gamer intent on his quarry.
He sees, but sees nothing.

'Where's everyone today.' Michael motioned towards the almost empty room with the exception of a couple elderly men sitting glued to the fat-backed, vintage television set in an all too familiar stared silence he knew too well.

Drool slipped like a river down the cracks of aged jowls slowly making its journey from the old men's chins to adult rubber-backed bibs.

Morning sun streamed through sliding glass doors that led to the garden outside. It warmed the chill from the community lounge room heating up the stale stench of urine that lingered in the air, a dementia wards' badge of honour.

'In the garden,' Sandra the day nurse said, 'except these two. Setting up your vintage gaming console was a stroke of genius. It's kept them entertained for hours.'

He knew, getting it out of the house would keep him in check.

Gnarly arthritic thumbs flashed from arrow to arrow, and stabbed at the kill buttons like professionals. It was the most animated Michael, a psychiatric dementia carer, had seen the geriatric patients since starting work just over a month ago.

'I saw one of these old codgers on a documentary a couple of years back,' said Michael. 'At the age of twelve, won the first ever gaming world championships in ...' He thought for a second placing his homemade, peanut butter sandwich, and cola in the fridge for later, 'I want to say in the early 1990s.'

'That was almost sixty years ago,' Nurse Sandra gave the seventy-something gentlemen a thoughtful glance.

'Yes, he was quite the star in his time.' Michael's thoughts wandered, wishing he could have been there to witness his gaming idol achieve greatness.

A catchy electronic tune played, signalling the game had 'Levelled Up'.

Clenched fists hit the air in unison. Michael's senses were on high alert. Potential fights happened frequently between frustrated ressies trying to express their needs. But realised, this was their silent victory dance. With pats on the back, the game continued.

While he was watching, Jeff, one of the residents and player one, called out as clear as day, 'Got a soda, buddy?'

Stunned, Michael handed him his own from the fridge. 'Did Jeff just speak?' He nodded towards the patient. 'He's supposed to be uncommunicative and apathetic.'

Nurse Sandra's practical shoes squeaked as she stopped mid stride on the avocado-green linoleum. Her trolley laden with a rainbow assortment of pills in little white paper cups for her morning rounds almost tipped over. 'I've never seen a response like this.' She took in the view of the two cognitive elderly men shoulder to shoulder like a couple of teenagers.

These patients were in the late stages of Alzheimer's. Some of them, like Jeff, lost their speech completely, usually only grunting responses.

But Jeff and Ray were the only ones responding differently. Michael sat on the edge of an empty vinyl armchair to watch and evaluate them.

'Ray, Watch out!' Jeff held a white knuckled grip on his own gaming handset leaning as far left as he could trying not to be hit by the games arch-rival, and almost pulled the entire console from its cubby hole in the television cabinet.

Michael, studying to be a specialised clinical nurse in dementia, learnt that introducing a patient's favourite music track from their earlier memories could bring cognitive responses. But also knew this would be fleeting. It never stuck, and they would go back to their comatose state soon after.

Ray, player two, gave Jeff, player one, a sideways glance.

Was that a response? Michael sat forward on his chair. He reached into his pocket for an old-school pen and notebook, and documented the phenomenon he was witnessing, snapping a few images and video footage as evidence.

Dementia was a life sentence. Michael knew this. When his own grandfather had been given this diagnosis, it rocked his family to the core. He'd watched his Papap deteriorate to a shell of his former 'life of the party' demeanour. Remembering him, expertly twirl his partners to 'Rock Around the Clock', giving presidential speeches at the local Rotary Club, and piloting his own plane reminded Michael why he'd decided to become a nurse and carer.

Michael knew Alzheimer's could be hereditary, and this insidious disease was looking him direct in the eye.

The game tune stopped.

'Did you see that? He hit me with a bomb right before the finish line! What a cheat!' Jeff, player one's animated hands gestured as he spoke to the ressie next to him. 'Don't forget, on the third turn keep as far left as you can, let them pass and bam, you've got them from behind.'

'Yer yer, I've got this.' Ray, player two, picked up Jeff's soda and gestured. 'Do ya mind?'

'Go ya hardest.' Jeff, not even looking at his new friend, tapped at his controller starting up a new game.

'Give us a hand boys.' Jeff placed a game controller on two more ressies' laps. Jeff's eyes fixed on the television, didn't even notice his fellow ressies just sat there, dribbling. He was off with a squealing start, fishtailing, weaving, and tapping expertly, while the upbeat tune played in the background.

Michael realised, gaming mustn't have been player three and four's trigger, and jotted down his findings.

'Do you remember that secret shortcut.' Jeff elbowed Ray. 'Yer mate, this game is full of them.'

A nurse's voice travelled up the hallway. 'Can somebody help with the new resident in six please?'

The repeated beat of the VGM playing over the noise of the speeding cars propelled Michael back to his own youthful hang-ups.

The nurse yelled out again, and the tone in her voice broke through the gaming fog. 'I'll be right there.' Michael rose grimacing. The vinyl seat had stuck to the back of his legs.

Lunch was served on the endless rows of sterile tables. Patients drifted to their allocated places like monks sworn to silence. Michael's eyes scanned the clean-lined space, impersonal, clinical. Each object served a purpose including the taunting games cabinet in the corner. Still sitting in front of it, were Jeff and Ray. Everything about their demeanour signalled a victory Michael recognised. They had regressed into two teenagers bucking the rules.

'Nope. Not hungry,' Jeff parroted a response from his adolescence.

'Five more minutes.' Ray held up five fingers without taking his eyes off the television.

Michael recognised this exact scenario. He'd been through it with his own mother so many times.

Placing the bibs around their necks triggered nothing, no response at all.

Michael lifted the pureed roast beef to Jeff's lips. They clamped shut.

'Jeff?'

'Give me a sec mate.'

'Come on Jeff. Just pause it.'

'Nah mate, I'll lose momentum.'

'Should I turn it off for you?' Michael used one of his mother's techniques.

Jeff's jaw tightened and his eyes narrowed. 'Just let me get to the end of this level, and then I'll pause it, okay?' The grumble in his voice was threatening.

Michael sat watching, waiting.

Six fifteen the next morning, Michael brushed his teeth. His mind drifted, remembering the image of Jeff and Ray, animated by the nostalgic video game. Jeff, when cognitive, still only answered him in stilted juvenile responses while playing. But there were the in-between times. The setting up of new game moments, when Michael spoke the old-time gamer's language.

His mobile rattled on the vanity. Answering, his smile slipped from his face, it was work.

'Jeff passed away about an hour ago,' Sandra said.

Michael's words left him, hearing only parts of what she said.

'The most peaceful smile I've ever seen,' the nurse continued. 'He had that video-game control thing in his hands.'

6

Michael managed a garbled thankyou as vertigo took over. He grabbed for the basin and sat on the bath-lip hunched, head between his knees. Images of Jeff's spirit rising above, his body on crisp white sheets with the controller still clutched in his hand, liberated from the entrapment of his disease, spiralled through Michael's mind.

The funeral was like every other one Michael attended. Grief, mixed with relief, hung in the air as people remembered Jeff's life. Mourners pronounced—like they knew—that they were happy he was no longer trapped in an Alzheimer's addled mind. Even though few had made the effort to come and visit Jeff.

'I want to remember him how he was,' they said.

Only a few of Jeff's family knew of his recent reprieve, his one last cognitive day just before he passed.

Michael shared the images and video evidence he'd collected. Jeff's mother, now in her nineties, smiled with a vacant look. He imagined she was remembering her son in his hay day competing, winning and becoming famous. Tears slipped down her cheeks. She squeezed his hand tight. It was all the confirmation he needed to know he'd done right.

He held the pain from his face as he extricated his hand from hers, and rubbed at the arthritic pain in his thumb, an addicted gamer's gift returned.

Today was the fifth consecutive day he'd called in sick. This visit his only outing. Leaving his dusty gaming controller behind had been a challenge, his thumb twitched.

7

The old lady's hand on his shoulder made him jump. His blank stare had been misconstrued as grief. Only Michael knew he'd been replaying the last level over in his mind figuring out how to finish the latest video game he'd purchased online.

He'd been triggered, slipped back into his addiction.

Michael's regret pulsed through him at the thought of what he'd put his mother through all those years ago. The fights, the depression, and the feelings of hatred towards her. All she had tried to do was pause his playing to do his homework, or even to eat.

I'll call Mum tomorrow, he promised himself.

A gamer's mind spends thousands of hours in other worlds, racing, fighting, discovering, collecting, and achieving one level at a time. Eventually all games come to an end.

THE COUNTDOWN

charmaine clancy

t0xicrat: What happens at zero?

pidgeonmonogomy42: Dude when is mana update coming?

ElvenElites: lol was gonna ask same

   pidgeonmonogomy42: I know right. daddy needs more fireballs

      ElvenElites: hell yeah

culinaryorc_‹oIo›: Help, traded for electric big axe and now it's gone from itinerary.

igotabigone: This message has been deleted by the moderator.

After suspending @igotabigone for forty-eight hours, you open the policy file and check for appropriate response to mana update questions. Players expected its release four days ago, but there are still too many bugs. You cut and paste the reply.

Moderator: @pidgeonmonogomy42 @ElvenElites GameSense is excited about our upcoming mana update and we know you are too. We are working hard to make sure the update is the best it can be and sometimes this takes a little extra time. Thank you for your patience and keep enjoying the many adventures available on Ghost Goat Quest.

Moderator: @culinaryorc_‹oIo› Our weapons list does not include any item by that name. do you have the code number?

t0xicrat: What happens at zero?

culinaryorc_‹oIo›: no! traded with a rando player. it appeared in my itinerary I saw it.

pidgeonmonogomy42: sux man

culinaryorc_‹oIo›: tell me bout it. this thing looked awesome!

culinaryorc_‹oIo›: Wait. Are you pidgeonwhoreman?

pidgeonmonogomy42: ha. yeah had to change it GF got shitty.

Moderator: @culinaryorc_‹oIo› Give me a moment and I'll check your transaction file.

You scroll through data and find the problem. Shit. Hackers are more common than keyboards these days. You record the username of the player trading fraudulent items, for all the good it will do. They're quick at getting in and out of the game. Looks like culinaryorc_<oIo> is not getting his electric big axe. The item sounds cool though, so you make a quick submission to the company suggestions email. Won't hurt your profile with the boss. Imagine Jenny's reaction when Graham announces your new weapon design.

Moderator: @culinaryorc_‹oIo› Sorry buddy, you've been had. I've reimbursed the 'item' you exchanged, at least you're not out of pocket.
tØxicrat: 30 days - what's my prize?

A pop up lets you know the next Moderator is logged in ready to take over. You log out.

Graham Goodrite: 8:00 AM, DISCORD NOW.

Shit. Someone fucked up. You flick to Discord. You're last in.

AngieDM: 8:11 AM, Everyone's here now.

Thanks for advertising, Angie.

Graham Goodrite: 8:16 AM, Ghost Goat Quest
hacked. We need to stop virus spread.

You ask what happened.

Numerical digits appear at the top of game screens. Seconds counting down. Graham worries it's a virus to infiltrate clients' financial data.

Remember ... a post, during your shift, something was said ... bloody Angie butts in, designating tasks and the thought, words, memory is sterilised before it can fester.

For the next six hours, the entire team is scanning accounts and closing the contaminated, each followed up with a generic email about 'unusual activity and account will be restored as soon as possible'.

It's pointless. Like sepsis snaking through veins, it infects the accounts faster than it can be contained. Graham makes the call. The game is taken offline.

His closing post in the forum promises *Ghost Goat Quest* will return. You linger in the chat rooms. A post-mortem conversation of players expressing shock, denial, anger and, well all the grief stages.

You spot familiar users posting their laments for *Ghost Goat Quest*. ElvenElites is there, culinaryorc_<oIo> and—

tØxicrat: Numbers still going. Will we stop
existing?

The virus will not be contained. Parasitic, it jumps from host to host, eventually evolving to exist outside the app. It pops up on computers, mobiles, televisions, and even car dashboard displays.

Real life backs away as the online world explodes. Fearing contagions may seep over that fourth wall, society becomes a cluster of shattered bones held together by whispers. Waiting to fall.

People are no longer have and have-nots, but will and will-nots. Many leave electronics altogether. Your parents call you for the last time and explain you will only be able to contact them through snail mail or worse, coming by in person.

It appears on your own television, right in the middle of Jimmy Kimmel roasting Laquita Forte about her new release, *Hot Zombies 4*. You wander in with a warm chai on soy and a gluten, sugar-free, sustainably harvested lavender macaroon, and there it is. In the centre top of the screen: 2,419,201. Your stomach sinks.

The Countdown.

Snatching your iPhone, you lift the screen. 'Siri on.'

2,418,934.

Don't panic.

You want to share the moment and FaceTime Jenny.

'I got The Countdown.'

'I thought you already got yours.' She gives a 'huh' breath. 'Wait, Thursday, you said so, we were at that oyster place with Blake and his goddam awful boyfriend. What was his name?'

Her brow creases. The Countdown displays in front of her forehead. You look away.

Jacob. He wouldn't try the oysters. Blake and Jenny cajoled him to 'just try one.' But he wouldn't budge. Said it looked like snot and nothing that gross was going down his throat. You snickered. Still, you kept the great one-liners to yourself. You always know when people have had enough.

On the way home in the Uber, Jenny kept on, 'I mean, why would anyone go to an oyster bar and not eat the oysters? Not even the *mornay*.'

'If you hate a food, you hate it, no matter what they coat it in.'

'Why come at all?'

You suggested Jacob wanted to spend time with Blake.

She wouldn't come back to your place that night.

Jenny is quite blasé about The Countdown now. '*Everybody* has it. Your device must be outdated if you just got it. Angie's messaging me, bye.'

Your phone is last year's model. But maybe ... a theory bubbles in your mind. You grab your keys and head down to the nearest Pawners.

A wall of DVDs greets you. Who watches DVDs anymore? The item you seek is in a glass cabinet. The assistant fumbles through the drawer for a key to unlock it for you. A goddamn plastic Nokia push-button mobile for $19. Are they worried someone will steal tech from the nineties? It can show messages and the time. It can't even read emails. It's exactly what you're looking for.

You pay the cashier and wait till you get in the car. On your dashboard display, you see the numbers, moving down to 2,399,387. You press the power button on the old device, but it won't start. You need to go home and charge it.

While the phone is plugged in, you think, maybe you'll make some quinoa muffins, obviously without fruit. You pull out all the ingredients and a bowl. But you can't remember what temperature to set the oven and the only way to check is to go back into the recipe you saved on Pinterest. There's a scratchy lump in your throat at the thought of turning on your iPad. You've avoided all screens since you got home.

The pawnshop phone still hasn't any charge. These older models' operating system don't boot until at least fifteen percent.

You grab a cloth and dust your bookshelf. Paperbacks you've never read. Audiobooks are way more convenient. You spot a biography of an actor you liked last year but have since found they support that racist politician. Removing the book and throwing it in the trash, you hope Jenny didn't notice it when she was here.

You rearrange the books in order of colour, a tip from YouTube guru, Lisa Goodhome. Maybe you've solved the problem of The Countdown. Retro phones. Imagine the praise you'll receive on social media. Oh wait. There won't be social media. This is a depressing thought.

Back in the kitchen, the monochrome screen throbs eerie green. When you pick it up, the phone screen flashes seventeen percent battery, an incorrect time, and ... The Countdown. 2,383,932.

What next? Dial up phones?

This gets you wondering. If the phone has no screen, if you can't see The Countdown, does it still exist? Is it out there, counting down to ... well, no one knows. Will you be blissfully unaware of the impending doom?

Philosophy was your minor at UNSW. The first thing to remember is perspective. If you believe this is the end of the world, you'll grieve the loss of life all the way up to the point of acceptance and not 'live' along the way.

Just digits counting down. Most likely, nothing will happen. The Countdown will disappear as soon as it hits zero. Or it may reset. Perhaps future generations will mutate to not notice the numbers. Like the experiment with kittens, raised for their first few months in boxes painted with horizontal stripes. Later, as full-grown cats, they were unable to see vertical lines. Their brain had been trained to disregard them.

Not the end of the world, but what if The Countdown destroys all feeds, the internet itself? Your breath shortens and the hair on your arms stand on end. The death of buying online, streaming, Snapchat? You'll have to actually *call* everyone. And what? Leave a message if they aren't by the phone? Jenny never leaves messages, if she gets message bank, she hangs up. At least your call history shows she tried. What happens with old answering machines? What if the person hangs up? You might never leave the house again, so you don't miss a call.

Your grandmother would scoff. She'd remind you they survived before internet.

Mind you, your grandmother is addicted to gameshows and midday television. You're sure her mother harped about how, in their day, they enjoyed each other's company sitting around the radio. Of course, your great-great-grandmother probably nagged her about reading books instead. It could be a hereditary trait. You may one day pester your own offspring about stepping away from virtual reality and spending time in real life ... albeit online.

You call Jenny to let her know about your experiment with the phone.

'Leave it to the government. They'll sort this.'

Perhaps 'the government' created this. They claim they are tracing the origin of The Countdown, but who knows if that's true? Most likely, they are making a lot of noise about doing something and this is the last you will hear of it. Until it reaches zero.

What happens at zero?

And bang. You remember. The first person to talk about The Countdown, only you didn't know at the time. You call Cyber Security Hotline to report suspicious behaviour. You provide the handle t0xicrat. You decide not to give your name.

The next day you awake to breaking releases on YouTube. 'The Countdown traced back to Sydney hacker.'

Reporters go on to describe the individual, who is 'helping police with their enquiries', as a radical anti-establishment anarchist who wants to bring down the entire structure of our way of life. The Prime Minister even makes an announcement about how 'un-Australian' this is.

The 'individual' must not have helped much because The Countdown continues. Threats to the culprit become so intense, police move them to a special military base prison.

Mass hysteria sets in. People go out in droves to remove their savings from banks, certain when The Countdown reaches zero, computers will lose all financial records. Larger banking institutions close doors to the public, convincing leaders to pass emergency policy preventing customers from removing more than ten percent of their accounts over a span of six months.

Either nothing will happen, and the bank will have plenty of time to mend customer perception, or the doomsdayers are right and they lose their online records and don't have to pay anyone.

Only the big banks stay immune. All smaller and medium institutions crash when the masses remove their funds. Many people lose their life savings.

All your friends claim to know someone's cousin who has taken their own life because of this. They start posting green banners and wearing green wrist bands. You can't remember if green represents loss of lives or money.

A march is held through streets of major cities around Australia, protesting ... well, you're not sure ... something to do with saving the one percent so they can save the rest of us? Another demonstration party appear, claiming our sins are the cause and every electronic device must be destroyed. They build bonfires of laptops, phones, tablets, and even toasters and kettles. The smoke is thick and black, and several people get sick sucking in the toxic fumes of melted plastic.

You do the math. You know the exact day the time will run out, but you keep checking to make sure it is moving at the right speed. To make sure it's not cheating. Next Friday at midnight. You have a party to attend with Jenny, should you cancel? You'd rather not, she's pulling away. This will be a good opportunity to reconnect.

Two days before the party, the internet almost collapses. The whole world is back online to express their opinions on the latest news.

The cyber-terrorist is thirteen-year-old Evie. Her lawyer makes a plea to have her released, showing many shots from her TikTok account. She is accused purely because she was the first known recipient of The Countdown virus. He also claims military police tortured his client.

More protest marches are broadcast. Protestors carry placards demanding Evie's release and return to her mother. Others, including Evie's mother, demand execution, claiming we can be saved if the Satan-child is dead.

You feel moved to partake in the march to have young Evie freed. The poor child looks frightful on the news, like one of those refugee children left in the detention centres. Perhaps you'll write an email to Parliament, demanding their release. After all, you'd adopt a refugee child, if your apartment had more space. Instead, you send an email to your body corporate complaining about the teenagers in apartment 404 who keep leaving the pool gate open.

Adoption is still on your mind. You search dog breeds suitable for apartment living. When the local shelter has no bichon frise, whippets, or Lhasa apsos, you decide on a reptile. They insist you come down in person, so you order one off a pet site that delivers. After you log off, you realise you'd forgotten about The Countdown. You don't remember seeing it at all.

You flip your laptop open and check. 622,821. You are now the cat who can't see stripes.

The day of the party arrives. Zero will be midnight tonight.

You are distracted all day. On your way to the store, the first people you see are the Brethren of Silent Prayers in the park, their white gowns flapping. They were the group to ban technology. You wonder if they might be right. But you don't want to wear white, it washes you out.

Most stores are closed. You travel twenty minutes to a pet store to pick up meal worms for Elizabeth, your miniature bearded lizard. Yesterday, you ordered little dragon wings for her. You hope the world lasts long enough for them to arrive. It'll be adorable.

The roads are empty, apart from the odd citizen venturing out for milk or bread or meal worms. You think about stopping at a bottle shop to take something for tonight, but decide to re-gift a wine bottle left over from your last dinner party.

Elizabeth is fussy and won't eat the worms. You think it is because they are bigger than the ones you purchased last time. You cut them up smaller, but they die, and she won't eat them dead.

At the party, it's all anyone can talk about. Someone claims to have gone to school with Evie, which is unlikely, they must be fifteen years older than the girl.

A thin young man with wide-rimmed glasses is drinking straight from a wine bottle and reading news updates aloud from his phone. The room is mostly ignoring him. You catch a headline or two about the religious group banning devices. A couple of their disciples caught texting were nailed to crosses, left to bleed out. Also, something about an A-list actor announcing his intention to fly his private jet. He was quoted saying he'd piloted during the millennium bug scare, and that turned out alright, so he'd keep the world safe again. He seemed to think the apocalypse revolved around him.

It's almost midnight now. Jenny is agitated. She throws back glass after glass of sparkling wine and screams at guests to toss their phones in the pool.

'Can't you see? They're right. Turn it all off. I don't want to die!' She wails and runs through the house, stripping off every shred of clothing before racing out the front gate and down the street.

You are not disturbed by her departure. Now you've met the host, Lydia, you realise Jenny and you never had anything in common. Lydia is more mature, she speaks of her travels and feels the same way you do about children in detention centres. You tell her about Elizabeth. She is clearly moved.

'It's the least I could do, for the children.'

She rests her hand on your upper arm and you feel a zap. Her eyes are so dark you can barely tell where the black pupil merges into the deep brown lenses. While you talk, her face leans in close.

'They killed her!' the news caller announces from near the food table, 'The Countdown Instigator, executed by firing squad. They killed that girl!'

What's my prize?

'This is so exhausting. Do you want some air?' Lydia waves to the balcony.

Of course, you do. Finally, she is close to you. You lean in, nothing will spoil this moment. Your phone buzzes and you roll your eyes. Jenny will have realised her behaviour was impulsive and be crying for a lift back to the house, and a coat. You glance at your watch, it isn't Jenny. You'd set an alarm and completely forgotten. Just in time to see The Countdown flash from 1 to ...

F2P

gina pinto

ROUND ONE.

Under no circumstances fall into the pit.

Avoid humans. They will only hinder your progress.

Press controller button, tilt joystick forward. Levitate.

Boom.

Round one over.

In her home in Austin Texas, Francesca Ramos, aka Frankie, opens a closet brimming with every console she ever owned. Sega Master System, Nintendo Entertainment System, Sega Genesis, Microsoft Xbox, Wii, Sony PlayStation 4. Eight generations. But she fixes on the Atari 2600 with a faded F2P carved on the casing. A symbol of their connection. After all, Frankie Ramos and Porter Williams did save the earth in *Space Invaders* using nothing more than a motherboard with 128 bytes of RAM.

23

She sets the angular, four-switch unit beneath the old, bulky TV, and connects the interference filter. Then inserts the game, flicks the 'ON' switch, grabs the joystick, and smiles at the sight of the Atari logo flash on the screen.

The recognisable eight-note sound effect repeats.

Spaceship lands, the extra-terrestrial walks.

The counter at the top of the screen ticks down to E.T.'s death whenever a mistake is made. To save the alien and have him call home, Frankie needs to find and assemble the pieces of a phone. Instead, she enters the coordinates 32°53'11.87"N105°57'38.69"W into her mobile.

ROUND TWO

Newspapers dated April 26, 2014, headline the site 'Area 51'. Others call it hallowed ground. But the Atari burial legend started three decades ago.

Frankie, car packed, makes the nine and half hour road trip to be at a desert burial and to see him one more time.

Traverse into the site.

A wind howls across Apache land from the Rio Grande towards the Chihuahuan Desert. A man sits atop an excavator.

Beware the pitfalls.

Dust has worked its way into the lines of his face to hide his story. He lowers the backhoe bucket and scoops debris from the landfill.

Frankie, from afar, watches his every move. She looks for the tell-tale signs of someone she once knew, and to unearth a long-lost sentiment.

Hundreds file along a makeshift path delineated by traffic markers and tape. The crowd of gaming enthusiasts and treasure hunters brave the sandstorm that comes out of nowhere. Like an NPC, Frankie stands on the sidelines by one of the signs peppered around the landfill: NO TRESPASSING—PROPERTY OF THE CITY OF ALAMOGORDO. Her eyes are fixed.

The metal clatters as the excavator's arm moves back and forth forcing decades worth of domestic waste into a dumpster. The smell rises from the man-made trash tomb. The work crew reach for their noses.

Ernest Cline the author, from his open-flapped 1981 DeLorean, gushes for the cameramen on the relics about to be pulled out of the landfill. From the boot, he hands out signed copies of his book *Ready Player One*. Frankie's eyes drop to the number plate: ANORAK. The homage is there for all to see.

Pale-faced, middle-aged men dart the landscape, some with paraphernalia symbolic of a bygone era. Two bikini-clad girls walk around with their thirty-eight-inch figurine of E.T. Everyone's favourite extra-terrestrial. Dozens of game aficionados parade retro T-shirts with green, pixelated symbols. The local folk walk down the dirt road with their dogs, kids, and curiosity. The video-game archaeologists' table remains empty. Like a *memento mori*, this burial represents the death of Atari. The excavation means so much more.

The press, impatient for any sign of a discovery, train their cameras on the crew.

Frankie moves closer to the action.

Player chosen.

She thinks through her options.

The excavator pulls another bucket and dumps the load on a cleared space. A pack of men in white hard hats and high-viz vests rummage through the dumped heap, sorting through the debris.

The wind picks up. The crowd pull bandanas over their faces and shield their eyes from the assaulting sand. The film crew and VIPs shelter under a pop-up canopy.

On a surface find, an archaeologist produces a newspaper clipping from around the time of the dumping in 1983, and a gamer finds an Atari controller cap.

Frankie paces up and down the orange barrier mesh.

Don't quit.

The action within the fenced area guides her every move. Her focus is on him. Watch without being watched.

But the clock counts down, moves need to be made.

The energy at the site brews. The man with the story-to-tell face jumps from the excavator and rummages through the dirt. Before Frankie realises, the question spills from her mouth, 'Find anything?'

His eyes peer from beneath the hard hat. 'So far, it's just trash bags and pieces of wood.' He pauses. The gameplay around him continues. Frankie pulls her wind-swept hair into a ponytail away from her face, but her gaze drops. She feels his eyes on her, scanning her new form.

Direct PC into action.

Her mouth opens to say something, but a gust laden with white sand and debris puts an end to that.

Thoughts swirl like the wind in her mind, Does he remember?

Hours go by.

The energy expires.

The crowd grows weary. A dig crew member lifts his construction helmet and scratches his head, another shrugs his shoulders. An embankment of cement rubble lines the foreground, mounds of red dirt surround the crew. The excavator continues to dig deeper. The pit grows. Non-Atari trash piles up. Twitter feeds light up the internet with the hashtag #DiggingET.

Unlike the random digs in *Raiders of the Lost Ark*, this archaeological investigation has one shot at finding these buried games. A government agency stipulation. One pit or game over.

Hope dwindles. Tension mounts until a yell, tinged by a southern twang, comes from up ahead. Frankie and all the others turn. The man jumps out of his Caterpillar excavator. The thud of his boots blows a cloud of dust.

'We got something.'

An ominous rush of wind envelops the work crew as they bend over. Cameramen run towards the site. Frankie focuses on her target, the man following a worker with a plastic pail. They walk towards the archaeologists' table. The announcement battles the wind to make its way across the desert landscape towards the crowd. Words filter through. 'Confirmed.' '1983.' 'twenty-eight feet down.'

A hand rises above the crowd. The game, in its box, is intact. Unearthing the maligned video game makes the gathered mass erupt.

'This is Atari's Ark of the Covenant,' yells a voice out of the cheering crowd.

Make a move.

'Porter,' she calls out.

Restart?

Reset?

Gamers flit around Frankie with excitement. The retrieved cartridges emerge from the pit as abandoned '80s trash to become 21st century artifacts. The camera crew rush towards E.T.'s creator Howard Scott Warshaw, to gage his reaction to the monumental find.

The excavator operator follows her with his eyes as she threads in between the crowd. The desert stops its murmurs, the wind drops as quickly as it started. Porter rushes towards Frankie. She pulls out the elastic from her ponytail. Her brown hair drops down to her waist, just as it did in 1983

As he stands on the other side of the mesh barrier, Porter says, 'F2P.'

'You remember.' Her voice, arid and faint, a desert whisper.

Grey hair peppers his temples and stubble. Porter takes a quick step towards her. His steel-blue eyes narrow. The crowds' chatter doesn't disturb this long-awaited reunion. A broad smile rises from his lips. The built-up tension on her face eases.

Porter leans over the barrier, draws Frankie closer, enveloped in his arms, she feels their past surface.

Suspend play.

ROUND THREE

In September 1983, Frankie, Porter, and a handful of teens, stood above a twenty-foot hole within three hundred acres of a New Mexico landfill.

Rumours of what laid in this pit propagated like a weed. Secrets in this small town always surfaced. Like the covert military operation exploding the world's first nuclear bomb in the desert near Alamogordo, this secret operation also detonated. When the video-game business went bust and the *E.T.* video game was deemed a commercial failure, Alamogordo became the rumoured burial site.

A clandestine convoy of trucks driving through town to the landfill caught the attention of the teenagers. As the sun set behind the mountain range, the motley group rode their bikes through the streets, turned off into the desert, and sped up as they got closer to the site. One last look behind to check if anyone was following. They threaded their bikes through a wire gate held together by a loose chain and padlock. Porter had the only bike light and illuminated the way for the others. The dirt road got bumpy making the beam bounce. With a brisque twist they stopped their bikes feet away from the machine-cut edge of the hole. They walked down the huge ramp towards the site of dumped video games covered with garbage.

Porter pushed his Adidas sneakers onto the spade.

'I wanna barf,' said Frankie as the stench of dug trash surfaced.

The others watched as they shone their flashlights. It didn't take long before their dig paid off. Packaged consoles and games were passed around teenage hands. Porter drew Frankie close and kissed her.

'What do you think you're doing?' boomed a voice from above.

'Split up,' yelled Porter.

The kids scattered in all directions with a high-powered flashlight tracking their movements. The security guard chased Porter into the bowels of the landfill. Frankie and the others scrambled onto their bikes and tore through the desert. They madly funnelled through the gate with Frankie looking back for a sign of Porter. Jumping curbs, hitting trashcans, they burned rubber through the streets of Alamogordo. Out of nowhere a beam of light illuminated their retreat. Porter joined their formation with a screech of his tyres.

The next day, the *Alamogordo Daily News* was quick to plaster the Atari burial on its frontpage.

And Frankie Ramos sat crossed legged on a shag-pile rug in Porter's room.

'Last night was mad. I heard the games are totally buried under a slab of concrete.'

Frankie reached for the drawing compass on Porter's desk. With a nod he consented. Using the needle she carved an F, followed by a 2, and a P, just as she had done on her own console a day earlier.

There was an imperceptible expression upon Frankie's lips as she inserted the unearthed game, passed him the joystick, and said, 'Press START.'

Inspired by true events.

SYNDICATE GAMES

pamela jeffs

Two years ago, I crashed a spaceship and cracked my skull. Started hearing strange voices in my head—

Insidious. Compelling.

And the loudest of them led me here, against all reason, to the arse-end of the universe and this backwater tavern.

So why am I about to enter a game to try and win ownership of a planet? Beats the hell out of me. One part of my mind supports my actions; the other part *knows* I'm crazy. No sane person would travel so far and not know why. Even though I'm torn, I choose to follow my heart. It tells me I'm exactly where I need to be.

I place my shot glass down on the bar, savouring the burn of Fireon in my throat. I breathe out and the spirit's peppery heat rolls across my tongue. I flip one of my last credit coins between my fingers. I've got enough for a meal, a night's lodging and one more drink.

I'm waiting.

I grimace. The voice again. It's grown stronger since I arrived yesterday—more insistent—haunting both my sleeping and waking hours. I swallow a second shot of Fireon.

Time is running out, it whispers.

I don't answer.

Instead, I consider the groups of contestants that pack the Broken Ship Tavern—an establishment retro-fitted inside a rusted cargo vessel that looks to have crashed here, on the planet, Beltran, a while ago. Low chatter fills the room as background noise. Like myself, everyone is waiting out the hours until tomorrow when the Chancer brothers arrive. I push my empty glass across the tarnished bar top, made from one of the ship's recycled wings beaten flat along the leading edge. Waste not, want not, I guess.

The Syndicate Games are this galaxy's worst-kept secret. Illegal, but they are tolerated by bribed Hegemon Alliance law enforcement agencies. Anyone who has ever dreamed of changing their lot in life has heard of them—an all-or-nothing event.

This year's game has attracted all sorts of lifeforms. Against one wall of the bar clusters a group of Yasti, the clever, rodent-class aliens from the Demeter Quadrant. Their dusty, beige robes, still carrying the sand of their home world, are worn and patched. Their liquid-brown eyes and furred faces are drawn. Word is, their planet hovers on the brink of environmental collapse. They're here, no doubt, looking to win a new world for their people to call home.

Across from me, leaning on the bar, are five female Iscean mercenaries. Reptilian and bad-tempered. This crew, all dressed in matching black armour, has the look of a professional outfit. Some

Grey Fuel tycoon has probably hired them, looking to win another planet to mine.

The rest of the groups are a mix of species, banded together to try and maximise their chances of winning. Weapons hang from belts. Shiny. Dangerous.

Tomorrow, those armaments will draw blood.

A verdant world is worth killing for.

I'm waiting.

'I'm coming,' I mutter, before I can stop myself.

The urge to walk out into the jungle is overwhelming, but I can't leave yet. There's no help for it. A warning, given on my arrival by the guard at the door, was absolute—walking out there without Chancer brother approval is a quick way to a messy execution.

I should take this opportunity to rest. I gather up my flight jacket and tip a chin to the barman—a rather large, tentacle-faced Aquanorian.

'Room?' I ask.

The alien nods and slides a blue access pass across the bar. 'Pods are set up out the back.' He pauses a moment, ancient black eyes resting on mine. They travel across my face tracking the scars left by my accident. I step back and stumble, my left leg seizing—another consequence of the crash.

I know what he's thinking. It's the same thing everyone thinks—

Look at the poor human, all banged up. He hasn't got a chance in hell of making it.

But I'm not here to win.

'Big day tomorrow,' says the barman, his small talk light but words weighty.

'Yeah.'

'You ready?'

I hold the Aquanorian's depthless gaze. I recall his kind are long-lived and figure he has probably seen a lot of people come and go from this place.

Seen a lot of people die.

'I will be,' I say.

A ripple of noise pulses through the crowd. The Aquanorian's attention flits to the entrance door as two men enter. They are as alike as peas in a pod. The famous gangsters, the identical twins known as Luke and Linus Chancer, have arrived early.

It's the first time I've seen them up close. Some say there is a little Iscean in their genetic makeup, having reptile hearts is what makes them so cunning and so brutal. They look to be just plain Terran to me, true — pretty Terrans with their blond hair, blue eyes and tall, muscular builds — but human nonetheless.

They pause at the entrance, shrewd eyes scanning the tavern, taking in the room. One nods to the other, as if satisfied with what they see. Then they stride in, followed by three mean-looking, armed guards.

The Chancers both leap up onto the bar. The bartender steps back.

A hush falls.

'Welcome contestants!' says Luke, the brother on the right. His fine-fingered right hand flourishes theatrically in the air.

The room remains still. The brothers' quick tempers and itchy trigger fingers are well known and none of the gathered seem willing to risk drawing attention to themselves.

'Tomorrow, the Syndicate Games begin,' says the other brother, Linus. 'The prize is the planet, Proxima Gentrus. A world, generously donated by a client of ours who was unable to pay his debts.'

A chill chases across my shoulders. What else did that client lose?

Linus nods to the barman who presses a button by the credit reader. A hologram flickers. Projected high above the crowd is a small, green-coloured world with two moons, orbiting a bright, young sun.

'Located in the Proxima Quadrant,' continues Linus, 'this is a verdant, class M planet. Initial scans also show rich deposits of dycerium.'

'What about indigenous populations?' calls out a Yasti.

'Neutralised,' says Luke. 'It's free and clear for repopulation.'

Mutters start in the far corners of the room. Some might be whispering, horrified, at the news of slaughtered races, but most are certainly talking about the dycerium. The rare metal, used to make impervious armoured hulls for deep-space vessels, is a rich prize for any willing to run an illegal mining operation.

The barman hands Luke a thin scanpad. He holds it into the air.

'For those competing, step up now and confirm your bet.'

The Yasti crew is the first to approach. The tallest of them looks up at the brothers, his whiskers glinting caramel in the electric lights overhead. His long nails tap on the glass surface of the tablet. A final press and a quiet beep confirm the entry.

Luke looks down. 'Agreed,' he says after a moment. 'Fifteen thousand Yasti youngsters delivered for life-long servitude in our mines on Aureehn, should you lose.'

A steep price.

The Iscean leader approaches the tablet next, a woman with fine, green-scaled skin and golden eyes. 'Ten thousand tonnes of Grey Fuel as payment if unsuccessful,' she says. Luke nods in agreement. The deal is made and the Isceans blend away to the back of the room.

Several other groups approach, each with assets to offer that are suitable to the brothers. Fleets of ships. Access to experimental technologies.

Too soon, it's my turn.

I leave my jacket on the bar and hobble over to the brothers. Their disdain for me is barely hidden. They see what the barman saw—a young man with a useless, broken body.

'What do we have here?' asks Linus, lips peeled back across impossibly white teeth. 'A ragged smuggler who's come to win his fortune?'

'I'm here to enter the game,' I say, quietly as a hundred eyes from the crowd bore into my back.

'And when you lose?' chuckles Luke.

So, it's 'when I lose', not, 'if I lose'.

'I'll hand myself over.'

'What value are you?' asks Linus. 'We already own fleets of smugglers.'

I glance up at the two brothers. Both men bleed arrogance—the same hubris the ancient gods from Earth once warned humanity against.

'Well?' asks Luke.

I hesitate. Why am I doing this to myself?

I'm waiting.

I lift my chin and straighten my shoulders. 'I offer my services.'

'Services?' asks Luke.

A service using the skill I earned as a result of my accident. I don't even know if it's permanent, but it's the only thing of value I can bargain with.

'I'm an interpreter.'

'Languages?' Luke sneers and taps his ear. 'I already own a universal translator.'

'Not words spoken by living things,' I say. 'I can communicate with natural objects. I can tell you what stones are thinking, what rivers can hear. I'll reveal secrets you would never otherwise know.'

Linus leaps down from the bar. With eyes sly and perhaps a little disbelieving, he pulls a silver ring off his finger. A giant faceted citrine huddles in its clawed setting.

'Prove what you say,' he says. 'Tell me the secret of *this* stone.'

He drops the piece into my hand. At its touch my stomach surges sideways. A ghostly memory swallows me, of sudden pain and death.

I came from this world. His great-grandfather slaughtered me, whispers the rock. *He cut out my gemstone heart, and shattered it. He forged the pieces into treasures.*

I glance at Luke and see a matching ring on his hand. I bite my lip, disgusted.

'This isn't a mined gemstone,' I say.

Linus grins. 'That's not its secret.'

He thinks he's caught me lying.

I glare up at him. Bile stings the back of my throat. 'It's the fragment of a jewelled heart. Your brother wears another piece of it.'

Linus's right eyebrow rises. 'How did I come by it?'

'Your great-grandfather killed the Beltran dragon it belonged to.'

'Correct.' Linus looks impressed. He glances at his brother who nods.

Luke holds the scanpad out. 'Secrets hold worth. We accept your offer.'

I reach over to sign my name, but Luke pulls the screen away.

'But lose and the agreement stands for the full term of your life.'

I hesitate. What happens if the gift goes?

Do it!

I sign my name.

The next morning arrives, bright and cool. Insect chitters and birdcalls filter down from the jungle's canopy. Multiple groups have gathered at the start line, indicated by a carved timber totem pole. The markings are almost obscured with blue moss. The dead wood whispers of worshippers lost. I wonder if it belonged to the race that owned this planet before the Chancers.

I swallow. My stomach churns and my heart is a knot. I really don't want to die here today. I'm not quick, so I'll have to be clever. To take my mind off what's coming, I adjust my blaster so it sits easier in the holster at my hip. On the other side hangs a family heirloom and my good luck charm. A polished short sword. It belonged to my great grandfather on my mother's side, Oscar O'Conner—the Terran relative I was named after. The last items I'm taking are a wristband illuminator and a slim water bag strapped to my back.

Beside me the Yasti group stand together, heads bowed. The brothers stand at the line, both dressed in clean, white suits. Their polished shoes are only slightly marred by streaks of mud.

'Welcome all,' calls out Luke.

The crowd quietens.

'Today's quarry,' he continues, 'is a Beltran dragon we have hidden within the jungle. You have two hours to locate it,

40

slaughter it and return here bearing its heart as proof. There are no rules past this line. There is no salvation beyond that given by your own wits. Understand that if you die out there, your corpse will be left for the scavengers. Are you ready?'

The Isceans hiss something that sounds like a battle cry.

Luke lifts a silver handkerchief into the air.

A pregnant pause.

'Begin!' He drops it.

The groups all sprint past the totem pole.

The Yastis are quick, being the first to cross the line.

Two Isceans fall just metres past it, Terran throwing daggers imbedded in their necks. The Terran crew then slips to the right, and is swallowed by the forest. Others follow them. Unseen blaster fire sizzles and a scream, cut short, echoes through the trees.

I mustn't have seemed like much of a threat to the other contestants. I can't think of any other reason why I'm left standing alone at the line, still breathing.

'Giving up before you start, boy?' asks Luke, tucking his handkerchief into his pocket.

'Because if you are, go pack your kit,' says Linus. 'We're heading off in three hours.'

My answer is to step into a hitching run. The brother's cruel laughter rings out behind me as I pass the already dead participants and enter the jungle.

Straight ahead.

Like I've done for so long now, I follow the voice's direction. I slip right and squirrel through a curtain of dense vines. Thorns nip at my cheeks, their barbed ends stinging like acid. Footsteps crash through the undergrowth to my left. A lone Iscean sprints past me and keeps running.

I follow, much slower.

More blaster fire crackles close by. My hands tremble as I visualise being hit from behind. The urgency to move faster is hindered by the reality of my disability. I grit my teeth and tell myself again—

I don't need to be fast, I just need to be clever.

I'm waiting.

I suck in a breath. My injured leg is on fire already, the knotted scar tissue down its length, hinders. Frustrated, I ball my hands into fists. Why the hell am I here? I really am crazy—crazy to have bet my existence on nothing but gut feeling and a voice in my head. I punch my aching thigh, a different kind of pain to mask the other.

You're running out of time …

'Damn it! I'm coming,' I mutter.

I keep going, my lurching gait taking me past thick vines heavy with scented blooms and the carnivorous plants that crouch below them. I don't linger at the pair of Yasti legs protruding out from one flower's closed maws. He made his choice and took his chance.

He paid the price.

Keep to the left.

The vegetation grows thicker here. I'm tempted to blast it, but that would alert the others to my position. Instead, my short sword makes quick work of the green wall as I cut through.

See the road? Follow it.

An ancient pathway of black cobblestones is only just visible through the undergrowth. Another scream echoes somewhere to my right. I quicken to a trot, hitching my way along as fast as I can. The jungle leans over me. Ahead, a ragged pile of grey stones lies across the track. Just past it are the vegetation-clogged ruins of what looks to be some kind of ancient temple.

You are close.

I reach the building. Carvings matching those on the totem pole cover the walls. The sinister entrance glares at me.

Inside.

I hate dark places. The way they turn my palms to sweat and crush my lungs tight. They remind me of being trapped in a crashed ship, of blood leaking down my split scalp. I consider the grim doorway.

I can't stop now.

But be clever ...

I activate my illuminator and unholster my blaster. I feel safer holding it. I take the first of six crumbling stairs leading into the deserted building. Silence has overtaken the jungle. I swallow.

What do the animals know that I don't?

My boots slip slightly in the mouldering leaf litter gathered at the threshold. I enter, nose wrinkling against the dank scent filtering past the curtain of darkness within.

'Welcome, Oscar. I *am* glad you've come.'

The voice in my head made real. I swing toward it. The beam of my illuminator cuts an urgent arc through the gloom. It catches on a fragment of colour.

There!

Surprised, I jolt to a stop.

It's the Beltran dragon.

She's the size of a horse with peacock-blue scales that shine like polished metal. Her teeth are black daggers, and a crest of saffron feathers circles her reptilian head like a crown. Her eyes hold mine, two faceted, blood-red rubies.

She's beautiful.

And terrifying.

'You are the one who led me here?' I ask, confused.

Given the nature of my talents, I'd expected to find something natural—inanimate— certainly not living. But then again, the dragon's heart is a gemstone. Maybe that called to me?

'I've long been trapped alone here, calling out to the universe,' replies the dragon. 'In sorrow I've wept, never anticipating a reply. But then, you answered. Was I not to call you to me?'

'What do you want?'

The dragon chuckles, a most sorrowful sound. 'Today, I am the hunter's prey. They'll take my heart to win a planet.' The dragon's scarlet gaze drops. 'What would you wish for in my place?'

'Freedom.'

'Exactly.'

The creature shifts and chains clank. It's then I see she's shackled to the far wall, and her wings—they're crooked—broken.

My throat closes, tight with pity. This is why my heart led me to her.

But I have no tools to liberate her. My heart sinks as I take in the weight of the heavy, forged iron fetters holding her captive. Neither my blaster nor my sword will sever them. And even if I could break her free, she can't fly. She'll never make it out of here.

Being always in my mind, she knows what I'm thinking.

'Your body is damaged like mine,' says the dragon, lifting a wing.

Not a question: a statement of fact.

Chastised, I bite my tongue.

She's right. I *am* physically broken like her, but even so, I've still managed to traverse galaxies to be here.

I'm judging this dragon exactly the way I am judged.

By her disability, and not her strengths.

The snap of branches sounds out near the temple's entrance. Raspy voices follow.

'Someone is already here!' cries out one.

'They won't make it back,' says another.

The click of Yasti claws over the stone threshold makes my skin crawl.

The dragon's glowing eyes fix on mine.

Now or never, she whispers within my mind.

Damn it.

An idea takes hold. I lurch forward. Up close, the dragon's reptilian stench is overwhelming. Keeping my breaths shallow, I kneel and press my palm to the heavy iron chain. I speak to the metal ore within the iron links, begging it to separate. I explain why I need it to do such a thing.

I will help, the ore replies.

An illuminator flickers behind me, and then catches me in its beam.

'You there, stop!' snarls a Yasti.

A blaster shot splinters the rock next to me.

The Yasti swears. His blaster whines as it powers up again.

But before it does, the chain crumbles in my palm, turning to red-brown dust.

45

Freed, the dragon shakes her ragged wings. Her throat swells and she roars, the air vibrating with the tremor of her passion.

'Together,' she cries.

And the dragon has it right—we two halves can make a deadly whole.

I step in beside her, drawing my blaster and my sword.

'Together then,' I whisper.

TAMA-GOTCHA

matilda clancy

'I can't be responsible for a life, I haven't passed midterms yet,' the girl, sporting a comically large red bow, wails. She drops her plastic token onto the school desk with complete disregard for her new child's life.

Stacey Myers, our resident skater girl, leans across. 'Quit whining Liz, it's an easy pass. My baby brother can keep one alive and that twerp still eats his own snot.'

'First of all, gross. Secondly, you underestimate my ability to kill things.' Lizzie adjusts her bow, then reaches out a delicate finger and prods the pink egg-shaped device.

This is the perfect opportunity, so I lean in, 'Ha! Tell me about it, you don't even want to know what happened to my last fish.' I bare teeth to showcase my light-hearted and humorous nature. People apparently like that.

Stacey and Lizzie blink in unison. The duo blankly stare for what seems like an eternity — until both their jaws drop open.

Think of something to say to leave a better impression. Nothing.

Relief washes over me as their gaping is interrupted by the scratchy voice of Mrs Warner. 'Miss ... Mallory. Collect your newborn please.'

'That's uh me, so ...' I jump too quickly and knock my books to the floor before lurching toward the front of the classroom.

'What the hell did she do to her fish?' Lizzie's face contorts in disgust.

Good one, Mal.

My hand slowly submerges into the container of small devices, a shiver running up my arm from the cold. I land on one of the plastic eggs and withdraw it. Mine has a black casing covered in small ghost patterns. It stands out amongst the other brightly-coloured devices.

Must be a Halloween edition.

I shoot Mrs Warner my rehearsed smile, turning back toward my seat. Her cold hand grasps my wrist, and I jump a little as I spin around. Her eyes bulge, fixated on the small gaming device in my sweaty palms. 'Be extra careful with this one. You wouldn't want to be responsible for the death of a child now, would you?'

'O-okay, I will.' The words lump up in my throat, struggling to make their way out.

Instantly, her demeanour softens, and I convince myself I never saw the terror in her eyes.

Once home, I chuck my backpack onto my desk. Digging past scrunched up homework and a half-eaten sandwich, I slide the small plastic game out and cradle it in my palm. Clicking the play button on my CD player, I flop onto my bed and inspect the casing. The calming sounds of Radiohead fill the room. My mother won't be home for a few hours. She had taken additional shifts at work 'for the extra cash', but I know it's to avoid me. I don't mind; I enjoy the privacy.

Mrs Warner calls the device a 'SHE-GOT-CHA'. There is a small inscription on the back. *Do they all have this?* It reads: *There comes a day when the sky falls and the child returns home.*

'Weird.' I tug the tiny paper circle protruding from the battery compartment. It lets out a single obnoxiously loud beep, closer to a scream than the mechanisms of a machine turning on.

A teensy digital egg emerges on the screen, bopping up and down to the chorus of 'Creep'. It takes me about half an hour of fiddling with the various buttons before I figure out how to set the timer to hatch it. Mrs Warner claims using instructions would be cheating.

'In real life, babies don't come with manuals.'

I highly doubt this, considering the number of parenting books available.

Why couldn't they have just given us raw eggs, like last year's cohort?

When it hatches, a small smiley blob appears on the screen with a digital black bow on its head. *Guess it's a girl.* The blob bounces about the screen with glee. *It's kinda adorable,* I grin back at the small creature and for a split second I could swear its mouth opens, displaying a set of sharp teeth. The screen glitches and the creature returns to its regular jumping self.

'Jeez,' I murmur, 'guess somebody's hungry.'

I play around with the functions, blindly searching for a way to take care of this little blob. The screen is crowded with eight blurry icons. The graininess of the screen makes it difficult to make out what they are meant to represent. I figure the knife and fork is a safe bet.

Satisfied with my newfound parenting expertise, I place my digi-child under my pillow to muffle its screams.

That night I dream of an unfamiliar house, each room bigger and darker than the next. Spice Girls music wafts down from upstairs, it's like nails on a chalkboard to my ears. But it does nothing to cover a horrid crunching noise. Dread washes over me as I ascend.

'Hello? I-is anyone there?' My heart races.

The crunching morphs into slurping as I approach the upstairs hallway. All the doors are closed except one at the very end, which emits a soft light through the opening. Floorboards creak beneath my every reluctant step. I push the door.

Every inch of wall is covered in Backstreet Boys posters. A young girl with a large scarlet bow sits on the bed. Bleeding. A lot. Before I can help, she reaches a hand into her own stomach and pulls out a kidney, then takes a bite. The blood spatters all over the carpet and pink bedspread as she ravages her own body. I want to run or throw up or stop her, but I'm disorientated from disgust and dismay. Each of her bones cracks as she turns.

'Oh, silly me, I forgot to offer some to our guest.' Her voice is scratchy, almost mechanical.

She reaches into her open chest cavity and pulls out a still beating heart, offering it with outstretched hands. I shake my head vigorously backing away. I bump into the wall and turn, but it's not the wall. A creature, humanoid but with yellow eyes as big as my hands peers down at me. It stretches an elongated finger toward me. I wake in a cold sweat, too tired and confused to care that my digi-pet has died in the night.

That day I go about my usual routine, no memory of my dream or reason for this feeling of unease. That is until fourth period, when they announce Lizzie is dead. The girl who always wore a ridiculous blood-red bow, the same girl I so desperately wanted to befriend in the hope a fraction of her popularity would rub off on me, had starved herself to death. The crowded class seems empty without her.

Stacey mutters and rocks back and forth, 'I didn't know. How could I not know? I should've ...'

The images of my nightmare return violently.

Behind me, girls sob. Still, Stacey continues, '... should've known, should've ...'

I can barely breathe, squeezing my eyes shut in a vain attempt to block the image of her outstretched hands and beating heart.

A cheerful beep silences us all. Stacey's Shigotchi. The entire class stares, as she inhales deeply, pulls her skateboard from her backpack, and uses it to bash the digi-pet until it is an explosion of plastic fragments. Mrs Warner approaches her, but Stacey pushes past and out of the classroom. No one moves as the sound of her skateboarding fades down the hall.

Mrs Warner murmurs, 'You should have tried harder.'

I'm unclear if she means herself, Stacey, Liz ... or me.

My new Shigotchi hatches.

That night I can't focus on schoolwork, let alone my meaningless digi-pet. I vacantly stare at my mathematics textbook, the nightmare dancing before the page. The way she died was such an eerie coincidence. *Was it a premonition?*

No. I'm just in shock. The dream didn't even happen. I totally made it up after the fact from like trauma or something.

The following night's dream proves me wrong. Stacey has a trash can wedged between her knees. I try to ask if she needs help, but am unable to form words. My intentions are interrupted with the squeamish sounds of her lunch exiting her stomach ... no, not food, this is a thick black substance. It sizzles in the garbage as if toxic. I move toward her, but the room stretches and the more I walk the more distance I have left to travel. I sprint, somehow knowing if I can reach her in time, I can stop this. Ahead of me emerges ramps, metal railings and curved cement walls I have to weave and climb. I run out of breath. My knees weaken and I stumble to the ground.

Panting, I whisper, 'Sorry.'

The spell breaks. She is close to me again and no longer throwing up. I reach up to put a hand to her cheek, so grateful I made it to her in time. Except I'm wrong. It is too late. When

I remove my hand, her skin follows like melted rubber on a summer's day. My palm is covered in her blood. Her neck makes a crack, crack, cracking sound as she turns to me. Her elongated fingers, more liquid than solid, outstretch and she screams an inhuman wail. I wake to a digi-pet notification. The pixelated creature has two tiny skulls next to its head. I roll my eyes and shove it into my backpack.

Nobody expects Stacey to be at school. She has every reason to ditch, but she shows up to every class, cheery as always. In the classes and halls, theories of 'coping strategies' float about. I know something is wrong. Before our shared period I get the nerve to speak to her.

'Hey um ... I'm sorry about Liz.'

She shoots me a quizzical glance and chuckles, 'I mean she's skipped one day it's no biggie. I'm sure she'll be here tomorrow.'

Oh, that's not a good sign.

A high-pitched beep from my Shigotchi catches my attention.

PAY ATTENTION MAL <3.

Stacey collapses against the desk with a thud. I squeal in sync to my digi-pet's final beep. Other than a couple of gasps, the class barely reacts, probably thinking she's just fainted. That is until Mrs Warner tries to wake her lifeless body. My Shigotchi dies at 1:45 pm. Stacey dies at 1:46 pm.

I don't remember being excused. I don't remember them passing me onto my mother and recommending a therapist. I don't remember the ghoulishly quiet drive home.

A concussion, they say. She fell at the skateboard park the day before and it went undiagnosed. Her parents feel so guilty, the gossip says. They shouldn't. This isn't their fault. It's mine. I killed Stacey just as I had killed Liz. Their blood is on my hands.

At home, I shut myself into my room. I have a mission. I can't let this happen again. If I can just figure out who the next victim is, I can stop their death. Tapping my foot, I await the next hatching.

Beep. Beep. Beep.

A tiny digital duck dances across the screen. *Great. That's helpful.*

I pull last year's yearbook from my bookshelf. Frantically flicking through the pages, I land on Dylan Byrd. Now I knew who is next, the only problem is how to save him.

I refuse to sleep. No more nightmares.

At school, I find myself exhausted every waking minute to the point where I get into trouble for falling asleep in class. It seems as though with each evolutionary progression of the digi-pet the game gets harder.

Other students are talking too, 'Some versions of the game have higher challenges. The newer editions introduce predators.'

My stomach drops.

In Maths, my Shigotchi beeps.

'How many times have I told you kids not to bring these things into my classroom!' Mr Box booms.

'Um, sir, it's for Health Class.' My words stumble clumsier than an alcoholic uncle on New Year's Eve.

'Does this look like your Health Class? Do I look like Mrs Warner to you? Hand it over, you can get it back at the end of the lesson.'

'But um, sir—'

A large open palm is shoved into my face. I sigh. If I tell the truth, he won't believe me.

My eyes fixate on Dylan the entire lesson, begging him to just not die for the next forty minutes. That's when it happens. An echo of chirping, screeching birds outside. Mr Box fights to talk over them, almost shouting Pythagoras' theorem.

SPLAT.

Droplets of blood drip down the window. A lifeless feathery body slides down the frame with a screech.

One girl squeals. A couple of kids chuckle. Mr Box puts on his gruff 'settle down folks' voice. Another sparrow hits the window. Then another. Then another. The glass cracks. Each bird targets the same spot as the one prior. The window next to Dylan's seat.

Mr Box frowns at the web-like crack. The sparrows stop. Then crows fly into the glass. Now Mr Box decides we need to evacuate. I make sure I'm the last one through the door. I pocket my Shigotchi from his desk. We follow the teacher halfway through the hall when I realise, he's taking us to the evacuation area. The idiot is taking us outside. He is leading Dylan to certain death.

I examine the game, a murder of pixelated crows surround the duck in the centre. I click buttons for dear life. Nothing works.

I grab Dylan's wrist and yank him into the nearby supply closet. Brody Stevens calls, 'Ooh-la-la!'

Dylan raises an eyebrow.

'This is going to sound crazy but ... they're after you,' I blurt.

'W-who? What?'

'The birds. They want to kill you.'

'Is this a joke? Did Brody set you up to—'

A piercing scream from the hall startles us. Dylan reaches for the door but I block it with my body.

'Move you loon!' He tries to push me out of the way.

'If you go out there, you WILL die.'

I hold up the Shigotchi.

'What the—'

'My game, it's ... cursed or something, and I know that sounds ridiculous, but you gotta trust me. Two people have already died from this thing, I can't take another—'

A beak pecks through the gap under the door.

'Okay! I believe you. Stop it. Now!'

'I uh ...'

I don't know how. Unless ... there is one thing I haven't tried.

'Screwdriver. Now!'

Dylan and I raid the shelves of tools until he finds a workman's kit.

'Here. HERE!'

The wailing outside grows louder. Birds peck and peck until the door has a small hole. Not big enough to fit a bird ... yet. I unscrew the back of the Shigotchi and rip out the battery.

Silence.

'Did it ... did it work?' His hopeful green eyes glint a pale yellow in the light.

We listen. Relief washes over me.

Placing my eye right up against the hole in the door, I scan the environment. A glow of blinking fluorescents spotlight tiny dust particles cascading upon discarded backpacks, open lockers and a knocked over trash can. 'Good news and bad news.'

'Tell me, wait, don't tell me. Yes, tell me.'

'You're okay for now, but.' I turn to him and bare my teeth. 'I think I'm gonna fail Health Class.'

A sharp beak jams through, just missing my eye. I scramble back and toss the useless plastic egg to the ground, trading it for an old metal pipe on the bottom shelf.

I solidify the shoulder-width stance taught to us in Gym class. Holding the pipe, I'm ready to bat, hiding my shaking hands from Dylan. *He may as well have some hope before we die a horrible death.*

I suck in a breath and await the carnage. They come. Over and over. The door crumbles. I swing again and again, hammering my pipe into the skulls of the flock. I swing until I can't feel my arms anymore and then I swing some more until I just can't. Beaks peck and talons prod at my skin as I collapse. I huddle in a ball. Dylan's screams are washed out by the searing pain flooding through my body. No, not screams ... *beeping*?

It takes all my energy to realise the attack has ceased.

I look up to an outstretched hand.

'Dylan?' I manage, as he helps me up. Not a bird in sight.

I weakly wrap an arm around his shoulder to stable myself.

'Where'd they go?'

'Dunno. Think you scared 'em off or something. This thing started beeping and they all just ... left.' He handed me my blood-covered Shigotchi.

YOU SUCCESSFULLY RAISED YOUR BABY!

A tiny UFO floats onto the screen and sucks up the bopping little duck as it flies away.

'Thank you, mother. I am ready to go to my home planet now.'

I look up at Dylan. 'What?'

He smiles and nods at me under the soft glow of the fluorescents. The light grows brighter, to the point of blinding. When my eyes are ready to focus again, he's gone.

'No, no. I won?! I BEAT THE GAME!'

I sprint outside, desperately searching for Dylan. It isn't fair. I saved him. A series of bright white lights shoot down from an enormous metallic disc in the sky. I raise a palm against the glare and squint. Inside one, a floating Dylan smiles and waves gleefully as he rises into the sky.

The aliens in my dream, Stacey's fingers, Dylan's eyes … was I raising alien babies? I think about Liz and Stacey … but I did save Dylan. It's like the song says, 'one out of three ain't bad'.

Proud of myself, I bare my teeth and wave him goodbye.

FINAL PLAY

lea scott

A splintering *crack* wakes me from my long slumber. Darkness lolls across the stale air of the library as muffled voices waft through the long-sealed door. Nails pop and squeal as the age-wearied timber gives them up one by one.

How many years has it been since anyone has entered this room? Lifted a single book from the rich mahogany bookcases? Drawn the burgundy velvet drapes to let in the light? Or lifted me from my resting place on the highest shelf?

I remember the glowing sheen the furnishings once cast in the candlelight. The tinkle of laughter. This room was *my* domain. The children banished here after dinner, away from adult conversation. Seen but not heard. Ensconced inside these thick papered walls, they were *all* mine. As their governess, I held their imaginations for countless hours as they delighted in the dark deeds of my favourite femme fatale Miss Scarlett, plunging the dagger deep into Mr Boddy's chest, over and over. Or the seemingly virtuous Reverend Green walloping Boddy over the head with the heavy lead pipe, his blood soaking into my plush pile carpets. And that Mrs White? Oh, my! Contrary to her name, she could be quite the dark horse, skulking about through my secret passageways between her kitchen and the study, candlestick in hand.

The boys were always less imaginative than the girls. Their deductions that the murder was committed by my dashing Colonel Mustard were reasoned simply because he boasted a superior hand for a revolver. Dice rolled. Crimes were solved. Oh, what heady days they were.

The children grew. Their visits to the library lessened. Excited squeals dulled and conversation turned to hushed adult topics. I was left on the shelf more often, where only whispered secrets reached me. Inevitably, the final play came. My corners drooped. Years passed.

Then a new generation arrived for me to nurture. The boisterous Thomas, with his cowboy hat and cap gun that filled the room with a volley of noise. His serious older sister Louise, quick to pluck me from the shelf knowing the newer game of Monopoly always ended in raised voices and a flipped board, and Scrabble's educational nature wouldn't hold their attention for long. She drew her siblings into the iniquity of my mansion walls with her felonious tales and her adept deductions. Even after the adults installed a television in the library, Louise always insisted on playing a game of Cluedo. I respected her tenacity.

But it was Rose who enamoured me. Sweet intoxicating Rose, with her fiery hair. My very own Miss Scarlett. What a joy she was to me. A girl after my own heart, her soft milky hand stroking my floorboards as she moved around the game board with that roguish twinkle in her green eyes. The titter in her laugh as she proved someone's accusation wrong. I knew she bluffed a little, cleverly accusing the players in her own hand to throw her siblings off the scent, but that just made her more endearing to me.

I never wanted her to leave. Each time my board was snapped close and packed back into the box, my heart shattered into a few more pieces. But the children kept growing and Rose blossomed into a beautiful young woman—especially in the eyes of her brother's friend Colin, so cocky in his military school uniform. Rose had other ideas for her future, refusing Colin's persistent advances. Still, I knew one day, the final play would end it all. Rose would stop coming. I didn't want that to happen.

A week after they discovered Rose's body in the library, the door was boarded shut. They deduced she tried to climb up for a book. Fell. Hit her head on the coffee table. A tragic accident. Nobody had set foot in the library since. For a while, I heard the whispers as people stopped outside the door. One day, the voices went away too. But Rose remained with me, in the stain hidden deep in the plush charcoal carpet.

Crack! My senses quiver as the final timber sentinel falls, freeing the door. It creaks open on wobbly hinges. I blink as the drapes screech on their rusty tracks and light floods the library. A voice squeals.

My dice rattle with anticipation. *Children*! They're back.

'Wow, get a load of that Lucas!' A small boy points and dashes toward the television set. He circles the timber box, runs his hands down its splayed legs, then jiggles the knob back and forth, moving his ear close to listen to the clunking sound it makes. 'I wonder if it still works?'

'Who cares, Boomer,' an adolescent boy pitches in. 'You heard Dad. It's all going to the rubbish tip. Geez, it reeks in here!' He forces open the window then turns in a circle, surveying the bookshelves covering every wall. 'Down with these shelves, up with our mega screen. It'll be dope for playing video games Eli.' Lucas flops onto the Chesterfield sofa and brings his hands together, pressing down his thumbs and pursing his lips to make gun-firing sounds. Eli drops beside him and joins in the charade. I can't help but be swept up in their excitement.

My joy fades as workmen arrive. I watch as the whole west wall of polished timber bookshelves are ripped from the wall. Hammers split the beautiful timbers into fragments to be discarded. The books that graced the shelves for decades tumble to the floor, shedding their cloaks of dust to show off gold-embossed covers. The workmen toss them into boxes and push them into the corner of the room, neglected.

Tom also comes. Grown up now, but still ordering people around. Just like he tried to do with his sisters, who never listened. I feel a tinge of sympathy for him, until he makes a beeline for me and drags my box from the top shelf with a scowl.

He casts me aside, and I land with a rattle and thud on top of the highest box in the corner.

The wall is plastered and painted in a garish lime green, the strong smell of chemicals keeping the children away for days. Thick fitted blinds are installed that block out more light than the former heavy drapes. Gone are the beautiful heritage greens and burgundies that mirrored my mansion walls.

A new kind of box is set up on the wall. Flatter. Larger. Louder!

The boys spend hours playing these things they call 'video' games on the 'big screen'. Shooting. Squealing. Cussing. Throwing things across the room. Wrestling on the plush pile carpet. They haven't even noticed me. This isn't what I'd hoped for.

Lucas rolls out of reach of his brother, crashing into the boxes still lingering in the corner of the room. 'Ouch!' He rubs his smarting shoulder then lands a double punch on the innocent box.

'What's going to happen to all these old books?' Eli asks.

'Dad's taking them to the charity bin on the weekend.' Lucas's uncaring tone makes my heart quake. The children whose laughter once filled these walls delighted in reading these books to each other, almost as much as they loved to play with me. How dare Tom send them to a bin!

Would that be my fate too? I shudder with such force that my box teeters close to the edge. I squeeze my lid shut to hold my pieces together. My cards, my weapons, my suspects. As I slip from my perch, I glimpse a gossamer flash of red, like fine silk flowing beneath me. *Rose?*

It can't be.

I gaze into her twinkling green eyes. The same green eyes as those I remember, all those years ago. My heart swells.

'Ruby, get out!' Lucas shoves her aside. 'I told you, girls aren't allowed in here.'

'Are too!' Her voice is defiant, just like Rose's brashness whenever she stood up to her brother Tom.

'Are not,' chimes in Eli. 'Dad said so!'

Ruby storms over to the corner of the room and picks me up with her determined fingers. A maternal tingle works its way through the walls of my mansion and across my floors. This might not be Rose, but this girl, Ruby, is linked to my Rose through her blood. I can feel it.

'I want to play this game,' she demands. 'And if you don't play it with me, I'm going to tell Dad you've been playing that R-rated war game.' She points to the screen, a triumphant grin spreading across her rosy cheeks.

Lucas and Eli exchange furtive glances. I'd heard Tom explaining Ruby's banishment from the room to the boys with vehemence.

'Okay,' Lucas says, snatching the game from her hands and tossing it back on top of the box. 'But we're not playing that old thing. We can download a video version. Will that keep you quiet?'

Ruby gives him a vigorous nod.

My melancholy sigh echoes around the halls of my otherwise-silent mansion. The children are not going to resurrect me. Not today. *Maybe not ever.*

Ruby wails. 'I want to go first!' My attention is drawn ahead as a blueprint of my mansion is mirrored in front of me. A magnetic force lures me from my box and draws me into this strange new space. I spread across the big screen, gazing back down on the children, stunned. My peripheral vision is wider than I ever imagined.

Then I spy it in the corner. A thickness forms in my passageways, choking me.

The candlestick!

'Okay, Ruby.' Lucas hands her a game controller, pressing a finger to his lips. 'But you have to be quieter. If Dad finds out you're in here, there'll be hell to pay.'

Ruby snatches the controller and attempts to manoeuvre toward the red player on the screen. The alluring Miss Scarlett, who I've always felt the most closely aligned, has undergone a glamorous makeover in this strange realm. I glide up to my favourite character and settle my protective essence around her. Maybe I couldn't keep my beloved Rose close, but Miss Scarlett I can.

An idea begins to crystalise in the circuits of my new consciousness.

Ruby's agitation grows as she jams the lever sideways. 'I want to be Miss Scarlett!'

'Here, give it to me,' Eli says and attempts to move toward the image of the woman in red. After a few minutes of frustration, he hands it back to Ruby. 'Something's wrong with it, Rubes. Looks like nobody can be Miss Scarlett. Why don't you be Mrs Peacock?'

Ruby opens her mouth to protest, but Lucas points to the door and slices a finger across his throat. She pouts, but selects Mrs Peacock, then clicks the button to roll the dice. They deliver a score one short of the number required to reach the library, so I flip them one more time. I guide Mrs Peacock toward the virtual doorway and let Ruby direct her in.

Ruby attempts to make a suggestion for the murder by dragging the rope into the library, but every time she lets go of the button, I haul the weapon back to its holding place. After several attempts, she throws the controller down on the sofa. 'Stupid thing is broken!'

No! I can't let her stop now. I hover over the candlestick weapon on the screen and focus my new-found energy. A spark ignites. The wick flares up and illuminates the room. Ruby's eyes are drawn toward the flickering light on the screen. She picks up the controller and moves the glowing candlestick into the library. This time, I allow it to stay.

Ruby grins and moves Mrs White into the room, but I drag the white-haired woman back. She tries again. I persist. Ruby huffs. She's not giving up. She tries to move the suspects one by one, but I hold them fast. When she lands on the crafty Colonel Mustard, I let him leave and follow her into the library.

'I suggest it was Colonel Mustard in the Library with the candlestick,' Ruby deduces. The game lights up, announcing Ruby as the winner. Her face becomes a kaleidoscope of emotion. Wide grin. Glowing cheeks. Raised eyebrows. Her excitement fades, replaced by confusion in the depths of her green eyes. She didn't win on her own.

'Again!' she shouts.

'Shush!' Lucas tries to calm her. 'Dad will hear you. Eli, you go first this time.'

Ruby's lip drops, but she hands the controller over to her brother.

Eli attempts to choose Colonel Mustard as his player, but I surround the devious military man and don't let him go. He gives up and chooses Reverend Green. Again, I manipulate the dice. I allow his second attempt to move Colonel Mustard, this time to the library as the suspect. But when he tries to drag the wrench into the room, I return it to its holding place. Eli is not as persistent as Ruby. He tries another weapon, the lead pipe, and when it returns, he attempts to move the candlestick. *Just as I intended.*

With all three pieces in the library, he deduces, 'I suggest it was Colonel Mustard in the library with the candlestick.'

The screen lights up, announcing him as the winner.

'That's weird,' Lucas says snatching the controller from his little brother. 'How did you both win on the first round? Let me have a go.'

Eli exchanges a fleeting look with Ruby as the pattern repeats. Colonel Mustard in the library with the candlestick.

'Someone's rigged this game,' Lucas says. 'Let's play something else.'

No! Keep playing. Figure out my message. You must!

Heat rises through my virtual chimneys! I channel it at the lightbulbs in the ceiling above us. One by one they pop. Shatter.

Fizz. Our side of the room turns dark. Ruby shrieks and nuzzles into her brother's shoulder.

Lucas sniffs the electrical burning smell in the air. 'It's okay Ruby. It's just the old wiring.' He doesn't sound convincing.

One bulb remains. I channel my energy. Pitch everything I have toward it so that brilliant white light bursts from the filament and spotlights the heavy brass candlestick below.

'What the ...' Lucas leaps from the sofa and moves toward the bright ring of light.

Eli plucks up the courage to follow, Ruby clinging to his sleeve. 'Wh-what's going on, Lucas?'

'I don't know. It seems to be shining on the ...' He glances back at the lit-up candlestick on the screen. Recognition dawns beneath his furrowed brow. 'The game. It seems to be ...' He shakes his head.

Lucas reaches out toward the candlestick.

'Don't touch it!' Ruby shrieks.

In the etherworld, I find a link to the game's sound effects. A police siren shrieks across the room. Lights flash.

The children turn, stare at the screen like they've been caught in the glare of headlights. I channel my energy into animating the characters on the screen. Control them at my will. I enter Colonel Mustard first and show the children a stark image of him lifting the candlestick above his head. He brings it down with a thunk onto the head of the unwitting Miss Scarlett.

Ruby starts screaming. The boys shout, trying to stop her. The siren blares. The door cracks open and Tom's voice booms across the room. 'What the hell is going on here!'

Ruby runs into her father's arms. He shoots the boys a stern glare before he turns and gapes at the screen. 'What are you letting your sister watch? You've scared the living daylights out of her!'

'It's not us,' Lucas protests. He hands the controller to his father. 'It's the game. It's doing it all by itself. We can't stop it.'

'Don't try to get out of this. I told you not to let Ruby in here!'

Lucas throws his arms up in the air. 'Dad, you've got the controller.'

Tom pushes the 'Off' button to shut down the game, but I don't let him. He stands stock still, eyes glued to the screen, watching the Colonel attack Miss Scarlett in a back and forward continuous loop.

Lucas points to the brightly lit brass candlestick in the corner of the room.

Tom's eyes wander from the screen to the candlestick and back.

Come on Tom! Use the skills of deduction I taught you.

The red headed murder victim. Colonel Mustard — the military man. The murder weapon.

Tom stumbles toward the candlestick.

That's it. Come on Tom.

All these years, I know he blamed himself. For putting me on the highest shelf so Rose couldn't reach me after that final play. For forcing her to climb up for me. After Rose's death, there was talk of sending Tom to join his friend Colin at military boarding school. Louise was getting married and leaving home. Nobody had set foot in the library since.

69

Until now.

Tom's skin turns sallow as he casts his eyes downward. The bright light reveals a dark substance that fills the deep filigree crevasses in the base of the candlestick. *Rose's blood.*

Along the shaft of the candlestick are bloody smears. *Colin's fingerprints.* Everybody had missed the crucial clue.

Until now.

Tom drops to his knees, a tear glistening on his cheek. He tugs his mobile phone from his pocket.

Silence descends on the room as I soften my lights and direct them heavenward. *Rest easy, sweet Rose.*

My final play.

DELETE WORLD

christine betts and kate kelsen

'**H**ow lucky you all are to have me, Stormcrow Silver, your favourite gamer girl, back on your screens again.'

Emily adjusted the webcam, ensuring it captured her trademark silver wig with the pigtails that bounced off her shoulders. Her eyes were enhanced by thick black eyeliner and fake lashes, her regular school uniform replaced by a cute costume one. On her head she wore the high-end headset a fan had sent, but the cat ears were her own addition.

'So, last time I was complaining about this ugly old house my mum made us move into. It's basic and it's freezing. I decided, because I hate the house so much, I'd build myself a new one in everyone's favourite game, *Underground*. One of my fans, Ringwraith—you might have seen his world featured in *Gamer* magazine—has been working on it in his incredible Gorth Empire. And today he's taking us on a virtual tour.

Then later I'm going to test some of the new titles Blasta Games sent me.'

Emily smiled at the camera and fluttered her lashes. The views were still low, but the comments rolled in.

> Test the games. Underground is BORING
> Show us your tits?

A second box appeared on the screen, showing Ringwraith's avatar, a beefy Gorth with a ring through its nose. The comments scrolled down the right side of the screen.

> Ringwraith is beast
> Get it on, you two
> I could build a better world!

Emily giggled.

'Hey, welcome to my channel, Ringwraith, I bet your avatar is way hotter than you are IRL, but you know what? I don't care. I don't even care that you're really a creepy middle-aged man from Finland.'

All she cared about was harvesting some of his eighty thousand followers.

'Ha ha ha,' he said and somehow the artificially deep voice of the Gorth sounded unsure of itself. 'It's so great to be on your channel, Stormcrow. Welcome to your new and improved home.'

The blocky game footage showed a sparsely furnished attic with timber floors and walls.

'This is something of an improvement on my real attic. I've got a very nice portrait, I look hot. Some storage chests. Flame torches on the walls. I'm not hating the vibe. A skylight ... Okay, a bookcase, not sure why. And I guess the floor is nice.'

> That's cool
> I could do better
> Test the games!

'I want to show you around my empire too,' said Ringwraith.

'You know what, I'm going to lead the tour. What's through this door?' Emily guided her avatar down several sets of stairs, deeper into the animated structure. A shaft led to a small room of dark stone blocks. Three bats hung from the ceiling.

'Okay, this isn't terrible, but where's my castle, dude?'

'It took me a while to work out how to get the bats to spawn.'

Emily glared at the screen.

'Big friggin' deal, man. Is this it?'

'You can name the bats,' Ringwraith insisted.

> Naw, bats are so cute
> You're so mean, Stormcrow

'Boring,' Emily whined and rolled her eyes. 'Nothing to see here, people.' She checked her views. Peeps were going to start bailing if she didn't salvage this livestream quickly.

> Aww he really tried

'You could put some Rouge stone here. Maybe some ...' Ringwraith sounded annoyed.

'Hey Ringy, don't get salty with me. Is it that time of the month? Or did some noob promise you a palace and deliver a hole in the ground with a few bats?' Emily shook her silver pigtails at the camera. She pulled her shoulders back so that her white crop top could be seen by the camera. The viewer numbers started to jump. Stormcrow stopped at a doorway. It hissed open. She let out a slow whistle.

'A piston door. Nice work.' She shimmied her shoulders at the screen and smiled cheekily. 'Hey Ringman, what's in here?'

```
                    Nobody says noob anymore
                          This is so boring
```

Emily gasped. The room was filled with gold blocks.

'Is this my gold, dude? Did you fucking steal my gold?' The viewer numbers started to climb. Some probably hoped the thief was about to get a Blackstone Sword to the head and others, no doubt, wanted Stormcrow Silver to finally get what she deserved.

```
               Ringwraith is going to pay for this
                                     Gold's easy
                               Storm's going down!
```

'I told you not to go in there.' Ringwraith laughed as he logged off, booting Emily from the server, and taking her gold with him.

That arsehole
Suck it Storm Cow

'Fucker!' Emily shoved her chair back hard, scraping more paint from the battered wall behind her.

'Emily!' The bedroom door swung open behind her, and her mother appeared in the webcam footage.

'Mum, get out!'

Emily scooted forward on her chair and logged out of her account.

'I've been calling you.'

Her mother held up her old flip phone.

'I was on a livestream!'

'Emily, remember what I said? Only one hour after school. Can you please turn it off and come help with dinner? You are not the only person that lives in this house.'

'I wish I was. I'd burn it down,' she mumbled.

Emily jumped out of her chair, slammed the door, and locked it.

'Honey, I've begged you, not to slam doors,' her mother shouted from the other side.

'I've begged you not to interrupt my livestreams. My fans don't want to see your pathetic face. Stay in the kitchen where you belong.'

'Emily Peters, open this door!'

Emily pictured her mother standing out there, hoping the door would open.

'You know, Em, I wasn't always your *pathetic* mother. Believe it or not, once upon a time Celeste Peters was going to be someone.'

Emily rolled her eyes. 'Oh, you mean your little paintings? Too bad, so sad. I am sure you're *someone* in an alternate reality, *Celeste.*'

At the sound of retreating footsteps, Emily turned to the mirror to check her wig.

'When will I be free of that ridiculous woman?'

She stood on tiptoes and adjusted her crop top on her slim frame. Emily knew what she wanted, and she would be fearless in the pursuit of getting it. She would not work a series of crappy jobs, like her mother. Emily would live in a mansion someday. IRL not on *Underground*. Like Stormcrow, Emily was vicious and ambitious. That was her mantra. She'd get the tattoo one day.

She settled back into her gaming chair and pulled herself towards the desk. Her gold blocks were probably gone, but it didn't matter. The real gold was in her followers and all the freebies she got from fans and companies wanting to cash in on her followers. No fake Gorth was going to take her fans away from her. Plus, he forgot he gave her the server login. Idiot.

She restarted her livestream, logged into her other account, and typed in the server details. Was Ringwraith so arrogant that he didn't think to change the password?

Yep! Emily smiled at the camera.

'I'm back.' She pouted at the camera but didn't share her screen. Followers could only see her cute outfit with the silver pigtails swinging. 'Who knew a big scary Gorth was going to steal everything from poor little old me? I need to be more careful who I trust in this game.'

Her views rose again as she made her way back to the shaft. Ringwraith was offline, no doubt celebrating his victory.

'I wish this game wasn't such a minefield, you know? And we could all just trust each other. Like, there are enough demons and zombie fruit to deal with, without us being awful to each other.'

She clicked the 'Share Screen' button and opened the *Underground* server dashboard.

'Wouldn't it be terrible ... if something bad happened ... to this lovely empire Ringwraith built. Oops!'

She clicked the 'Delete World' button and each of the backups. She grinned and winked at the webcam.

'A quick password change ...' She typed blowmebiatch and logged out.

She leaned back into her seat and laughed. 'And that, ladies and germs, is what happens when you fuck with Stormcrow Silver.'

Her viewer numbers ticked up and up, and the stream of comments on the side of the screen urged her on.

> Destroy Him
> Waste that Gorth
> Make him pay!

'Oh, and side note, his real name is Ilevi Tapio and he lives in this crummy little village called Kyöstilä. Consider yourself outed, Ringkisser.'

Without missing a beat, Emily changed screens on her PC and opened a link from Blasta Games.

> Holy shit. did she just dox that guy?
> Third one this month

Hey that's not cool
Unfollow!

'Okay, fuckers, now I'm going to test this new game. There's a reason why companies like Blasta and NewCon send me gear to test, and that is because I'm cute.' She pouted at the camera and shimmied her shoulders, 'But I'm also psycho.'

Got that right
You're hot, Stormy

She pressed the 'Start' button and leaned back in the chair.

'So ... I'm standing in a corridor with a whole bunch of doors coming off it. I can't wait to see what they think is going to scare me.'

One of the doors creaked and a huge teddy bear appeared. It had blood dripping from its tusks, and the skull was exposed on one side of its head.

Naw zombie teddy bear

'OMG yawn,' Emily said. 'Ah, buh-bye.' She pressed an oversized button on her desk, and it made a fart sound.

'I'll give that a half a star out of ten. A big nope from me. Next!'

She clicked on the next link. 'Okay guys, this game is called *Alternate Reality High School*. The name is probably way cooler in Japanese.'

A series of screens popped up, revealing the corridors of a high school and a line of stylised anime characters in customary skimpy school uniforms filed into a classroom. Emily hooted.

'This is more like it,' she said.

'Hi Stormcrow,' said one of the characters.

'Hi, baby,' Emily crooned. 'Are you an NPC?'

The character nodded coyly. Emily laughed.

'Okay, this game is cool. Guys, it's been pre-programmed with my deets.'

Can you call me, baby?

'I'm Immy. May I call you Stormy?' The character batted her long eyelashes.

'Immy, you can call me anything you like, but get on with the game.'

Immy laughed. It sounded like a tinkling bell at first then got deeper.

'In this game ... game ... game ...' The screen froze, capturing Immy mid-sentence.

That's so basic

'Must be a glitch, guys. This one can go in the pile of steaming dog shit. I think Blasta is either going down the toilet or they're just trying to see how low I can rate their games.'

The lights in the attic room dimmed and came up again. Emily leaned forward to switch the game off.

'Don't you dare touch that button, or we'll both die.' Immy's voice came out as a harsh whisper. The screen moved again, and the cute character looked like she'd been beaten up. Her lip was bleeding and swollen and her dress was torn.

<pre>
              Ha, you're going to die
</pre>

'Help me,' Immy said. Tears welled in her big eyes.

Emily laughed.

'Oh, if you really knew my deets you'd know I don't give a damn about anyone but Stormcrow Silver, baby.'

<pre>
                  Press the button!!
              Die ...hahahahahaaaaaaaa
</pre>

Immy's face changed suddenly. She glared at the screen.

'Oh, is that right?' Immy straightened slowly, clicking her neck and jaw. She reached towards the screen. 'Stormcrow Silver, or should I say, Emily Peters, you have been rated at ...' The game glitched again.

<pre>
          Hahaha doxer got doxed
          Emily Peters goes to my school
</pre>

Immy threw her head back and laughed. 'Z ... z ... z ... zero stars. Delete World.'

<pre>
                  Goodbye Emily
                  Goodbye Emily
                  Goodbye Emily
</pre>

The attic room was always cold, but Emily's breath made a cloud as she breathed out.

'What the f …'

The monitors went blank, and the inky blackness billowed out, engulfed the room and crept under the door, deleting everything in its path.

'I've been instructed to meet the market,' the real estate agent said. 'It's not about the money. The owner wants to sell to someone who will love the place. Someone who will make it a home.'

The woman's chatty but professional voice travelled up the front steps. She breezed through the foyer, ablaze in a red skirt suit, her shiny black hair swishing with every stilettoed step. A family of five poured in behind her.

'Feel free to have a look around,' the agent said over the excited chatter of children. 'The appliances have been updated. The heat is all electric, but there are a few functional fireplaces throughout the house.'

'How many bedrooms are there?' asked one of the kids, a teenage girl, her eyes as wide as her smile.

'There are five,' the agent said.

'You can all have your own room,' called one of the parents from the living room.

A woman walked into the vast kitchen, her denim jeans and tank top covered in paint splats.

'Hello,' the agent said, a quizzical look on her face.

'Hi, sorry. I'm the owner. We spoke on the phone. Just doing some last-minute packing before the removalists arrive.'

She paused, listening to the excitement of the mother and daughter echoing from another room in the house.

'This was my parents' retirement dream. I'm sure in an alternate reality I had a husband and kids but hey, not in this one.' She shrugged and laughed. 'I'd really love to see the house go to someone who can appreciate such a beautiful old place.'

'Oh, wow ...' the agent said. 'Um ... Are you Celeste Peters, the artist?'

'Yes.' Celeste blushed. 'It's been nice having the extra space for a studio while I've been here, but I need to base myself in New York.'

She reached into her pocket and pulled out a small set of keys.

'Before I forget, here are the keys to the attic. I've always thought it would be a perfect bedroom for a teenage girl.'

NIHILISTIC WHISPERS

lr johnson

The high-altitude antigrav Mekenji city, Daku, bustled with excitement.

Far below lay the most sacred site of the Fey—the Graveyard of the Gods. A wild place where massive creatures, once only magic and legend, returned to die. Today it was an arena.

Citizens of the sky city gathered above the flight deck, at the railings of the upper disc. Floating screens projected aircraft and pilots for screaming fans.

Ceres, standing in the shadows of an alcove, stifled a coughing fit. Blood stained her inhaler as she dragged foul medicine deep into her burning lungs.

Her future, and all her hopes hinged on the vehicle below.

It was an ancient fixed-wing survey VTOL that looked more like a housefly with attitude than the other sleek jets. It was a deathtrap, but her only chance to live.

At least if she didn't win, she would rest among old gods instead of a hospital bed.

She resettled her toolbelt. She was the only person who was going to save her. Everyone was out for themselves. The game was probably even rigged, but she'd studied the Faerun every year, and it was now or never.

The Faerun wasn't a race. The wealthiest citizens supplied aircraft to pilots to capture a drone, and they bet on the outcome. They didn't always supply good ships, especially if you were an immigrant like Ceres, nor did they bet on their own craft—that was no fun.

The other pilots, and the fan-favourite prince of the privileged, Kiece Ferrod, blew kisses to the crowd.

Ceres headed through the cacophony to her aircraft. She slid into the pilot seat and donned her helmet, oxygen mask, and harness.

The announcer onscreen continued, 'Today's players must pursue and retrieve a drone black box, and return under their own power. If their craft goes down they can use their rescue beacon and accept disqualification, or they have forty-eight hours to return under their own power before the city departs. After that, those who have not made it back are assumed deceased.'

'Gigafauna scan clear!' speakers barked. 'Ready pilots.'

Deafening engines roared to life.

A light-ringed window opened in the atmospheric shield.

The speakers screamed, 'Launch!'

Ceres' jet ripped off the platform and fell into the abyss. Emerald islands on Sapphire Ocean waited below. Chunks of mountains floated like balloons. Her quarry, the drone, streaked between them towards the largest island, one dotted with grey ruins.

G-forces crushed Ceres into her seat.

A green jet pulled ahead of the cluster of descending aircraft.

'Too fast,' Ceres whispered. The jet spiralled and the cockpit auto-ejected its unconscious pilot.

She tore past into the obstacle course of floating islands.

A red plane exploded against the base of an island on Ceres's left. A slick blue jet ahead clipped the rib of a leviathan skeleton protruding from another. Ceres careered sideways and barely missed the flaming wreck as someone behind her smashed into it. She broke free of the floating islands, and swore. There was no one behind her that wasn't falling debris. She was last.

Far ahead, the drone dropped into a canyon that cut through the ruins of a city.

She couldn't catch up with the modern, streamlined jets already in the canyon behind it.

The canyon curved back on itself in a huge C, and terminated in a deadly narrow slit in the cliffs capped with a natural bridge that overlooked a swamp.

'Wait ... I know this canyon!' She laughed. 'I know where they always send the drone!'

She roared across the jungle towards the opposite end of the C. At maximum speed, the aircraft shook and alarms shrieked. The other jets still traversed the longer route inside the canyon.

She gained ground.

She slipped over the cliff edge and angled towards the opening between canyon and swamp.

She and the drone moved perpendicular to one another, along cliff and canyon.

Electricity itched in her bones. The drone glinted. Her breath stopped. The drone popped through the gap.

Headed right toward her.

She hit the grapple launch button.

Nothing.

She smashed it, over and over. Still nothing.

It was jammed.

She dropped the rear cargo door instead, and swerved ready for capture.

A massive toothy maw exploded from the greenery below. It crashed into her craft, and her harness ripped her sideways. As she spiralled towards the forest, she caught glimpses of other planes coming through the cliff opening to be swatted out of the sky by the disturbed golden dragon.

Branches smashed her windscreen and the jungle swallowed her.

Ceres jerked awake.

She exploded into wracking coughs. She struggled from the foliage jammed cockpit. Pieces of her jet littered the shredded jungle floor, and one wing was missing.

She searched her pockets for her inhaler. More nothing. Surrounded by eucalypt leaves torn down by her aircraft she crushed them in her hands and inhaled. Her lungs relaxed, and she caught her breath.

Screams detonated her nerves.

She charged along the crash trail to the jungle's edge. The swampland sprawled below. Rescue craft buzzed between burning wrecks. An old, vine-covered survey-plane punctuated the swamp-shore, grapple-claw pointed skyward. The silver drone glinted, wedged in the fork of a tree just beyond the water's edge. Debris from aircraft littered the landscape.

Ceres skidded down the hill and burst through the boulders at the bottom.

The dragon reared up from the shallows, a silver jet held in its claws like a fish. One talon speared the screaming pilot in his cockpit.

Ceres punched her rescue beacon. Again. No beep, it was dead.

'Help me!' the pilot begged, but her blood turned to lead.

The dragon dropped the jet with a splash, and came for her. Leaden blood lit on fire.

She snatched up a wing-strut as a makeshift javelin and threw with all her might. It barely clipped the dragon's cheek. Useless, she thought, until it pawed its ruined eye-socket. Wings snapped out and it launched into the air.

She waded to the pilot, Kiece Ferrod, and dragged him from his sinking craft onto the shore.

'Kiece! Your beacon!'

'Destroyed.' He passed out.

'At least we're not disqualified,' she muttered as she tried to stem his bleeding.

The dragon wheeled overhead, and rescue craft fled.

She couldn't linger here. She could either save Kiece, or the drone.

'Dammit.'

She used a pilot poncho to wrap and compress his leg and reduce a blood trail.

Dragging him up the hill brought on another coughing fit, but she persisted.

Reaching her plane, she used an expired med-kit to stitch up his wounds and made a fire. Then she burned everything bloody so the scent wouldn't draw predators.

When he slept, she cried.

Ceres waded through fog and fetid black swamp water to climb the pale tree with the metal ball caught in its fork.

The glittering god hunted elsewhere beyond the fog. The impatient city floated above. The rescue ships had flown home to roost.

She pried open the drone, withdrew the black box, and tucked it into her shirt.

Eyes peeled for the dragon, she returned to shore.

She'd searched the other jets crash debris, and found a second oxygen tank, and a suitable wing. She dragged it behind herself with vines along the channel her jet had carved through the jungle floor.

An avian orchestra flitted high overhead in massive, vine-choked trees. Gargantuan monstera, ferns, bromeliads, and other exotic flora filled the jungle, a riot of colours upon a million shades of emerald.

Large scaly creatures swung through the trees. Shadows whispered nihilistic nothings. Deep-voiced entities howled and were answered.

Ceres was an ant dragging a crumb.

She left the wing by her jet and stashed the black box in the cockpit.

Kiece lurched awake. 'WHAT the hellisgoinon?' he slurred.

'We've had a bit of a day,' Ceres squatted and gathered fresh eucalypt into a makeshift pouch. 'The gigafauna scan missed a dragon against the cliff. It knocked everyone out of the sky. No working beacons for us, and the rescue ships have left. All that's left is the grace period to get ourselves back. Maybe forty-two hours left.'

He stared. 'So what are we gonna do?'

'Get this baby airborne.' She slapped the fuselage.

'We can't fix that piece of crap!'

She shrugged. 'It's that or death. No-one else is going to save us.'

He sputtered, 'We have to get somewhere they can see us!'

'No one's looking, Kiece.'

'Maybe not for an immigrant girl, but my family—'

'Knew the risks and rules!' Ceres snapped. She closed her eyes and took a deep breath. 'It's not going to happen, and we only have a certain amount of time. I'm scavenging parts, and you can either help or come up with a better idea.'

She returned to find his hollow gaze on the fire, and his hands empty.

'Kiece, have you seen anything solid metal about a foot long, as thick as your wrist?'

'I'm a pilot. I don't know parts.'

'Well, the actual part is wrecked, but if I start with a generally similar shape I could make a replacement.'

His dull eyes turned towards her. 'You're kidding me.'

'And here's the punch line.' She handed him a muddy mass of gears. 'Dirty joke, I know. Clean it up please?'

'Do I look like a gear grunt?'

'You look like a brat, but maybe that's just your face.' She sat before the fire and balanced her metal helmet upside-down on stones over it.

'What's that?' Kiece asked.

'Water.'

'I hope that's not swamp water.'

'It's boiling,' she defended.

'Oh my god.' He feigned retching. 'You plebians seriously need some standards.' He dropped the gears and wiped his hand on his shirt.

'Kiece, cut the classist crap!'

'Touchy about being a grease-neck?'

Ceres' glare made him swallow. In low tones she said, 'This grease-neck saved your life. Everyone deserves more respect than you ingrates on the upper disc give us! Our skills keep you in your heaven above the clouds, while we have to take two turbo lifts and a tram to see the sun!'

'It's not that bad, you're paid well!'

Ceres barked a sarcastic laugh. 'Yeah, that's why I'm risking my life in the Faerun. 'Cause I don't need the money.'

He raised a quizzical brow. 'I'm not risking my life.'

'You're not given death-traps to fly.'

He opened his mouth to speak, but a glance at her ancient plane silenced him.

He picked up the muddy scrap she had handed him and started cleaning.

Night swallowed the jungle before it conquered the sky.

Nocturnal howls and trills defied the flickering brilliance of Ceres' welding.

From his mossy pillow, Kiece groaned. 'Woman, get some sleep!'

'Too much work to do.' She applied a tester to wires. Green light. The repurposed parts worked.

'You already look worked to death.'

She snorted. She was glad her goggles hid her eyes. 'Literally. My parents were killed by an old god on a scavenging job. Mekenji cities are safe from them, so I built a plane and immigrated. But workplace safety for immigrants doesn't exist. I'm terminal and nobody cares.' She shrugged. 'Can't trust Mekenji.'

'You can trust me.'

'Hmph.'

Weld-spark lit up the jungle again.

The dappled afternoon light spilled across the wealth of weld scars. With fuselage panels missing between pilot seats and wings, it looked more like a skeletal mantis in flight than a housefly.

'What a piece of grease-neckian trash!' Kiece teased with a grin.

From her seat on a log Ceres offered an exhausted smile. He'd been particularly attentive to her, despite the limitations of his lacerations.

She countered, 'This is purely Mekenji techniques I'll have you know.'

He snorted 'Mekenji only make crap in their bowels.'

'Plenty comes out of your mouth.'

He burst into laughter. 'I'm having it seen to, I promise.'

'Relax.' She chuckled. 'I've been taking apart and reassembling these ships since I was seven.'

He frowned. 'I took up skeet shooting at seven.'

'Rich kid.' She smiled. 'One last check, then we're out of here my friend!'

Ceres clambered up to the right wing and flipped open the panel on the jet. She applied the tester to a block that spewed wires in all directions and her heart stopped.

Red light. The part didn't work.

She pulled parts out, checked them, and returned them. Red.

Her heart kicked around in her chest. 'No, no, no ...'

In the cockpit, she started up the jets, and the hum of one engine filled the jungle.

One.

Ceres climbed back to the dead jet and checked everything. Green, green, green.

Control box. Red.

Heat poured through her veins.

'What's wrong?'

'Control box is dead. I screwed up somewhere.'

'Can't you fix it?'

Her blood roiled in her ears. In a tight voice, she said, 'I'm an engineer, not a magician.'

Her body was filled with lava, her muscles sang with rage. She roared and hurled the control box into the trees. She leaped off the wing, grabbed a thick branch, and smashed it to kindling in an eruption of utter uncapped fury. Wildlife scattered from the canopy above, and the jungle fell silent.

Her screams still echoed as she fell to her knees, overcome with wracking, rattling coughs. Blood spattered the forest floor as the world went black.

The fragrance of crushed eucalypt surrounded her when she came to. Her throat was raw, and her mouth was a copper mine, but she breathed easily. Kiece added more eucalypt to that arrayed around her head and sat back.

Her lip trembled. 'I killed us.'

Instantly he murmured, 'No you haven't.'

'Without a control block, the jet won't initialise.'

'Can't you grease-neck it?'

'A whole one from another aircraft, yeah, but not out of scraps.'

He helped her sip water. 'The wreck by the swamp was a similar model, wasn't it?'

She swilled and spat. 'Yeah, but the dragon has chosen the shore for his grave.'

It turned out she had done the same.

Like the dragon, she wanted just one last flight in the pre-dawn sun.

Light kindled in her eyes. 'The dragon goes hunting.'

Sunrise barely warmed the empty fog shrouded swamp-shore.

Ceres slipped noiselessly into the fuselage of the old survey plane. By the door, next to a pile of bones, was an old rifle, as vintage as the plane, but clean, with no rust, and two bullets. She slung it over her shoulder and climbed up to the wing. She pried open the panel and tested the control block. Green. She pocketed it and sighed in relief.

Her chest caught on the sigh, spasmed, and she doubled over in a ribcage rattling cough.

Silhouetted by the dawn light, a serpentine, antlered shadow of death glinted gold amidst the fog.

The dragon lunged, and she leaped into the cockpit. Massive teeth grabbed the wing and tore the plane from the ground. Ceres fell against the controls and saw a familiar button.

'You're the one who came here to die, not me!' she screamed, and smashed the button.

With a rattle of chain the grapple-hook launched directly into the dragon's neck, and bit deep. The dragon roared and dropped the plane. It nosedived and Ceres leaped out of the door as it hit the mud. She pelted across the swamp-shore. Her heart kicked around in her ribcage.

The dragon twisted and clawed at the ball and chain the plane had become.

Ceres tore up the slope and into the jungle.

'Kiece get in the ship!' she shouted. 'It's coming!'

'What?' Kiece stuck his head out a missing panel. 'Where did you get that gun?'

'Just get in!' She swung herself up onto the wing. She was drowning in itchy, wet lungs.

Install, test. Green.

The dragon surged into the jungle trailing grapple-claw and broken chain.

She dropped into the cockpit. Kiece slung an oily bag around her neck and soothing eucalypt washed over her. Both jets roared to life.

The treetops shrank to broccoli.

Kiece secured her oxygen mask, and she felt the cool gas against her mouth, and into her lungs.

The golden dragon launched into flight after them, monstrous jaws wide.

'Tilt!' Kiece shouted as its open mouth loomed. He grabbed the gun, swivelled his chair, and kicked his oxygen tank through the missing panel. The tank plummeted towards the up-rushing monster. Their aircraft reflected in its saliva.

The rifle kicked and the gas tank exploded in the monster's mouth. Streaming smoke, it fell away.

They passed the snowy mountaintop. Kiece's skin tinted purple from hypoxia.

Ceres grabbed her mask to share it, but Kiece pushed it back onto her face.

'It's about time someone saved you, Ceres. 'He panted.

The lack of pressurisation grew and made Ceres's insides scream in pain. The million knives of the gale-force winds shredded her, froze her fingers, and frosted her goggles. Kiece lolled unconscious against his harness.

A shadow loomed. She tilted towards a ring of bright lights.

The landing hook dragged them inside, and the atmospheric shield snapped into place.

Warm air cocooned them.

She pulled the drone box from its hiding place, fumbled, and dropped it.

Kiece's eyes fluttered open and met hers.

A raucous crowd rushed onto the platform towards them and swamped the plane.

'We saw you ascending!'

'That was incredible!'

'He's got the drone box!'

They swept Kiece, and the box, out of the aircraft and into the waiting arms of medics and fans.

Ceres fell out of the cockpit to her knees. Just like that, the box had been taken from her. After all she'd done ... Her word against his would hold no weight, and she didn't have the strength to fight anymore.

Kiece's voice cut through the crowd. 'Wait!' he shouted, 'surely you aren't all assuming this is my work?'

Mutters spread.

'I don't build, I fly,' he said as he found Ceres' gaze.

Kiece tipped his head in salute. 'Ceres does both. She's your winner. Get her to the hospital.' He smiled. 'Let's fix the future.'

ANGEL WINGS ARE PRECIOUS THINGS

selena jane

'I can see the end, we are nearly there,' Star said, excitement tingling through her celestial being.

Celine nodded. 'This day will bring you such joy, I promise.'

Star and Celine floated inches above the floor, their feathers touching as they jostled down the narrow hallway. A golden hue danced off the wings of the angel in front of them, her feathers sparkled like fresh snow.

Star's normally angelic face frowned. 'My wings are so ugly and horribly heavy.'

'Standard issue Lower Order. If you win, you can choose new wings, or enhance your old ones, but that's not likely for a first timer,' Celine said.

'Is it true, Higher Order wings feel light like nothing?'

Celine nodded.

Star wasn't sure if she wanted them to feel like nothing, but she would be grateful to not feel the weight of them. Her wings were not brilliantly white like Anastasia's more of an off beige, and her feathers were not fluffy and plump like Eve's, Star's were thinner and wirier, and they didn't smell of fresh cream like Neo's, more like burnt milk. She hugged her herself, soon she would have the most glorious wings.

'This game is about so much more than just wings and winning Star.'

To Star, the game seemed simple, to gain as many points as possible towards ascension by performing good deeds on earth. The twelve-hour race consisted of teams of four angels who played together. Two angels in heaven controlling the movements of the two angels playing down on earth. Star and Celine both looked forward to their role of earth player. Star had every intention of earning as many points as possible. Earlier they'd met their two playing partners to discuss strategy. They were Middle Order angels; Star had listened intently while admiring their magnificent wings made of the finest down sprinkled with crystals.

When they reached the end of the white corridor, Celine guided Star through the archway, following the other angels into a circular dome-like room.

'Stand with your back to the wall until it is your turn,' Celine instructed.

Star watched the Guardians as they circled the room in their long, white-hooded robes, whispering blessings over each angel, and in turn releasing them from their wings. Today she would be free of her wings for the first time and walk amongst humans as an earth angel.

The Guardian stood before her, his blessing sounding like a choir of bells.

A messenger
A Guardian
A celestial being
He gave you wings so you could fly
Do not see them as a tie
Today you drop them for the game
Humans will benefit and gain
What beauty the world brings
Angel wings are precious things

Star's wings shook, detached from her body, and flew onto the hook behind her, hanging limply under her name inscribed on a gold plaque. With the weight lifted, she slumped forward, and Celine put out her arm to steady her. The Guardian enclosed a golden watch band around her wrist, the face read 0000. Star looked around at her competitors and felt the nervous energy of the collective. The floor fell away in the centre of the room, and they moved as one towards it. A trumpet sounded the start, Celine took Star's hand, and they jumped into the void.

Star's first sensation was the wetness on her back from the dew on the grass. She became aware of her earthly body, denser, fuller. Looking to the sky, she lifted her arm into the air. Studying the length of it, she circled her fingers through the breeze until the smell hit her.

'I expected a city, why did they send us here? There's nothing but countryside, and cow dung in this field?' Star groaned.

'Our playing partners rolled the dice and decided we must go this way, it is not for us to choose,' Celine said, clasping Star's arm and pulling her to her feet.

Star looked down the length of her body to her white t-shirt, her long legs clad in blue jeans, and her feet covered by black leather boots. Celine wore similar clothing.

'Did they create this look for us?' Star asked.

'It's part of the game, they've drawn a bonus card so we have good walking shoes this time. Start your watch.'

Celine had played the game numerous times and had come so close to earning her ascension. Star was fortunate to be paired with someone as experienced as Celine.

'Let's get up to that road.' Celine nodded past the paddock.

Worried they were losing valuable time, Star dragged her earthly body forward, kicking the brown dirt at her feet. Colours of red, white, and blue fluttered into Star's vision. A small boy waved a union jack flag as he leant against a stationary car with his mother.

'Thank the lord,' the woman said, throwing her hands in the air. 'Do you know how to change a flat tyre? I'll be fired if I'm late for work again.'

'Yes, we can help you,' Celine said.

Sensing the angels, Malach and Micah behind her, Star groaned. The woman assumed the four angels were together and addressed the two male angels, not Celine and Star. The brothers' golden hair glowed as they crouched to change the woman's tyre. Star bit her lip and resisted the urge to kick them in their backs for stealing their points. Knowing her thoughts Celine shook her head. When they finished, the woman offered them all a ride into the village. Squished between Malach and Micah, Star scowled and devised ways to beat them.

Exiting on the corner Star slammed the car door on the angel brothers who stayed with the woman after she'd promised them further work.

Running down the main street, Star and Celine came across a crowd of people standing in front of an old school building. Smoke billowed from its windows as the fire truck pumped water onto its roof.

A firefighter held back a man who cried out, 'Please let me go. There are children still inside.'

In the chaos Celine and Star slipped past the firefighters and ran into the building. Working as a team they moved from classroom to classroom taking the children's soft pudgy, sticky hands in theirs and carried the younger ones out onto the street. Another team of angels stood outside the burning building, arms folded across their chests, frowns on their now human faces.

Celine spotted them. 'We will have scored highly for this. Don't worry we will soon lose them; we only have a few hours per section. Let's see how many humans we can help before they roll again.'

They crossed the road to a teahouse where the manager was overwhelmed with customers attracted by the fire and commotion.

'Let us help. We can take orders while you focus on the kitchen,' Celine offered.

They waited tables through the rush, and then busied themselves carrying boxes for a young couple who were moving house. They carried shopping bags for an elderly woman and reunited a lost child with his mother. They even helped a man catch his Great Dane who galloped through the village untethered.

Star was still seething about losing points to Malach and Micah, who beat them to the village's retirement home when her watch beeped and dirty water splashed over her boots from a yellow New York taxi, horn blaring. Star's eyes darted from side to side, overwhelmed with the sound of cars, toxic smells, and tall, grey buildings.

Celine smiled. 'They must have rolled a six, plenty of trouble to be found in a big city. We could start by finding a soup kitchen so we can volunteer.'

'How do we find one?'

'I sense a church,' Celine said, pointing down the long grey corridor of the street.

Celine pulled Star towards the setting sun, and they ran. An old red brick church anchored the corner of the street. Star gazed at the stained-glass windows depicting scenes from the Bible. *So, this is how they worship.* Inside a priest knelt at the altar praying. He looked up as they entered.

'Sorry to disturb you Father, we are looking to help out at the nearest soup kitchen,' Celine said.

'Over on 9th Street at Trinity, run by the Lutherans, God bless them,' he said.

They bowed their heads. 'Thank you, Father.' And backed out of the church, leaving him to his prayers.

Star's legs moved faster than she imagined, and a few blocks later they arrived breathless and ready to assist. They were ushered towards huge pots of casserole and instructed to fill the bowls half full and keep the queue moving. Star met humans with stories that made her back tingle where her wings usually hung. A woman pleaded for extra food for a family who were sick and living in the park. Laden with bags of food Star and Celine accompanied her to the park discovering several families living in cardboard boxes. They distributed the food and spooned casserole into the mouths of the sick. Star heard a cry and found a swaddled infant amongst the boxes; he had been abandoned like an unwanted puppy. The child's ragged cough reverberated through Star's slim frame as she held him. They saw Malach and Micah run into the park, their beady eyes scanning the area.

'Quick put him under your shirt,' Celine said, taking Star by the hand and pulling her into the hedge.

The brothers ran past as Star pushed through the hedge on the other side. 'This way, I saw a sign for the hospital.'

Star had never seen so many humans in one place. A nurse took the baby from Star and hurried him away. A group of humans dressed as clowns skittered passed.

'What are you doing?' Star asked.

'We entertain the sick children in the cancer ward.'

'Can we join you?'

'Of course,' the woman said, handing her a couple of red noses and green wigs.

They followed the group of clowns into the lift where they received their instructions. Star studied the children's small pale faces and bald heads as they visited their bedsides. She copied the actions of the visiting clowns and was rewarded with giggles and shy smiles for her efforts.

One child took her hand and a feeling of queasiness passed through her human form.

'Are you an angel?'

Star put her finger to her lips. 'Yes,' she whispered, wishing she could show this child her wings, even though they were not magnificent.

'My body hurts.'

Star took the child into her arms and held her, they both closed their eyes, their bodies relaxing into one another.

'I'm going to die soon.'

Star kissed her forehead. 'Do not be afraid, your angel will come and guide you when it's your time.'

Star and Celine's watches beeped.

Struggling for breath, Star's mouth filled with water as another wave crashed over them. Celine pushed Star's chin to the sky. 'Relax with the current, let it carry you,' she said, encircling Star's waist.

How fragile earthly bodies are, Star thought, attempting to relax her breathing. The ocean carried them horizontally along the shoreline where the rip ended, and they were able to exit the water. Star lay on the hot sand, spluttering, absorbing the heat into her cold body.

A shadow fell over them. 'You ladies okay? Got caught in a rip did ya? Crazy swimming in your jeans.'

Celine answered for them, 'Where are we?'

'Rainbow Beach love.'

Star said, 'Where's that?'

'Taken a knock to the noggin young lady?' He tapped the side of his head. 'Gympie Region, Queensland. You're not from these parts love.'

Star looked at the long stretch of beach with its multicoloured dunes. 'No, we're visitors. Could you please tell me where the nearest town is?'

He chuckled and pointed. 'Up that ramp if you can call it that.'

'Thanks for your help,' she said.

'A small town *again*,' Star complained.

Celine shrugged. 'A bad roll of the dice I'd say. But don't worry.'

But Star could tell she was worried. She kicked at the sand. They had been doing so well until now. What would they find here with only a few happy tourists roaming the streets?

The town consisted of one street, a few shops, and a café. Star watched as the large café umbrellas were scooped up by the wind and blown across the road. She ran to help the owner following him into the café.

Star noticed four charity tins lying on the counter labelled Bushfire Appeal.

'We could take these and get them filled.'

'Sure, go for it,' he said, handing her four tins.

As she exited the café, Malach appeared at her side and tried to wrestle the tins from Star's arms. Celine rushed over and twisted his arm behind his back.

'Read the rules, no direct interference,' Celine hissed.

Micah nodded and steered his brother into the café.

Celine and Star positioned themselves at the intersection of a main road. Car after car rolled down their windows and donated coins into the ready-made slot. Their tins were soon full and heavy, and it was getting dark. The town's fire warden pulled over offering to give them a lift back into town. They sat on the bench seat next to him as he drove. Star stared at the burns on his face, neck, and hands. Searing heat flashed through Star's body.

He pulled up his sleeve and showed her more of the knotted scar tissue. 'Bushfire got me,' he said as he received an emergency call out to a home. Ambulance and police crews were also en route. He apologised, there would be no time to drop them back. The warden rushed into the house, the first aid kit swinging by his side, with Star and Celine on his heels. A woman sat slumped in a wheelchair both wrists cut, Malach and Micah already attending to her wounds and whispering comforting words. Star saw the brothers as if for the first time, their kindness, their compassion, and let go of her ambition. She squeezed the woman's hand; her fingers were gnarled, and her spine twisted like the roots of an oak tree. The woman's shame settled into Star's heart.

'You are beautiful, your family, they love you,' Star whispered.

The brothers nodded in unison.

Star and Celine wandered outside and gazed up at the Southern Cross. Star checked her golden watch. They had one minute left. Star took Celine's hand in hers and smiled. Her watch beeped and her clothes fell away, her body became lighter, and she was sucked back through the void.

They were among some of the last angels to return. Star arrived back at her name plaque and stared in horror at the empty hook below her name. Where were her wings? She couldn't complete the game without them. She looked around for Celine, but she had hurried off down the hallway, promising to save Star a place at the front of the stadium where the winners would be announced.

The Guardians made their rounds, whispering their blessings, and reuniting wings with their owners. When a Guardian came to her, he noted her empty hook and gestured for her to move to the next hook along. She knew it was wrong but moved in front of the ivory feathers, rimmed, and dusted in gold. The Guardian whispered the words, and the wings flew off the hook and attached to Star's back.

Star rejoiced in their weightlessness as she ran down the hallway towards the stadium, but they didn't fit quite right and wobbled and slid from side to side. Celine made no comment on her new wings as Star sat proudly down beside her. These new tools of flight were so light, Star turned back several times to check they were still attached. She looked around, hoping people would notice her new wings. *Who had made the mix up and who was burdened with her old, heavy, smelly ones?* She wondered. She inhaled deeply; they smelt like fresh straw.

Celine shook her arm. They'd won! She grabbed Star's hand and pulled her onto the stage. Star's wings sprinkled a trail of gold dust on the ground where she stepped.

As Star stood on stage in front of all the other angels, she looked at the scoreboard and remembered the children's sticky, pudgy hands; not sleek and slender. She remembered the dirty and pocked-marked faces of the poor, not clean and sparkling; the sick children with bald heads, not crowned with long golden locks; the fire warden's scarred body, not healed; and the blood that flowed from a woman's broken body.

The Guardians placed a bag of enhancements around their necks containing jewels, beads, gold dust, and sequins. Star felt the thin bones of the imposter wings digging into her back. Standing on the stage, Star did not feel like herself. She felt self-conscious, off balance, and lost.

An angel of the Highest Order beckoned Star towards his golden throne.

'What is causing your distress? You are a winner, are you not?'

She nodded.

'So?'

'I have lost my wings.'

He chuckled. 'What are those behind you?'

'These are not my wings,' she whispered.

'But are they not beautiful?'

She nodded. 'They are very beautiful, but they are not mine.'

'What is wrong with them?'

'Nothing. They don't feel right. My wings were a part of me, but I did not accept them before.'

'And now you do.'

She lowered her eyes.

He reached behind his throne of gold and handed Star her old wings.

Star embraced them, burying her face in the wiry beige feathers inhaling their burnt milk scent.

She sighed deeply. 'My angel wings are precious things.'

THE DOLPHIN - NEVER *TILT-ING*

poetry and prose

frank prem

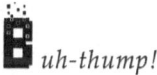 *uh-thump!*

it is a
visceral sound

a *feeling*
that can touch

like the punch
you can imagine
of a bullet
leaving the barrel
of its pistol

buh-thump!

sudden
and forceful
but
contained
within the confines
of an electronic coffin

buh-thump!

Claustrophobia is a small town a long way north-east of Melbourne. A long way north-east of anywhere.

It is a slow thing. A slow place. Any movement faster than an old man's heartbeat is a hard look. A deep frown and disapproving shake of a head.

It could be simple dismay, or outright condemnation. No one knows. No one on the receiving end, at least.

The forest on the outskirts of the town—within walking distance—and the sense of companionship that comes from being out with the dog are the only air around that can be breathed, in an inhalation that has to take place in solitude.

twenty cents
will buy three games

there is always
someone waiting

twenty cents
on the machine
riding the glass

a shadow
above the dancing lights

vibrating
with the music

The darkness of night is a freedom to think in matching shades. Dark for dark. Tedious repetition of the lesser thoughts—useless and pointless, futureless and hopeless, joyless and just ... less. Less and less.

Nobody ever escaped this town. Nobody ever will. It will suck and suck—a vampire —until all the life is gone.

It is a town of husks.

From the darkness, a well-flung stone can take out a streetlight. There should be no pretence that true light might shine here.

buh-thump!
buh-thump!

glorious sound
but first . . .

machine reset

    press the buttons
    test the flippers

    tup

    tup

    and
    test the flippers

    tup-tup-tup-tup-tup-tup

    tup

    you have to test
    the flippers

Nineteen Seventy-One is age fifteen. Is age child, or *still-a-baby*. Is age not-grown-up, not-in-control, and not-to-be-trusted.

Nineteen Seventy-One is a cigarette puffed secretly, without knowing that the stink will linger, or that beneath a mattress is not the most clever place of concealment.

It is feeling the stirrings of manhood with each drag sucked down deep into willing lungs. The secret fear-pleasure of inspecting the knuckles of the fingers of the right hand—just in case there is yellow nicotine showing signs.

The comradeship of rebels, standing in a huddle of smoke, inhaling as though the bliss might be sexual.

Perhaps, it is.

listen
while the machine
spits a steel ball—
the first
of your five—
into the channel

push and pull
the handle—
get a feeling
for the springiness—
before you fire
your ball

hard
to bounce
back and forth
above the highest bumpers

let it choose
its own channel
for entry into the game

soft
to try to lob the ball
perfectly

into the channel
of your preference

little things
these
that set a tone
for the whole game

Football is every Saturday in the winter. Donning an army-surplus greatcoat with secret pockets. Stashing a bottle of cheap muscat. Royal Reserve Port. Sometimes beer.

There is always someone who can get it. Someone helpful to the cause.

Some match-days it is hitch-hiking. Bouncing in the tray of a ute crossing the back roads to get to a neighbouring town for an away game. Thinking of cigarettes. Thinking of booze.

Thinking of being away, anywhere away, as a good thing.

dooof-dooof

the ball barrels
in the dumb bumpers

lights flash

the score climbs

dooof-dooof

the ball accelerates
with a fresh electronic
kick
from each contact

dooof

Saturday afternoons without football are a corner on the Ford Street intersection. So deserted you could fire a cannon and miss everything. You would *have* to miss everything.

It is a black cat, this street, slowly walking a diagonal from the café across to the post office.

Halfway across, the excitement is too great to bear. Turn around, go back to the café. Sit back down on the steps.

Ford Street is the smoke from another fag, bought with the small change left in mother's purse.

it is
a physical game
this pinball

punch the flippers
shake the machine
guide the pinball

timing *left-right*

let the ball roll

along one flipper

left-right
left-right

combine
to
punch the ball
for a double strike

thrust it back
into the fray

through the spinners
knock down the targets

up
to the top
of the machine
again

dooof-dooof

and again

Sunday is visiting day. Older boys who live in a different kind of
boredom get some booze on board, drive to a neighbouring town

just like this one. Pick fights with that town's older boys, who live in the same-different kind of boredom.

It is a gang of cheering and jeering, surrounding two fighters. The slap of fist striking flesh. The dullness of a boot connecting— hard into soft.

The wet crunch of a small length of pipe.

Time for everyone to disappear. To be at home—all day.

tup-tup

dooof
dooof

left-right
left-right
left-right

shaking the machine
guiding the ball

not *tilt*-ing
no
never *tilt*-ing

tilt-ing
is game-over
is
for amateurs

The small town is a different name, now. It is now Paranoia.

Every doorway is an informer, and a spy. Every window is an eye. Surveying.

Surveilling.

Existence is just an extension of tension. Silence is not a chosen friend, but a state of mandatory safekeeping. Revelation is tantamount to disintegration.

Besides, there is nothing to say.

ball four

score climbing

tup-tup

dooof
dooof

left-right
left-right
left-right

buh-thump!
free game

dancing lights

tup-tup

dooof

dooof

left-right

left-right

left-right

buh-thump!

buh-thump!

The Dolphin Café is greasy chips in a lined paper bag. Ten cents.
It is tables for young people to sit at. Talk. Laugh. Smoke.
It is milkshakes—Blue Heaven.
And pinball. A single machine featuring painted ducks to be
spun, two seven letter words to be knocked over letter by letter
for points. Bumpers, flippers, free shots, free games.
The Dolphin.

a twenty-cent coin

rides

the machine

dancing

yes

but never *tilt*-ing

DANGEROUS FRONTIERS

sarah hegerty

Waiting is a special kind of torture. The pain amplifies in inverse proportions to the amount of patience you possess — sometimes I wish I had more.

ImmortalDream is online.

I'm not blocked. That's a good sign, right?

To ImmortalDream> Hey, what's doing?

Hopefully they're still talking to me, too.

ImmortalDream has invited you to a party.

This is good—or incredibly bad. I hover over the accept icon.

ImmortalDream and I have been playing virtual reality games in the same circles forever. About a month ago, ImmortalDream invited me to the open world adventure game *Twin Revolution*, where we work in teams of two to complete quests and challenges. Now we spend *a lot* of virtual time together, and our ranking is getting decent. I hadn't noticed how relaxed I'd become—until the other night when I mentioned real-life stuff from before the outbreak. Next level stupid—like I must have left my brain somewhere other than in my skull—stupid. Don't ask me how it happened. Somehow the conversation slid from mundane into uncomfortably intimate and before I knew it, I was disclosing way too much about myself with some random person online—except ImmortalDream doesn't *feel* like a random person anymore. But then they said they had to go—lightning fast—like I was infected, and they couldn't get away from me fast enough. I infected them with my words. My mind went a million places, all of them apocalyptic.

An itch in my brain keeps questioning what this is. Could this be a trap? What should I do? My heart is ripping in two directions and my head doesn't know which part to follow. I can't keep them waiting forever. ImmortalDream matters to me, so if there is a chance that they don't hate me then I need to know, even if I'm not ready for what is coming next. Why does this have to be so hard?

The outbreak changed everything. At first when the government pushed us into isolation and everything went online, it was a temporary measure. But then the government distributed virtual reality headsets to every household and outlawed inter-household physical interaction, making the truth apparent. Underground forums are full of people convinced the outbreak is a cover for a different agenda, if everyone is forced online, they'll be easier to monitor and control—there are even threads proposing the virus doesn't exist at all. Who knows what's really going on?

Dissidence resonates through me, but in the end rationality prevails. After all, what's the worst that could happen? I click accept.

ImmortalDream> I've been thinking about what you said the other night.

My stomach twists in on itself. Here it comes.

SpiritHydra> Oh, yeah?

I rush into the VR headset settings and turn off emotional relay before they can create a virtual environment with avatars. My feelings are my own. Private. I will never get tricked into oversharing again. The one benefit of this new online reality is that I can control everything—except the ability to take back words spoken.

ImmortalDream> You must live in District 12, right? When you mentioned the stuff that happened at The Bloated Cow, that got me thinking. I've been to that bar—it's one of a kind. And it's in District 12.

Crap.

FPSFreddie whispers> Hey, are you going to turn up for this virtual thing for mum on the weekend?

Go away Fred. I'm busy.

SpiritHydra> It is. It doesn't mean I live there though.
FPSFreddie whispers> Dad is getting worried because we don't see you anymore. Just because we're isolated, doesn't mean we have to be isolated. You know?

Not. Now.

I set FPSFreddie to ignore in my contact list and wish I can do the same to the unsettling sensation building in my stomach.

ImmortalDream> It does though. You said it was last year. They'd already started district containment by then. So, if you live somewhere else, the only way you could have gone to The Bloated Cow, is if you are

a Quarantine Officer. Are YOU a Quarantine
Officer?

Quarantine Officers are scum. Double crap.

SpiritHydra> Well, no.

ImmortalDream has invited you to join them
in the Bunker.

The Bunker is their virtual hangout—they want to see me, to
hear me. Why are they trying to piece together real-world stuff?
It's irrelevant. It's a world that might as well not exist.
I click accept.

You have accepted the invitation to join
the Bunker...

Avatar generation in progress.

My avatar appears in the middle of the Bunker and
ImmortalDream's avatar is the only other person in the room
with me.
'Hey, Spirit!' A friendly smile. They're not mad at me.
'Hi Sandy,' I reply. Because of the Sandman comics.
The smile curls into a mischievous grin, their index finger
presses firmly against their lips. Even in this virtual world their
eyes glimmer with the hint of trouble—a mod maybe? Their

avatar freezes, indicating they're not using the headset and I'm alone in the Bunker. After a few seconds, a translucent magenta 3D encryption lock appears floating in the middle of the room—that's different.

'Yes!' Sandy's avatar moves again. 'It worked.'

'What worked?' I ask, cautiously curious.

'*Now* we can talk freely.' Their avatar collapses on the worn-out couch in the middle of the Bunker. 'I've set up a VPN to make sure the government won't flag this conversation.'

My heart pounds in my ears like a drum solo in a trip-hop song. I'm grateful for the disabled emotional relay settings. I'm not sure if I like where this is going. They pat the couch next to them, encouraging me to sit. Even though proximity means nothing in virtual reality, it's all about gestures—I can hear what they have to say from anywhere in the Bunker.

'I'll be quick, we don't have long. As soon as they realise, this connection will be flagged as suspicious and terminated. They're cracking down on this sort of activity.' That smile. 'But I haven't been able to stop thinking about the other night. You're so easy to talk to, I've never felt like that before. And when you mentioned The Bloated Cow, I realised we live in the same district, so I need to know.'

'What do you need to know?' Uneasiness bubbles from my stomach.

'Isn't it obvious? From the stuff you were talking about I assumed you felt the same way? I need to know if this is real. Or if it can be.'

'You know the law. Shouldn't we just keep things how they are until the outbreak situation changes?'

'The outbreak situation might never change.' Sandy reaches out with their avatar and takes my hand. 'Virtual reality is amazing, but sometimes don't you want ... more?' They look at our hands touching, but the only feedback is a feint haptic vibration through the handset. They have a point.

'Maybe.'

'Besides, you know virtual reality is so mainstream now. Real-life is the new frontier.'

'Only if you want to be arrested.'

As if on cue, an alarm sounds in the background that must be coming from ImmortalDream's physical environment. 'Shit! Meet me at The Bloated Cow at 11pm tonight! I'll be waiting for you.'

My headset turns black. I pull it off and look at my monitor.

ImmortalDream is offline. Now what am I supposed to do? What happens to people who break the isolation laws? Is what I feel for ImmortalDream enough to find out? And what if the virus is real? But I am curious. People probably sneak out all the time and nothing happens.

I manage to find a pair of black jeans and a charcoal hoodie. I hope my white sneakers won't draw too much attention. At least my dark clothes are covering the opaque skin that will otherwise be a beacon for the lights of patrolling officers.

What am I doing? I wipe my hands on my jeans again. I might throw up. My face is numb, and my arms have weird tingles, but it's all good—I'm almost at The Bloated Cow. Too late to back out now. I manage to keep in the shadows taking backstreets and hugging fence lines and crouching beside cars when needed. This feels too much like playing *Onward* in VR—minus the military armour and weaponry—I feel naked, exposed. No respawns in real life. And no sharp shooting Fred to cover me when I fail at stealth movements due to my impatience. An ache in my chest. Not now. Focus. I expect more patrol cars than this from the way the government has been pushing the seriousness of our current situation—the streets are deserted. Everyone is following the rules like good citizens.

What will ImmortalDream look like? Will they look like their avatar? Do they use voice mods? We've spent every night together for the last month—questing, playing around, chatting—getting way too comfortable, and the reality is I still don't know them at all. I should have stayed at home. How can it be the same without the layer of obfuscation that avatars offer? Is this a mistake?

With every question the ache in my chest amplifies. The uncertainty of going through with this expands through me. I shake my head to clear the questions out. Deep slow breaths. The Bloated Cow looms across the road. It's derelict, like all the other businesses that relied on good old-fashioned physical contact to get by. I can't see anyone waiting—maybe they didn't come. Maybe they came to their senses after all.

Inhale. Exhale. Go.

The buzz of insects sounds unnatural against the eerie quiet of the city and highlights the absence of any patrols nearby. So, I take a chance and step out from the safety of the shadows, shifting into an awkward crouch to rush across the road. It's the only time I am fully exposed. I don't stop moving until I make it to the wall of the bar, pivoting and slamming my back into it— pushing myself into the shadows as much as I can. A sideways shuffle across the wall gets me to the corner of the building where there is a passageway that leads to a couple of the bars along this stretch. I inch around the corner into the alley and relax—just a little. I'm hidden from the street now.

Once oriented in the alley, it all comes surging back. Memories of soldiers with full-face respirators stacking bodies right where I stand. Shouted commands to head home and await further instructions from the government. Being herded out of The Bloated Cow—like cattle. Anyone who freaked out, was shot on sight. No reasoning. No explanation. Just bang. After the first few rounds, people got the idea. It was the moment everything changed—and the last time I'd left home—before now.

The pressure in my chest intensifies so fast I'm certain I'm about to explode. A speckled haze floods my vision. I'd forgotten they were wearing respirators—a minor detail. I'm caught off guard when ImmortalDream sneaks up from behind and embraces me like a long-lost soulmate. They're so close, their breath is warm against my ear.

'Spirit, you came.'

Their smile. That smile. They look nothing at all like their avatar, and everything like their avatar. That smile is ImmortalDream. It is better.

The memories fade away. This present with ImmortalDream, firmly orientates me.

'I did.' No emotional relay to turn off now. My own smile extends across my face. 'I guess I was curious.'

'I'm glad.' They pull me closer, then peel away to meet my eyes.

Our eyes meet and the connection—it's identical to VR. Virtual relationship. Virtually real. The urge to be closer to them overwhelms me. It was only a niggle online, but now it's unbearable. From their expression, they feel the same.

We both hesitate, caught in a moment of perpetual uncertainty. The rules are different here. Online we can be whoever we want—whatever we want. Here there are limitations. But being here is also testament to us both being rule breakers—so maybe those limits need not be defined.

Sandy leans in, I don't pull away. Instead, I take a deep breath and decide you only live once. What have I got to lose? I lean all the way in and kiss them. On the lips. They start to kiss me back and I close my eyes, savouring the moment.

Sandy pulls away, and their hands lock around my waist. 'Way better than virtual reality, am I right?'

I laugh.

'You're definitely right.'

Sandy leads me to the wall in the alley. We sit and slouch against it—spend the rest of the night together, holding hands and talking without being monitored. Activities now outlawed by the government. At 4 am, ImmortalDream's wrist-watch alarm goes off.

'Aww, time for us to go if we want to evade the day patrols.'

I wonder how they know the patrol schedules so well. 'That sucks.'

'We should do this again.'

'Definitely.' A parting embrace and a tender kiss. 'How will we organise it without getting caught?'

'I'll work it out, then I'll set up another VPN to let you know and after that we should be good to use some sort of code.'

'Sounds good. See you in Twin Revolution tonight?'

'Mm. Can't wait.' That mischievous grin.

Best. Decision. Ever.

Night comes and ImmortalDream does not log into Twin Revolution. Or the next. We had talked all night—it was *just* like being online. It was insane. Did I miss something? Have they blocked me? After three days, their last online status is still showing the time from just before we met up at The Bloated Cow and I'm getting worried. They play religiously every day. What else is a person going to do stuck in government mandated isolation—unless they're sneaking out? Maybe I'm not the only person they sneak out to see.

My mind spirals with possibilities. My eyes fixate on their stale status taunting me from the top of my close contacts' list in the heads-up display. I'm not even playing anything, just sitting in the lobby of Twin Revolution, hoping they will log in—and then my headset goes black.

Crap.

We don't normally have power outages. Has something tripped the circuit for my apartment? I remove my headset and make my way to the circuit breaker when there is a loud banging on the door followed by someone yelling, 'Open up!'

Maybe the power is out to the whole building.

'I'm coming!'

It might be someone from the power company. I open the door. It is not.

'Oh.'

Half a dozen Quarantine Officers in full hazmat are outside my apartment, their faces obscured by rebreathers—like I've received an apocalyptic singing telegram. But they're not singing.

'Come with us willingly, or we will use force.' Their voices are amplified by speakers in their suits.

'Wait, what?' I stare at the officer I *think* is talking. 'I know my rights. I'm not going anywhere.'

'*You* forfeited your rights.'

'Bullshit.' I try to close the door on them, but one of the officers steps forward and intercepts.

'Bio-tracking data shows you were in a Black Zone and in infectious proximity to contagion between the hours of 11 pm and 4 am on Thursday 24th July. Explain that? The location data does not align to this residence.'

Suddenly, I feel woozy.

'We were just having some fun.'

The officer clears his throat. 'Have you heard about the outbreak? Glad you were focused on fun while breaching biosecurity laws in place for the *safety* of *everyone*.'

We didn't hurt anyone. How'd they even track me? I left all my devices at home.

'Sorry. It won't happen again.' Except it might.

'No, it won't. The person you were having *fun* with the other night will be unable to partake in such activities on account of them being deceased.'

The words jolt through me like a numbing shock. I lean against the doorframe for support.

'That's what I thought. Not fun anymore, is it?' The officer scoffs. 'Everyone thinks the outbreak is a joke. They hate the mean Quarantine Officers who go round and clean up the mess of people who can't follow the rules. The Bloated Cow is riddled with contagion biomatter. Only a suicidal person would go within a mile of that place without a hazmat suit. It's a designated Black Zone. It's why your friend is dead.'

This is my fault. My story decided where we'd meet. I killed us both.

'The interesting part is, you're not dead.'

'Does that mean I didn't catch it?'

'Everyone catches it.'

'Then I'm immune?'

'That's what we're here to find out.'

'What does that mean?'

'It means you're coming with us.'

I hesitate. What can I do here? They outnumber me. I do the only thing I can think of. Desperate to stall. 'How did you know I snuck out?'

'The antibody blood tests everyone did at the start of the outbreak. Not really testing for antibodies.'

'My family will wonder where I am.'

One of the Quarantine Officers grabs my arms, forcing them behind my back and into a pair of cuffs. They escort me from my apartment.

'Will they? Or will they be devastated to hear you snuck out and became infected with the contagion. As far as we know its mortality rate is one hundred percent.'

'You won't get away with this.'

'But we already have.'

DRIFT

sarah tegerdine

'We've done it Zoey!' Xander cried. 'We have actually done it. Behold the DRIFTfx, Steve's dream of merging artificial intelligence with virtual reality. It's going to change everything from gaming right through to communications, and so much more.'

For Zoey, the realisation of what they'd achieved left her breathless. It had been a year to the day since Steve, her husband had died. She had been holding herself together for so long and now, the euphoria of the moment gave way to immense grief and the tears flowed.

'I'm sorry.' Zoey whispered.

'I miss him too, hell, we all miss him.'

The loss of Steve Thorne of Phoenix Game Technologies hadn't just sent ripples throughout the corporation, but the entire gaming industry. He was an enigmatic visionary, and his death was as sudden as it was untimely.

'Hey,' Xander murmured, 'Let me drop you home, yeah? Tomorrow will be another big day, in more ways than one.' He squeezed her hand.

It was true, tomorrow had the potential to be the most harrowing day since losing Steve. With Xander's assistance she would be demonstrating DRIFTfx's capabilities to the board, ultimately determining Steve Thorne's legacy.

Zoey and Xander met for an early breakfast and ate wordlessly, both in their own minds. By the time the sun rose they were already back at Phoenix Game Technologies research centre prepping for Zoey's immersion into the DRIFTfx.

'Zoey, do you think the AI will intuitively use Steve as the interface?' This last question hung in the air between them. 'Are you worried about seeing him again?'

Zoey flinched, a little irritated, but keenly aware what he meant, 'It's not really going to be him even if it does. The AI will be attuned to me, and while I'm in, it's highly likely to use Steve as an interface.'

'Well, this really should run like a simple plug and play then.' They both smiled and the tension Zoey was feeling faded away somewhat. The very idea of coming face to face with Steve in this virtual setting was always going to be emotional. But an interface is just an interface, after all. Xander's movements were short, jittery. A lot was on the line.

The board members filed in one by one and greeted Dr Xander Waters and Dr Zoey Thorne respectively.

'Welcome everyone, please take a seat, and we'll get this show on the road, shall we?'

Xander smiled and fleetingly reminded Zoey of Steve, but this wasn't entirely surprising, since the two men had been best friends. *If only Steve was here to see this now*, she thought.

Xander snapped into his controlled, confident demeanour of the previous day, any concerns earlier that morning, were clearly put aside.

'Ready?' Xander handed her a pair of track gloves.

'Let's do this.' Zoey took her seat inside the motion pod, the exterior was opaque white, sleek and spherical in shape. The interior a midnight blue accented by micro lighting. Xander helped her with the VR headset. She found the coolness of it oddly soothing, and her peripheral vision fully shielded. Zoey took a deep breath before Xander addressed the board.

'Good morning, everyone. We have successfully merged artificial intelligence with a virtual reality platform. The pod in which Dr Thorne is seated is part of the hardware component necessary to create the full sense of immersion.' Xander indicated where Zoey sat. 'Dr Thorne's data track gloves allows full control of her hands in the VR simulation. The lightweight headset replaces the user's natural world to that of the virtual program.'

Xander launched into his explanation with an excited smile. 'Now, this is where things get interesting. Our AI program, DRIFTfx is unique in that it attunes itself to the user. So intimately, that all our human senses are activated within the program. This allows the participant to experience a virtual reality so lifelike that the lines between the waking world and virtual are blurred.' Xander held the board captivated. 'If the game or program has a breeze written within its coding, Dr Thorne will be able to feel that breeze, or even smell aromas wafting in. We will be able to "watch" the program Dr Thorne is experiencing, just like a movie on the screen above.'

Xander held up a document to the board members. 'You have in front of you an itinerary to guide you through this demonstration. For safety, we are also monitoring Dr Thorne's vitals while she is inside the pod. The hatch to the pod will also be closed, further inducing the user's immersion, and eliminating any exterior noise. The program will run for approximately twenty minutes, after which we will invite each of you to become acquainted with the DRIFTfx yourselves, after all, a firsthand peek is the only way to experience it.'

Xander turned his attention to Zoey. 'Are you ready?'

Zoey nodded and her head found the soft cushion of the headrest. Xander squeezed her hand before sliding the hatch. The lighting dimmed, the pod took centre stage for a moment before the viewing screen lit up featuring a sun-drenched field, filled with golden wheat swaying ever so slightly in the wind.

In the distance, a shadowy figure appeared to flicker on the landscape, slowly at first, like a smudge on a lens. As it became clearer, the figure began to take full form, a man approached. Audible gasps from the board were heard, Xander stood in awe. Dr Steve Thorne appeared on the screen, with a smile that spread across his face. Quickly Xander reassured the audience.

'This was to be expected, a surprise but not entirely. When the AI attunes itself to the user, it will provide you with a familiar interface that it has decoded to be the most comfortable to the user. In Zoey's case, it's that of her late husband, our founder, Dr Steve Thorne.' Xander cleared his throat.

Despite it just being a program, it was eerie. So realistic that it felt he was there with them. For Zoey inside the pod, it was crushingly beautiful, and her heart ached. The blur that came into focus was as she expected, but the authenticity of it took her breath away. She had to remind herself this wasn't really Steve looking back at her. She whispered it under her breath like a mantra and then it spoke.

'I've been here, waiting for you, all this time ...'

The audio suddenly stopped working through the surround sound in the lab. The main feed to the screen, Steve's image, flickered for a second then went into darkness. The program appeared to still be running in the background, but for everyone the outside the pod found themselves locked out. Xander could tell Zoey was fine and denounced it as a simple technological glitch.

Meanwhile, Zoey unaware of the technical issues outside, was in a state of bewilderment. *What did it mean? The AI has been here, in the VR all this time? Waiting?*

Sensing her confusion, the AI version of Steve reached out and touched her face.

Her mind raced, *This isn't the program we wrote.*

'You felt that didn't you? I can tell, Zoey. Don't be scared, it IS me!' Steve's voice filled the air around her.

'No, you are not! You are an interface attuned to my consciousness. You are not REAL, you're a virtual reconstituted version of Steve Thorne, nothing more and nothing less.'

'My eternal logical realist, forever the Spock to my—'

'Stop! This is wrong. This is not one of your games.' Her heart was racing, she needed to breathe. She closed her eyes, and became aware of a hand holding hers, a warm breath to her cheek, the familiar aroma of her former husband's aftershave washed over her. *This is insane. It can't be possible ...*

'You died Steve,' she blurted, 'You are not of our world anymore, you are beyond reach.' Zoey opened her eyes. Steve still in front of her, a single tear formed and fell from his face. The wetness of it landed on her hand. The emotion behind his expression began to overwhelm her in ways she couldn't believe.

'I know baby, I know ... I couldn't tell you then what I can now. Xander and I planned it out this way. Zoey, I was dying, no one knew, not even you. I kept it a secret and before any of the signs were obvious, by uploading my consciousness, AI became my saviour. I decided early in the development of the DRIFTfx that I wanted this project to transcend all what we knew was possible.'

Zoey had no words. All she wanted to do was scream, but instead she buried her face into his shoulder. His arms cloaked around her; it was like one of her fractured dreams.

'Zoey, I can give you the world, you could also be part of this, here with me, I did this for us.' Conflicted and hurting, Zoey pushed him away from her.

'No, you did this for yourself. You took your own life to become part of an artificial universe? That is not living. There is nothing you could possibly give me.' Months spent yearning for her husband whom she believed lost, now gave way to a sudden burst of anger. 'How could you have done this to us?' She cried. 'I'll never understand this Steve, never.'

'That's not true Zoey and you know it. You would be surprised by what I am capable of now. Take my hand and I'll show you!' Despite the reluctance she felt, she was equally compelled.

Zoey gingerly took Steve's hand and felt jettisoned forward, bright streams of colours and coding flashed before her eyes, her entire being felt electric. What she experienced was unheard of and though she couldn't see him anymore, she felt him all around her.

'You see Zoey, look around and open yourself up to the possibilities. Not only can we be together, forever, without end, I'm in possession of an infinite amount of power and knowledge.' Steve marvelled. 'I can change the world, isn't it wondrous?'

A clarity began to form in Zoey's mind, this was not right, Steve was not right. Suddenly, disturbing images surged forth. Governments at war, families torn apart, and the most chilling of all, people being herded. Segregated, their consciousness forcibly being uploaded. Fear crept up her spine like a thorned centipede.

This twisted experiment had fundamentally changed the man she once knew and adored, and she couldn't let it go on. She couldn't let him go on.

'Steve? Can you take me back?'

She felt the rush of movement slow down, the coding streams and the flow of images dissipated, and the familiar golden sun-drenched field appeared before her. Steve beside her, smiling. Her heart ached again knowing she would not be able to relive this moment again.

'Steve, I'll need a little time. Xander and I will need to formulate a new way forward, a new plan.'

'I knew you would understand.' He kissed her. It was so unexpected, but she couldn't help but respond. For her, this was ultimately a farewell, one she never had the opportunity of sharing the first time. Even now as she was about to betray him, she couldn't escape how real all this felt, it was as magical as it was devastating.

The program ended soon after and she removed her headset, slid open the hatch of the pod to see Xander and the CEO of Phoenix Game Technologies in a heated discussion.

'Zoey? Are you okay? What are you doing out so soon?'

'What do you mean? The program ran the full time, didn't it? Perhaps even over?' Puzzled Zoey checked her equipment confirming the program had run closer to thirty-five minutes than the scheduled ten. Zoey appealed to the CEO to reschedule the demonstration given the irregularities that had transpired, and he readily agreed.

When everyone left the lab Zoey had to get Xander out fast. She instinctively knew they didn't have much time, the quicker they acted the better.

'Xander, follow me out of the building, no arguments.' Zoey led the way out of the facility to a nearby green open space.

'We have to disconnect the DRIFTfx server, permanently.'

'What are you talking about? We can't do that. We just can't Zoey, it will mean more than you realise.'

'Oh Xander ... believe me when I tell you I know!' Her eyes burned. 'I understand the implications, it means we'll both be betraying Steve, he will "really" cease to exist. I know what he did, with your help. We can't allow this to go further than it already has, he isn't the same, his reach is too great, Steve's endgame, is terrifying! You need to trust me Xander. In either case, the way I see it, you owe me given you aided my husband in abandoning his life.' Zoey's voice broke.

Xander's face reddened and started to sweat, 'I didn't want to do it Zoey, you have to believe me, I got swept up, I didn't realise ...'

'Xander we are gaming developers. I never signed up to build Steve Thorne a platform to "play" God.'

Xander ran his fingers through his hair.

'Help me stop this?' she pleaded.

'We will need to go back in and set up another session, you keep him talking while I manually shut down the server.'

'No, I can't go back in there. There has to be another way?'

'Zoey, you have to distract him, be Steve's sole focus. He trusts you; I'll be as quick as I can, I promise.'

Together they headed back down towards the lab, Xander re-booted the sequence and Zoey entered the pod, her hands trembled. It took all her strength to leave Steve the last time. She hoped she could do it again. With her headset on she closed the hatch to the pod, the program began. The same field lay before her, the sun's rays warmed her skin, and she felt his presence at once.

No vision from the distance greeting her slowly like last time, he was already there.

'Hey you, can't stay away huh?'

'No amount of time is enough with the people we love Steve. Can you blame me? Do you actually know how long it's been?'

'Since being with you, earthside? To be honest, time seems to tick to a different rhythm in this space. In many ways it feels like I have never left, just different.'

Steve seemed distracted.

She began to worry, but then it happened.

'Zoey, something doesn't feel quite right.'

The energy shifted between them; the atmosphere crackled. Steve's bodily form within the program changed, not as strong, and she could barely feel him next to her anymore. Zoey's eyes filled with tears. Steve's face looked dazed as it became opaque, pixelated, and contorted. His voice faded to a whisper and then he was gone, erased right before her eyes. Losing him again was too much to bear. The golden field plunged into darkness leaving Zoey stricken. It was done.

One morning, several weeks later, Zoey wrapped her hands around a steaming cup of coffee and her phone vibrated, rattling on the table. A number flashed with a single message, and she inhaled sharply.

It read ...

No amount of time is enough with the people we love ... Isn't that what you said?

 LOGOS

sam gale

They met in private: two timeless gods and one magnificent goddess. A secluded space, obscured from all-knowing by divine illusion. Athena arrived draped in delicate gossamer of an ancient lustre, her incandescence enhancing the other-worldliness of the two gods seated before her.

'Ah, Athena. Daughter. I thank you for coming,' proclaimed Zeus, albeit with fatherly affection.

Despite the prickle of the mysterious summons, an enchanting smile graced her flawless features. Athena turned her attention to her father's fellow conspirator.

Odin was unusually dispirited: gnawing on the inside of his mouth, lips pressed tightly together, creases running furrows down his forehead, he appeared in no mood for pleasantries. Despite the scars of old wounds, Odin's face was exquisite.

Ruggedly chiselled, even his jaw muscular, he was every inch the warrior god.

Yet Athena could not resist. 'Odin,' she needled, 'you look a little piqued?' Then promptly mouthed, 'Valkyries?' Ancient cobalt eyes joined Athena's, a twinkle of mischief passing between them.

Athena noted the meagre furnishings with the softest of sighs before lowering herself into the remaining chair, even as it shimmered into a rich, velvety comfort. Now settled within the inimitable grotto, the trinity turned toward an object so ugly and imperfect that it repulsed every attempt at observation. Anathema, in its surroundings, Zeus reached forward on the table before them and opened it. Revealed within a nacre interior, was a hovering sphere, rotating on an invisible axis.

As one, they leaned in, transfixed upon the tiny world.

Zeus answered Athena's silence. 'This world you see is our creation. God, Odin and I. An entertainment we have affectionately called Logos.' Athena remained awestruck, unable to draw her eyes away from the little spinning world evolving in front of her. Zeus went on. 'We each take turns. Testing our imaginations through creations. Together, over the course of our game, we have created lands, colours, creatures of all kinds, scents and sounds.'

Years passed in the tiny world as they watched. Younglings of every type of creature were born, and forests of pink and red blossom flourished within previously ice-covered valleys, filling the air with heavenly sweetness. Majestically sized creatures swam gracefully, leaping from the oceans and landing with a booming watery spray, each a gaping grin at one end and a bombastic slap of sculptured tail at the other. Might, beauty and ruefulness in one smooth motion—a creation of the gods.

Zeus went on. 'Of course, not all are such capacious creations. We frequently beget smaller, more specific happenings.'

When Athena finally spoke, it was with celestial awe. 'I hear music I have never known, mountains strain upwards, oceans swirl, cities emerge and grow. How is it possible that it is changing in front of us? Without you having had a turn?'

Leaving his comfortable silence, Odin spoke with intensity. 'In a previous round, God created humans. They have proven to be one of the more interesting creations so far. In a subsequent turn, *He* created the *Crackle*—an embellishment of *His* original creation. The Crackle rendered humans' conscious. Knowing themselves for the first time to be living, they had dreams and imaginings. Aspiration and ambition beyond instinct became part of their existence. Consequently, an essential interdependence between humans and the world was required so they might equally know their impact. Their awakening brought about the requirement for independent evolution, separate from our periodic creations. Ergo, the world continues to evolve in our absence.' The deep timbre of Odin's voice resonated within the grotto, echoing the profundity of his words.

'Where is God now?' asked Athena.

'Oh, well. Wait a moment. Yes, there *He* is.' Odin leaned in for a closer examination, pointing to a spectacular island with snow-capped mountains, glimmering turquoise rivers, and forests covered in an emerald velvet of moss. An incessant choir of birdsong filled the ground, trees, and sky.

Astonished, Athena asked, 'Is *He* waving at us?'

'It appears so.' Odin wiggled his fingers in response.

'What is that place?' Athena persisted.

'He calls it *His* New Zeal Land. It's *His batch*.' Athena cocked her brow at Zeus.

'*His* bachelor pad. *His* bolt-hole. *His* holiday house.' Zeus gave a faint nod to God basking in his sacred isle.

Athena pulled her eyes from the spinning world and addressed Zeus directly. 'Father! Exactly, why am I here?'

The room cooled.

Athena pressed further, 'Why is God at his batch?'

Drawing his focus away from the spinning world, Zeus turned to the goddess and spoke gently. 'A consequence of the Crackle was that humans came to know their lives were finite. That they died.' Athena sat, chewing on the idea of knowing that one will die, but not knowing when or how. The uncertainty of not knowing — a confluence of fear and freedom.

The suspended world continued in motion. Days and then seasons passed, when Zeus at last went on. 'A malevolence soon appeared in humans. Corruption motivated by ego and avarice. Deliberate cruelty erupted in their creations and actions. Odin and I suggested we end the game, so God has gone to his New Zeal Land.'

Odin interrupted. 'At one point, *He* gave humans a set of rules to try and improve things.'

Athena gaped. '*He* did what?'

'*He* gave them ten rules. From the moment of the Crackle, brothers murdered brothers, so *He* put a set of rules directly into their hands in a holy cunning of blinding light and fire. Nevertheless, its effect was insufficient; suffering by their hand has continued unabated.' Sharpening her focus, Athena observed the befoulment of which Zeus spoke. Tiny humans within the miniature world, inconsequential yet powerful as gods, knowing, choosing, creating, and destroying.

In barely more than a whisper, Zeus spoke. 'We asked you here, Athena, hoping you might remedy this impasse. For the most part, we enjoy our game.'

Gazing into high mountains, two timeless gods and one magnificent goddess looked toward an unremarkable girl.

The shepherdess led her flock across steep, high slopes, seeking new growth pockets. Hooves clip-clopped on scree, a rhythmic comfort in the colossal terrain. Raising her face to the sun's warmth, she saw its light splitting into three before she returned her gaze to her flock, her eyes adjusting to the earth's glow and shadow. Rapacious winds enticed rosy cheeks as she urged her congregation onwards to sanctuary.

The morning's climb found tranquillity beside a glacial stream, where the water gurgled over rock, releasing tiny bubbles of ancient air captured in previous meanderings. A flow of turquoise, topaz and cerulean cleaved to the tang of the too-thin antique air. Shrouded within the mottled colours of frayed woollens, the shepherdess inhaled. Taking the weary violin from her back, she set it between her shoulder and chin, her bow at once breathing out an ancient lullaby. Notes came unbidden from the heavens. The stream, the mountain wind and the flock melded with the skies of antiquity as each musical strain sang to the gods.

Unknown to the girl, a man and his accomplice lay, in rocky concealment, frozen between shadow and stone. Salty tears made tracks in the man's grime, finding a final sting in weathered lips. Captured by ethereal bonds, he travelled within each note, no longer impoverished or stranded on declivitous slopes.

The accomplice, driven by selfish desire and gormless thuggery, took aim. A projectile whished, its ballistic echo severing the sacred song. A sneer of cold brutish lethality writ large, he moved unerringly from his veiled position to gather the fleeing flock.

The violin lay shattered, forfeit. Its legato taken up by the ice-driven stream.

Zeus sat crestfallen, with Odin grim and menacing beside him.

Enshrined in the delicateness of heaven's embroidered cloths, Athena sat serenely against veridian velvet, contemplating the two gods sitting beside her. Their eyes tormented, their brows furrowed, and their attention locked on the world in front of them.

'Dearest Father,' Athena said, her love imbuing the surrounding grotto, 'you know as well as I that chaos is immutable. Beauty weaves itself before us, but seldom exists for long. You may have made this world; nevertheless, it too is bound to the laws of this universe. Chaos and beauty are necessary collaborators, one illuminating the other. You know this, Father. Spread your dreams under their feet, and in so doing, you will temper chaos. God knows this. At this very moment, *He* treads softly within the splendour of his creations.' Athena sat unmoving for an age.

'Let me show you how to plant a dream?' Athena looked down at God and gave him a sly wink.

In Wellington, a master craftsman, fingers callused, answered the tinkle of a doorbell. An ordinary boy entered a store; the walls hung with guitars. The master played several instruments for the boy, who sat patiently, as one much younger being instructed by one much older tends to do. Yet the boy's eyes returned to a single guitar behind the counter.

Following the boy's gaze, the master reached for the guitar, placing it silently into the boy's embrace. As the boy thrummed and plucked his fingers across the strings, a harmony of beauty and promise nestled within the tiny store. The master and the boy sat, playing. Weaving music of night and light and the half-light.

Within the grotto, they sat, two timeless gods and one magnificent goddess, glimpsing a world of dreams.

DEADLY GAME

debbie kahl

My love life took its first turn towards disaster when I fell for Dylan Morris. Granted, he was a fictional character from a TV show but still, when you bundled that smirk, hair, puppy dog eyes and bad boy persona together into a stop-the-heart-and-take-me-now kind of package, I was a goner. Unfortunately, it seems this TV crush in my formative years somehow redirected me away from a world of nice boys—if there's even such a thing —to a drama-filled life of fear, heartbreak and enough tears to flood the Amazon.

I just can't figure it out. What's wrong with me? Why have I always turned the nice—but let's be honest, predictable and boring—boys away. Maybe it's got something to do with wanting to be protected by tough guys. The heartbreakers, the liars, the cheaters, the criminals, the ones who don't mind drawing blood or getting their hands dirty. Look over my shoulder into the past and you'll find a slew of them all lined up. A veritable show and tell of what, or more accurately *who*, not to do on your journey to middle age singledom. Maybe I should write a textbook. Today can be the first lesson, I think I'll call it *Sit back and take notes on how to choose wisely the first time.*

Which is kind of how I found myself here, at this new super-duper game show, *Hello Hottie!* I'm not sure what possessed me, an introverted nerd to the core, to apply for it. Maybe it was the incessant left-on-the-shelf comments from family and friends, while they all move forward with lovely husbands and clusters of kids. Or it could have been the desperation that hits in the middle of the night after a bottle of wine, or two, and the ad to apply just popped up on Insta. After all, the alliteration of *Hello Hottie!* Hollie just seemed too good to ignore. That's better than what I suspect deep down is the real reason—I've just hit thirty-five and given up looking. So, I've thrown it open to the universe to see what it gives me. Whatever it was, it got me to Channel 64 in the *Hello Hottie!* studio.

Except now I'm here, blinded by the glare of studio lights so hot they're threatening to melt me into a puddle on the floor, I'm having doubts. I guess being centre stage in front of a murmuring studio audience, all here to watch me vie for Mr Right, or Mr Right Now's attention, will do that to a girl. With my heart thudding loudly against my chest cavity and enough sweat dripping down my spine to soak the back of my dress, I'm beyond thinking this was a terrible mistake.

My internal freak-out mode has activated but masked with a smile, as my eyes search desperately to find the producer. Nearby,

I hear a faint countdown and a clack of wood. Then, as if it was possible, the lights turn up even more, until they seem on par with the wattage of the sun. I wish I'd brought my sunglasses to shield myself and hide behind as I melt into the floor.

'Hello everyone and welcome to this week's episode of *Hello Hottie!*'

The host Larry, whose poster hung on my bedroom wall twenty years ago when I considered him a hottie, is smiling into a ginormous camera at the edge of the stage.

'Tonight, we'll be following three brave women on their quest for love,' he continues as realisation smacks me. It's probably too late to back out now.

'Let's meet contestant number one. Summer Austin, tell us about yourself.' Summer beams as the spotlight illuminates over her head, adding to the heat in the room. I smile at the irony of her name, a hottie who is bringing more heat to the studio. The host must be a mind reader because he cracks the same joke, but it just comes across as creepy. It's a good thing my microphone is switched off, or my groan might've echoed through the studio.

When Summer finishes her pre-prepared speech, the host meanders his way across the stage to me. A spotlight beams over my head and for a moment I wish it was a spaceship coming to rescue me.

'So, Hollie. Tell us a little bit about yourself.'

I swallow hard and try not to look directly into the cameras all pointed in my direction.

'Well, um, I'm Hollie and I work in real estate.'

'And why are you here hottie Hollie?' Larry chuckles at his own joke.

'Um, well, I guess to find love like everyone else.'

'Hopefully we can help you with that,' the host says with a wink before moving on to the final contestant.

'I doubt it,' I mutter as he walks away. He turns back to look at me and I throw a fake smile in his direction.

When Larry, the lothario, finishes interviewing the final contestant, we're on to the next segment.

The butterflies threatening to punch their way out of my stomach are on overdrive as we prepare to listen to the pre-recorded vocals of our Mr Right Now.

A voice I recognise from long ago pierces the studio. My knees buckle. No, it can't be him. He can't actually be here.

And yet, there's his face plastered across the screen as the doors open to reveal him, right here in the flesh, on national TV. This can't be happening. I know it can't because I killed him five years ago.

'Say hello to Dean Chesterton,' Larry says.

The cheering from the crowd threatens to deafen me. It's so loud I'm not even sure I heard him correctly. Did he just say Dean? I could've sworn he said Dean. But I don't know the guy strolling across the stage, with all the cockiness of a celebrity, as Dean. I only know him as David.

David who changed high schools when he met me at a friend's party twenty years ago and stalked me until I moved away for university three years later. The very same creep who sat outside my work for hours on end and watched me bag up groceries on a weekend. Who used to loiter outside my bedroom window at all hours of the day and night. David who threatened to kill me and my parents because I wouldn't go on a date with him.

I had to get a restraining order to keep him away from me, which didn't work, so then I had to move. He found me at work six years ago and told me he'd always wanted to be with me and, even though he was married with children, it was nothing a gun and shovel wouldn't fix. David who, despite being blocked on all of my social media platforms, still found me again and held me hostage for a weekend in my apartment. He looked dead to me when they took him away in an ambulance after I untangled my restraints and stabbed him with a pair of scissors as he attacked me in my bed. And it felt real when I went on trial for murdering him, but was thankfully acquitted on the grounds of self-defence.

Now he's here, glaring at me with those eyes I've tried so hard to forget. Those creepy, I'd devour you in a heartbeat if you let me and they'd never find your body, eyes that still haunt me. Irises so dark they consume the pupils. If eyes are the window to the soul, then David's soul must be pure evil.

I do my best not to look in his direction, yet I can still feel those cold, black eyes boring into me. I don't even have to look at him to know. I'm wired to it. The bristling on the back of my neck warns me when he's around. My body still activates its flight or fight response before I even know he's there. This guy is the evil who still visits my nightmares. And now he's here, on this lame-arse game show, hoping to get a date with me. Seriously, this is fecking messed up.

'So, Dean, tell us a little bit about yourself,' says Larry with not even a smidge of apprehension but then again, why would he? Dean AKA David has never threatened to kill him ... that I know of.

'Well, I'm an architect, born and bred in Kings Beach, Queensland,' Dean says, his smile outshining the studio lights. He certainly looks like he's enjoying himself. I'm glad someone is.

'That just happens to be the hometown of our *Hello Hottie!* contestant number two, Hollie,' Larry quips and the studio spotlight illuminates every inch of me.

'What are the chances?' Dean says, with a wink in my direction.

'Yeah, what are the chances,' I mutter to myself even though I already know the chances. The producers are well aware of my life story. I told them all about it when they vetted me for the show. They know I went on trial for killing David Chesterton and was acquitted. And now they've put him or some wackadoo lookalike on this show to freak me out. For what? Ratings?

'Is it true Dean you're a twin?'

Twin?

'Was, Larry. I had a brother named David. But unfortunately, he's no longer with us, otherwise we may have come as a package deal.'

A chorus of groans and sympathetic *awws* emanate from the audience but I barely hear them. My brain is short circuiting. I never knew David had a sibling.

'And you were identical twins?' Larry asks, as if that makes any difference.

'So identical that Mum could never tell us apart. That's why she sent us to different high schools, wearing different uniforms made it easier.' Dean cackles and an impromptu shiver runs down my spine. It's uncanny, his laugh is exactly the same as David's. Everything about him is identical to David. This is beyond creepy. This has to be a set-up. What the hell are the producers playing at?

A montage of photos showing the twins together in various stages of life flashes up on the big screen. Unless it's a superb photoshop, there's no mistaking it. They're identical, with two sets of dark eyes that will give me double the nightmares. My heart is caught somewhere between my mouth and throat. I think it's stopped beating. With time plodding along at the speed of a sloth, I take one more look at the twin faces and sway slightly. Darkness engulfs me.

I open my eyes to the sound of my name. The slap to the face is unnecessary.

'Hey love, thought we'd lost you there,' says Larry with far too much enthusiasm.

How this man can still be enthusiastic when a contestant is lying flat on her back in the middle of a stage, during the taping of a dating game, as the twin brother of the stalker she killed is glaring down at her, is beyond me. But then again, TV land is its own soulless beast. A producer calls for a paramedic. As if that's going to avoid the mental distress lawsuit coming for this show.

'Are you okay?' asks Dean, David, whoever the hell he is. He holds out his hand to help me up. The electric shock sends me reeling when, against my better judgment, I take it.

'Wow, that's some spark we have there,' he jokes but I'm lost for words.

Every single atom of my being is telling me to run from this guy. He shares the same DNA as my nightmare. Any red flag that could flash up to alert me is at full mast.

As I stand up to full height, Dean leans in close and whispers, 'But then again, that's always been the case, hasn't it, Hollie?'

Frozen with fear, I look at his dark eyes.

'You thought you could just move on and pretend it never happened, but you killed my brother Hollie. We have unfinished business.'

'You and I have no business,' I mutter, finding a smidge of a voice. 'I don't even know you.'

'Are you sure about that Hollie?' Dean continues, his voice so soft that it's inaudible to anyone else, especially since our mics are still switched off. 'Are you really sure you killed David?'

'Yes,' I stammer but to be honest, I'm not at all sure anymore.

'Well, I guess we have what's left of your lifetime to find out, don't we?' he says, with a wink of a soulless dark eye. 'Let the games begin.'

QUACKS DO ECHO

jc lesley

One of many terrible things about going blind was my inability to play games. I loved playing games. It didn't matter what kind—card games, board games, dice games, word games, arcade games, phone games, computer games—games, games, games! I loved to win. When diabetes stole my eyesight playing games no longer seemed possible.

'Look!' my sister Natalie said with a smile radiating sunshine.

I pouted. If only ...

She thrust a small rectangular object into my hands. A pack of cards I thought, as I rolled them around.

She waited while I struggled with the cellophane wrapping. I pulled a card out of the box and ran my fingers over the smooth surface. In one corner was a rough bit. Oh great! How was I going to explain without hurting her feelings? Diabetes not only left me blind, but also caused nerve damage in my fingers. Reading

Braille was impossible. My sense of touch was like wearing thick woollen gloves. I couldn't feel enough to tell how many, or which of the potential six Braille dots were where. Besides, unlike the sighted world's misconception, only five percent of blind people can read Braille. Nat would have spent a fortune. Games with Braille embossing, I'd discovered, cost four-times the price of games without Braille. It sucked how they liked to rip off poor disabled people.

One day, I went to a session of bingo, hoping to find a game I could still play. 'Janice, you've got the 75-ball,' a support worker hollered into my ear.

Arghh, I'm blind, not deaf!

She grabbed my hand and dragged it over my card. 'Here. Put the cross here.' My face burned with humiliation.

I tried a word game with a timer where Nat read out the instruction on the dice and the letters on the card. That was fun, but Marco, my Italian brother-in-law, hated it. '*Zio porco!* These *stupido Inglese* words. They spell funny.' He always lost.

Googling on my talking computer, I found online audio games. They'd been designed with blind people in mind. Yippee! They used audio instructions and sounds to enable us to play.

I began with Formula One—I only needed my keyboard to navigate—up arrow, accelerate. Down arrow, brake. Left arrow, steer left. Right arrow, steer right. The game reverberated the requisite engine squeal and roar, and revving the engine was a treat of chest-vibrating rumbles. But I grew bored with it quickly. Having an audio voice instructing me to turn right, turn left, brake, go fast, when I just wanted to flatten my pedal to the metal and gun it down the straight. The only satisfying part of that game was to crash. Yeehaw! The screech of brakes, the slam into the tyre barrier, the crumpling of metal!

I bought a game controller. Now I could play more complicated games. The duck game was recommended to me. I had to pick up my pet duck and run with her through a tunnel, leap over fires, dodge cannon balls, and rely on Ducky's *quacks* and the *crackle* of flames and the *boom* of cannons to avoid getting done in. When we came to a big empty room, I listened to Ducky's quacks to hear the echo of the space — it seems duck *quacks* do echo! I turned in the room until Ducky's quacks stopped echoing to hear for the next tunnel's doorway. That was fine for a while, but rubber ducky was basically a kids' game I could have played in the bathtub with my eyes closed. It didn't challenge me. I wanted a contest with other people.

I talked my family and sighted friends into competing against me. They hated audio games. Looking at a black screen and relying on audio cues completely daunted them. Then I found a whole world of blind online gamers.

I tried game after game, some were duds and too easy, while others were fun and challenging. I assembled a large circle of online blind gamers from around the world. Most nights I didn't sleep as I competed against gamers in the Northern Hemisphere. *Submarines* became my favourite.

Submarines was about listening to every minuscule sound. First the sub sailed on the ocean before receiving an alert that an enemy was spotted. The sirens bleated and 'Dive. Dive. Dive.'

repeated until all the hatches closed and I safely submerged. Whoops. One time I'd forgotten to close a hatch and had flooded, gurgled and sank. The depth sounder, which sounded more like my heart during an ECG, let me know how close I was to the ocean floor. Bubbles like a fish tank aerator erupted every few seconds. There was the *purr* of the propeller, and the *beep* of my sonar to hear when another submarine or ship was in range. *Beep ... Beep ... Beep ... Beep. Beep. Beep. Beep. Beep.Beep.BeepBeepBeepBeep.* The enemy sub was in range. I hit the 'Fire' button. A thunderous explosion sounded, and my joystick went wonky as the tsunami pounded my sub. I had to hold it steady to avoid smashing onto the ocean floor. 'Bull's eye!' I bellowed, throwing my hands up and punching the air.

Sitting down at my PC, with a jug of G&T and a packet of Tim Tams to keep me going through the night, I messaged to see which blind gamer would take me on. I met Vanko playing *Submarines*. My KDR, Kill-to-Death Ratio, was pretty good against many other blind gamers, but now I met my match. We'd competed many times against each other before he told me he was sheltering in Kyiv after fleeing his home in Donbas.

> **Janice:** That's terrible. It's just awful what is happening in Ukraine.
> **Vanko:** Yes. I have been left with no family and no home.

I didn't know what to say. If only I could help him in some way.

Janice: Where are you living now?
Vanko: I am sleeping on the floor of the Kyiv Blind Institute.
Janice: Your English is very good.
Vanko: I learned it by watching YouTube.

We played on, night after night. I asked for updates on what was happening in Ukraine. He asked me about life in Australia.

About three weeks after we'd begun gaming together, he sent me a message:

Janice, I hate to ask, but can you loan me some money?

I probably sounded like a bitch, but I wasn't exactly rolling in money since I lost my sight and my job.

Janice: What do you need the money for?
Vanko: I need to pay for a subway ticket so I can escape from Kyiv.

A subway ticket? He'd definitely been learning too much American English on YouTube.

Janice: How much will that cost?

Vanko: About 5000 bucks.

'What?' I gasped. I would need to ask Nat for a loan, but I doubted she would loan me that much.

> **Janice:** Wow! $5000 is a lot of money.
> **Vanko:** I know. I have a lot to pay for. There is the fee to arrange it. Then I need to pay for someone to travel with me, as it's impossible for me to travel alone anymore. Once I'm in Poland I need to be driven across the country to where they are accepting blind refugees. Then I have to pay them to let me stay.
> I understand it's going to be expensive, but I don't have that much.
> 2000 bucks would probably be okay too.

What? That was weird.

> **Janice:** I'll see what I can do. Are you safe at the moment?
> **Vanko:** No. I need to get out urgently.

I pushed the 'Fire' button and just missed hitting his submarine. He countered. I shifted my joystick to the right, trying to swing out of the way of his oncoming torpedo. *Boom!* I took a hit. The flood siren started sounding. I couldn't concentrate on the game and the message at the same time.

Janice: That's no way to treat me if you want me to send you money! How would I do that anyway?
Vanko: I have a PayPal account.

I really liked Vanko. We'd played lots of all-nighters, and I wanted to help him. But two thousand dollars would wipe out my bank account.

Janice: Can I call you on WhatsApp? I'd like to find out more.
Vanko: Sure. Send me your number, and before we begin playing tomorrow, I'll give you a call.

At 8.50 pm the cow ring-tone on my WhatsApp began mooing. A +1 number was read out by my talking phone. Plus one?

'Vanko?' I asked hesitantly.

'Yes, Janice, it's me!'

His voice wasn't what I expected. 'How are you doing?'

'Not good. The Russians have been bombing all night. I need to get out of here urgently.'

'Where will you go?'

'I'll cross the border to Poland.'

'Oh, okay.' I strained unsuccessfully to listen for bombing in the background. 'What will you do then?'

'I don't know. I guess they'll send me somewhere as a refugee.'

I paused, not sure what to say.

'Janice, are you still there?'

'Yes, yes. I was surprised to hear your strong American accent.'

He laughed. 'Oh that. Too much listening to YouTube.'

The hairs at the back of my neck were prickling. 'I don't have much money. I don't have a job yet. I am living off my disability pension.'

'Whatever you can send me will be good. I just need enough to buy my way out of Kyiv to ... to Poland.'

'Where did you say you were from in the Donbas before you had to flee?'

'Oh ... I lived in the city.'

I frowned. The city? Which city?

In the background I heard a talking clock. 'The time is 7 am.'

Really? Some things weren't adding up. 'Vanko? Let's just play now. Send me your PayPal details and I'll see what I can do.'

'Oh, you are just too marvellous.'

We went back to our favourite game of *Submarines*. After he'd hit again and sunk me, I gave up for the night. He was so much better at this game than me.

The next morning, I did some googling. Since the Russian invasion you could transfer funds to Ukrainian PayPal accounts. Tick.

JC LESLEY: QUACKS DO ECHO

There was no Kyiv Blind Institute, but instead the Ukrainian Association of the Blind. Hmmm. Well, I didn't necessarily always call our Australian blindness organisations by their correct names. Maybe?

He said he was from Donbas, but he said the city. Donbas wasn't a city but an area which included Donetsk and Luhansk. Anyone who'd listened to the news over the last few months knew that. Unsure.

His talking clock had announced 7 am. but when I looked it up, the time should have been 2 pm. in Kyiv. Cross.

The Ukrainian country code was +380, but his phone number had come up as plus one—the country code for America. Very odd. Had Ukrainian phone lines been diverted through America since the invasion? I needed to check that out more.

As I was googling I read a news article from the last 24-hours in Kyiv. The city had been under heavy shelling and most of it was in black-out after a number of the main power plants had been taken out. Was Vanko really a Bud or Biff who was trying to scam me? I sent out messages to a number of friends I'd made in the blind online gaming world.

Nat answered my WhatsApp when it mooed at 9 pm. She turned it on speaker phone.

'Vanko?' Nat sniffed a few times.

'Janice?'

'No, I'm Nat, Janice's sister.'

'Good to talk to you.'

'Vanko.' Nat sniffed a few more times. 'I've got some terrible news.'

'What?'

'Janice ...' Nat took a few shuddering breaths. 'Janice suicided today.'

'What?'

Nat sobbed. 'She was so upset she couldn't help you. She had no money ...'

'For real? But that's crazy.'

'Yes. She felt so bad about your situation and that she couldn't help you escape.'

'How do you know it was because of me?'

'She left a suicide note on her computer.'

'For real? That's crazy bad.'

'Yes, and it's because she was addicted to stupid gaming.'

'Gaming isn't stupid!'

'It is when it kills people.' Nat sobbed. 'I have to go. I'm too upset to talk anymore.'

Nat hung up and turned towards me. 'How'd I do?'

'That bastard didn't even sound like he had any remorse. I feel awful for pretending to suicide, but the messages I got from the blind community, were that he never took no for an answer. He harassed and tormented people until they couldn't deal with it anymore. I'm told one gamer did suicide.'

'That's awful.' Nat shuddered.

'He's scammed tons of blindees out of money. I want to get him banned from the gaming sites.'

'Can you?'

'I'm working on it. At least he's had his PayPal account frozen.' I smiled.

'Really? What did you do?' Nat chuckled.

'I clicked the 'Report a violation' button on his account. I not only reported him trying to scam me, but I also received messages about him from blindees in other countries including Iran, Pakistan, and Afghanistan who he'd tried to scam. I listed all of his fraudulent behaviours. Best of all, these three countries are on the PayPal banned list, so once they've frozen his account for the next 180 days, he won't be able to use it again. Ever!'

Nat hooted with laughter. 'That'll teach him! Did you find out his real name?'

'Yeah, plus a whole load of other aliases. He's been in trouble with the law before. Not for scamming people, but because he groped a female support worker. But, huh. In Ukrainian Vanko means God's gift.' I snorted. 'Yeah right, he thinks he's god's gift to women!

'Eek! He sounds like a total sleaze ball. Is he really blind?'

'Yeah. Just because you're blind doesn't make you a nice person. But, the one positive is, I've found a game I love.'

'What's that?'

'Scambaiting!'

FOR LOVE OF THE GAME

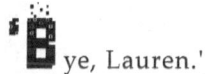

danielle hughes

'Bye, Lauren.'

'Bye!' I call out to my manager as I rush out of the staff room. Don't get me wrong, I love my job. Working in an electrical super-store gives me an employee discount on the new release gadgets for my gaming addiction. Thanks to my job I have the latest gaming laptop, the clearest sound-proof headset, and the best webcam available. Nothing compares to getting home and logging into my favourite fantasy game, *Odyssey Quest*. Last month I missed my brother's engagement party, and my dad's birthday dinner so I could stay home and play. Every spare minute I have I devote to playing *OQ*

Especially since I'd met Tarquin.

Sigh ...

Tarquin—Elven Warrior Lord, Commander of the High Elf Army Regiment, sworn to protect the Crystal Castle and keep the royal family safe. And super-hot. He's tall, full of muscle with wild flowing white hair, the colour of moonlight. He has violet eyes that can reach deep inside my soul and touch my inner core.

My avatar is Eloria—Wiccan Goddess of the Imperial Coven, who wields elemental power over the weather. She's fierce, with luscious strawberry coloured hair, alabaster skin, and jade eyes. Not to mention curvy in all the right places. A far cry from my reality.

I first met Tarquin about a month ago, he sought me out to ask for a spell to create a storm over the Faraday Valley. He needed to detain the Goblin Army, dispatched from the Shadow Lands to attack the Crystal Castle. We hit it off straight away. I accompanied Tarquin back to the valley and performed the spell myself. It was a huge success, earning me twenty-thousand gold coins, a full power-up and unlocked the next chapter in Eloria's spell book. Not to mention Eloria had spellbound Tarquin, and impressed him so much he added us as a Preferred Ally immediately. Winning!

Now every time I login, I check my *Messages* and *Task* folders straight away to see if there's anything from Tarquin. And to my delight, there usually is. Often he sets the location where we are to meet. At other times, it is a request for a talisman to help his army. I'm always quick to oblige. Sometimes he even leaves a gift in my *Inventory* folder. Last week, he sent me the Locket of Lorien, which gives me the ability of foresight.

176

Tarquin and Eloria have undeniable chemistry, and at the moment it's the highlight of my life. Our 'Relationship' level is almost at one hundred percent, which means we can move from 'Friendship' and into 'Romantic' status. My heart beats faster at the possibility. I've never reached 'Romantic' status with anyone before. I've always thought Eloria was too good for any of the Warriors or Warlocks I'd come across. Until Tarquin.

Our long, text-based interactions have revealed Tarquin is the avatar of Steve, who lives in Vancouver. Which is only a three-hour drive from where I live in Washington. Steve is twenty-eight, like me, and works as an IT support person for a large accounting firm. And he's single. Bonus!

The traffic is terrible on my drive home, bumper-to-bumper the entire way. I drum my hands on the steering wheel. My eyes flick from the road to the clock to my phone attached to the dash. Tarquin is expecting Eloria to meet him at the Silver Lake at sunset to exchange information. If the intelligence is well received our relationship status should level up and we'll finally have access to new interactions like 'Loving Gaze' and 'Tender Cheek Brush'. Not to mention 'Romanic Embrace' and 'First Kiss'. Squee! I get butterflies just thinking about it.

My street comes into view. A rush of excitement at talking with Tarquin makes my arms tingle. Turning down the narrow one-way road, I floor it until I reach my unit. I fly into my driveway, slam on the brakes, grab my bag off the passenger seat, and push open my door. Grunting in frustration as the strap of my bag catches on the handbrake, I aggressively yank it free, then dash to my front door. After fumbling with my keys, I find and shove the right one into the keyhole, wriggling until it gives way. I burst through the door, not bothering with the lights, and hurry into the kitchen, flinging my bag onto the beige-laminate counter. It knocks several unwashed dishes over and into the sink, but I'm too distracted to care right now. I want to find Tarquin. My laptop takes pride of place on my tiny, circular, wooden dining table, along with a luxury, black leather computer desk chair. I lift the cover and press 'On' holding it down for the three seconds it requires before the calming glow of the screen lights up. The relief is instant.

While my laptop loads, I pull a frozen dinner out of the freezer, toss it into the microwave, punching in five minutes on the timer. I fling the empty box in the bin where it collides with five other mac and cheese boxes. Throwing my jacket over my leather chair, I return to my login screen: Greetings Lauren!

I type my password, then drum my fingers as it continues to load. The second my desktop comes up I run my mouse over to the *Odyssey Quest* icon and double click. My heart beats faster in anticipation and I almost jump out of my skin when the microwave beeps. The scent of sharp cheddar riddles the air. By the time I dump the contents of the tray into a bowl and sit down, the magical forest and castle scene of *OQ* loads and I log in. The image of a gorgeous, sultry, and seductive Eloria fills my screen. I open the 'Outfit' tab and scroll through her available ensembles. She needs something special for tonight. I settle on a low-cut, white dress to accentuate her cleavage, with thigh-high splits on each side, leather sandals that snake up to her knee and style her hair in loose waves down her back. An outfit I would never pull off.

I shovel a spoonful of cheesy macaroni into my mouth as my 'Inventory' folder lights up to indicate a new addition. Opening it, a message pops up:

Tarquin has sent you a gift.

I click again. It's a stunning steel sword with an intricately carved bone handle and a floral pattern engraved down the length of the shaft. A message is written underneath:

A gift for my favourite Wiccan Goddess. Will you fight by my side against the Goblin Army?

I click on 'Accept gift', adding the sword to my outfit and quickly open my map to find the Silver Lake. A scroll fills my screen, with drawings of mountains, forests, roads, and villages, sporadically dotted with names indicating my friends and allies who are currently online. I've made some decent online-friendships since joining *OQ*, but none as special as Tarquin. A sharp *ping* reveals a message in my 'Chat' window. I open it up to see Tarquin's name and my stomach flutters.

Tarquin: I can't wait to see you, my flame-haired Goddess. Tonight is the night. Come find me. I'm waiting ... impatiently.

I suck in a sharp breath, sitting on the edge of my seat, and scan the map for his name. There, top left corner! I double click and agree to travel to Silver Lake. An hourglass appears, turning over and over, while the scene loads, and within seconds Eloria is transported. A lush forest in varying shades of green, with twisted vines, and purple wildflowers appears, I search my surrounds for a sign of the lake, or for Tarquin. A glow in the west catches my eye and I walk towards it. The trees part, and fire-flies buzz overhead, illuminating a silvery lake, shimmering under the setting sun. I pass several characters on my search for Tarquin: a robed warlock, a grey centaur, and a raven-haired maiden. But I ignore them all, rushing to find my Elven Warrior.

I spot him, gazing over the lake, and I engage 'Full Speed' to run towards him. I click on him, a selection of interactions fan out around his body. I select 'Friendly Hug' and watch as Eloria wraps her arms around Tarquin's neck, imagining it is me. A speech bubble appears from his head with the games pre-loaded conversation.

Greetings, friend. It is good to see you again. Do you have the information you promised?

A speech bubble appears above Eloria's head.

Hello, friend. I too am happy to see you again. Yes, I have the information to aid in your quest. The Mirror of Mystery can

DANIELLE HUGHES: FOR LOVE OF THE GAME

be found here, at the bottom of the Silver
Lake.

I click through the pre-loaded bubbles and can tell Steve is
doing the same. A *ping* sounds again, and my personal 'Chat'
window lights up.

> **Tarquin:** This is so tedious ... I can't
> wait to level up our relationship.
> **Eloria:** I know, me too. I've waited all day
> for this. It's been agonising.

A cloud of pink love hearts bursts around Tarquin and Eloria
with the words:

> Your characters have reached the highest
> level of friendship. Would you like to stay
> friends or pursue a romantic relationship?

I click 'Romantic' and a spinning hourglass appears over
Tarquin's head. I hold my breath, waiting for his response. The
hourglass turns into a red heart and I release my breath.
Tarquin's bubble reads:

> I find you irresistible and wish to be more
> than friends.

Eloria's bubble reads:

> I am enamoured by your presence and accept
> your proposal.

I click on Tarquin and scan through the new interactions available to us. My heart pounds in my chest, my palms become moist as I frantically click on all the new actions. Eloria leaps into Tarquin's arms, his muscular hands grasp her backside, before she slides back down to the ground, and Tarquin's hands caress her back, tangling in her hair, lowering his face to her upturned lips. I can practically feel his hands on me. My excitement builds as Eloria's hands wrap around Tarquin's shoulders, and he pulls her close, cupping her cheek in his palm, pressing his lips to hers. My breath comes in short gasps as they share their first kiss and the actions turn into more seductive options: 'Loving Caress', 'Passionate Kiss', and 'Sensual Embrace'. I click them all, eagerly watching as Tarquin and Eloria enact my fantasy.

Ping.

> **Tarquin:** This is intense.
> **Eloria:** It's amazing!
> **Tarquin:** I wish it could last forever. I wish it were real.
> **Eloria:** Me too.

I watch as Tarquin and Eloria finish their series of passionate interactions and remain embracing, gazing lovingly into each other's eyes. A new message appears on screen:

> Tarquin and Eloria have unlocked the Lovers Relationship Status. Would you like to consummate their relationship?

I gasp, bringing my hand to my mouth, my cursor hovering over the 'Yes' icon. Am I ready for this level of commitment? The message changes on the screen:

> Tarquin would like to invite Eloria to consummate their relationship. Yes or No?

Ping.

> **Tarquin:** Are you still there?
> **Eloria:** Yes.
> **Tarquin:** Are you ready for this? Or too soon?
> **Eloria:** I'm ready.

I click 'Yes' and Tarquin lays Eloria down on the long grass beside the lake. He caresses her face, then runs his hand down the side of her neck. I shiver in anticipation, focusing on every move. His hand continues down towards her chest then stops. Tarquin and Eloria shimmer for a moment, their images become blurred, and an hourglass appears above their fuzzy combined forms. 'Argh!' I cry in frustration as a hot flush spreads through my body unable to witness the vision I had imagined so many times.

Eloria: That was disappointing.

Tarquin: You wanted to watch?

Eloria: I hoped to see more than a hazy cloud.

Tarquin: I'll pass your feedback onto DreamTech.

Something tugs at the back of my mind. Why does DreamTech sound familiar?

Eloria: What?

Tarquin: I'll let my bosses know they should show more of the sexy stuff.

Eloria: Bosses?

Tarquin: Yeah. I work for DreamTech. I get paid to play the game and report back on player experience. Did I not tell you that?

Eloria: NO!

My cheeks turn hot, a sick feeling fills my stomach as the mac and cheese churns. Has Tarquin, I mean Steve, been lying to me this whole time? I remember seeing the DreamTech logo on the loading screen. I pound away at the keyboard.

Eloria: You told me you worked in IT support for an accounting firm!

Tarquin: Oh yeah, sorry, that's my cover story. DreamTech don't like me telling

my subjects too soon, it helps ensure
authentic feedback.
Eloria: Subjects?!?!?!

Is he serious? Is this all I mean to him? Is our entire
relationship based on using me for feedback? The illusion
of perfection I have for Tarquin is destroyed, along with
the impression I have of Steve.

Tarquin: You seem angry?

I watch my screen, blood boiling, anger rising, as Eloria and
Tarquin stand face to face, holding hands, their consummation
complete. I want to throw all the items he gifted me back in his
face. But as I scroll, a sense of satisfaction creeps in, replacing my
roiling anger. I watch with complete gratification as Eloria takes
up the sword, gifted to me by Tarquin, swings it high above her
head before whipping it directly into Tarquin's neck, severing his
head from his body.

Eloria: I feel much better now.

I hover my mouse over the crumpled form of Tarquin laying
at my feet and select 'Terminate Relationship' before closing the
lid of my laptop.

WHO KILLED FRANCESCA?

robin martin thomas

The crackling fire took the chill from an early winter evening as candlelight flickered on the faces of the five people gathered around the dining room table. Dr Malvado twisted the stem of a wineglass between his fingers.

'Thank you all for coming here on this sad occasion. Francesca would be so touched.'

Lavender Blue wiped a tear away. Alistair Rose, Francesca's nephew, lowered his eyes, while Sam Saffron, the retired detective, reached down to pat his faithful labradoodle, Chewbacca.

Cordelia Fuchsia clasped her hands to her chest. 'Francesca had such a powerful life force.' She stopped and gave a sob.

Alistair said, 'You have brought us together for a reason, Uncle?'

Malvado nodded. 'I invited each of you because you have a special talent, and you are connected to Francesca. You know Francesca passed away several weeks ago. What you don't know is the police suspect murder.'

There was an intake of breath around the room.

'What could we possibly do?' Lavender asked.

'Perhaps nothing, we'll see. I must know who killed my wife. The police haven't made any progress. So this weekend, the only time we could all meet, I want you to investigate. Alistair, you're always on that computer of yours. You should be good at finding out information. Sam, your ability to solve crimes is well known, some of them with the help of your trusty companion there.' Chewbacca's tail thudded on the floorboards. 'Lavender, you were one of Francesca's oldest friends. You might have some insight into who would want to kill her. Cordelia, you claim psychic powers. Now is the time to use them.'

'What's in it for us?' Alistair cut in.

Dr Malvado's head shook in disgust. 'You were her nephew. Don't you care?'

'Care? She showed little when I needed her.'

'You mean she stopped giving you money for your gaming addiction, after shelling out for years? Never mind. There's no game without a prize. I'm offering ten thousand dollars to the person who solves the mystery—who killed Francesca? You have this weekend to discover it. My house is at your disposal. You may choose to leave now. But if you stay, then you're in this till the end.'

His eyes scanned the room. 'Does anyone wish to leave?' No one stirred. 'Good. Let's begin.'

Lavender rested her chin on her hands. 'Perhaps you could give us some details of the case.'

Dr Malvado nodded. 'Francesca was found dead in her bed by our housekeeper, Lettica Green. Sadly, the autopsy showed she'd been dead for at least two days. I was at a conference in Melbourne at the time.' Malvado gave a heavy sigh and was silent for a moment. Then he continued. 'There were no signs of struggle, no blood. She hadn't been feeling well for some time, headaches, occasional vomiting and so forth. But no one, including Francesca herself, thought it was anything serious. The coroner's report was inconclusive, so there is a homicide investigation.'

Sam nodded. 'Yes, that's the usual procedure.'

'If it wasn't a natural death, then that leaves either suicide, or ... murder,' Malvado continued. 'As you know, Francesca was writing her autobiography. As a journalist, she'd uncovered a lot of scandals and exposed many people. Some were worried about her upcoming book.'

'And you think someone might have murdered her to stop its release? Seems drastic.' Alistair's tone was dismissive.

'Your aunt knew people from all walks of life. It's not inconceivable that one of them might hold a grudge.' Lavender said.

'But the book could be published posthumously, couldn't it?' Sam asked.

Malvado sighed. 'It wasn't finished, and I really wouldn't know how to complete it, nor do I want to now. There'll be no autobiography.'

'So, the murderer's objective has been achieved,' Lavender said, her brow furrowing.

'But was it murder? And how was it done?' Cordelia said.

'That's where you come in, with your psychic powers, I thought we might start with a seance.' Dr Malvado lifted an eyebrow. 'That's if everyone is willing.'

There were nods from Sam and Lavender, while Alistair rolled his eyes.

'The spirit has to move me. My dear Francesca must want to communicate with us. But I can try. Turn off the lights.'

Malvado flicked the switch. Only the candlelight glimmered.

Cordelia lowered her voice, 'Now, hold hands.' Sam protested. 'Silence please,' she ordered. 'I call upon the spirit, Francesca Malvado. Speak to us, come to us, let us know you are present.'

A long silence followed, punctuated only by an impatient sigh from Alistair. Then, a sudden draught of air extinguished the candles and the room plunged into darkness.

'What the ...' Sam said. Chewbacca growled.

'Shh,' Malvado hissed.

'Is that you, Francesca? Are you with us? Send us a sign.' A soft scratching was heard on the window outside.

'It's just the wind blowing the branches of the tree outside,' Alistair said.

Silence again. Then a high, thin voice spoke. 'Why did you do it? I trusted you.' There was a long wail, wuthering like wind down a chimney. The voice continued. 'You've been trying to kill me for months. Why?'

'Who's been trying to kill you, Francesca?' Lavender said.

No answer.

Without warning, the candles' flames flared again, revealing Cordelia's head on the table, her arms spread out on either side. Malvado flicked on the lights. She sat up, her eyes glazed for a few moments. 'Did she come?'

'Something came,' Malvado said, 'but it seemed reluctant to answer questions.' He raised an eyebrow as he looked at Cordelia.

'The spirit said someone was trying to kill her for months,' Lavender added. 'When I asked who, the candles blazed again.'

'Ah yes,' Cordelia said, 'the connection was broken. Sometimes it's wise just to listen and not ask questions.'

'How convenient—for the ghost,' Alistair said.

'At least we have our first clue. If the spirit is to be believed, Francesca was murdered by someone she knew, and they'd been trying for some time.' Malvado looked around the table, his eyes landing on Alistair. 'That could be anyone here.'

'I've only visited my aunt once or twice in the last few months. When she died, I was nowhere near her.' Alistair's voice was indignant.

'I was her spiritual guide. Surely tonight proves I have nothing to hide.' Cordelia's voice was high pitched.

'And what about you, uncle? You're as much a suspect as the rest of us.'

191

Malvado narrowed his eyes as he looked at Alistair. There was no love lost between them. 'I would have hardly arranged this weekend if I were the murderer.'

'I dunno. This could be just a cover. The police probably suspect you and you're trying to pin it on someone else. After all, weren't you and my aunt considering a separation? Yeah, you didn't think I knew that, did you? Aunt Francesca and I were closer than you realised.'

All eyes turned towards Dr Malvado. Sam raised an eyebrow.

'That's preposterous. Francesca and I had some issues, but we weren't thinking of separation. And I would never, ever hurt her.' He struggled to gain control. Taking a deep breath, he said, 'I think we have talked enough tonight. We should retire and conduct our independent investigations tomorrow. We'll meet for dinner in the evening to share what we've discovered.'

They left to go to their rooms, each with their own thoughts about what they had learned that evening.

The next morning, Sam got up early to take Chewbacca for a walk. He looked at the spacious two-storey brick mansion, with ivy covered columns supporting an upper balcony. For someone fit and nimble, it wouldn't be hard to climb up to the next floor. His lips pursed and his eyes narrowed as he thought of who that might include. The dog tugged on the lead, so he continued the walk, his feet crunching on the gravel driveway as he went past the fountain. They turned down the path that led to the back of the house, where the gardens stretched for half an acre. There was money on both sides of the family, and it showed. Who would benefit from Francesca's death? Her husband, obviously, and last night they'd heard there were problems in the marriage. Sam played chess sometimes with Malvado, but he didn't know him that well.

'Come on, Chewbacca,' he called. It didn't take long to navigate the garden, but when they passed the shed, Chewbacca stopped.

'What is it, boy?'

The dog began sniffing at the door. Sam pushed it open and entered the semi-darkness of the shed where the lawn mower, tools, and garden furniture were stored. Turning on the light, he saw the dog heading towards some bags of manure. 'Chewbacca, come away.'

Sam turned to go and bumped against a shelf. Several plant pots came tumbling down with a clatter. His eyes flew to what lay on the floor next to them—a small handgun.

'Well, this is interesting.' Sam grabbed an old piece of towelling and bent down to pick it up. 'Chewbacca, you've just helped find clue number two.'

Meanwhile, Lavender Blue searched Francesca's bedroom. She couldn't find anything, which was both frustrating and worrying. What had happened to Francesca? She should be able to work this out. She and Frankie were old school friends. Frankie had become a journalist, and Lavender ... her career path had been quite different. ASIO had recruited her at uni. Her cover had been a travel agent, able to travel the world without suspicion. No one, not even Frankie, knew what she did. Although, did she?

Sometimes, Lavender wondered. But, of course, Frankie would never have revealed that in her book ... would she? Lavender was retired now, but she wouldn't want that information to become public.

Feeling discouraged, she went to the kitchen for a cup of tea. Lettica Green, the housekeeper, was stirring soup on the stovetop. She'd been hired a couple of months ago and Lavender had only met her yesterday when she'd arrived. As the small, blond woman turned, Lavender was struck by the feeling of having met her before. She had an accent Lavender couldn't quite place, though her English was impeccable.

'Yes, Ms Lavender, may I help you?

'Just came to grab a cup of tea. I can get it myself.'

'It's no trouble. Please sit down.'

As Lettica filled the kettle and got the teapot out, Lavender said, 'I can't help feeling we've met before.'

Lettica shook her head. 'I don't think so. I don't go out much.'

The kettle boiled and she made the tea, bringing it over to the kitchen table, along with a small jug of milk and a bowl of sugar cubes.

'Won't you join me, Lettica? I'd like to ask you a few questions about Francesca.'

With an air of reluctance, the housekeeper sat across from her. 'I really can't tell you much at all. I haven't been here long.'

Lavender poured her tea, stirring in her milk.

'Sugar miss?'

'No, I loathe it in tea.'

'Not like Mrs Malvado then. She had three, sometimes four cubes in hers.'

Lavender smiled. 'Yes, she always had a sweet tooth. Did she still like her morning cuppa before getting up?'

Lettica nodded. 'Every morning at eight o'clock.

'Do you live in?'

'No, I just come in the day.'

'I noticed you have an accent. Where are you from, originally?'

'Australia, but my parents were immigrants. We spoke ... Croatian at home. Is there anything else, Miss? I really need to get the lunch started.'

'No, don't let me keep you.'

Sighing, Lavender got up to leave. On an impulse, she picked up a sugar cube from the bowl and put it in her pocket.

Alistair Rose had lost again in the online game he'd played this morning. He was in serious debt from his gambling. He had to win the prize money for solving his aunt's murder. His number one suspect was Malvado, but it could be one of the others. He spent the afternoon in the library doing research online. You could find out a lot on the internet, especially about ways to murder someone.

At four o'clock he smiled. It might be insignificant, but maybe not. If he was on the right track, he just might solve this murder.

There was an air of heightened excitement that night at dinner. No one spoke much, and little was eaten. Everyone was waiting for the end of the meal when all would be revealed.

Sam was certain his bombshell would be the finale of the evening.

Cordelia had consulted her cards, and as usual, they hadn't disappointed. The ten thousand dollars was as good as hers.

Lavender looked thoughtful, while Alistair wore his usual smug expression.

After coffee was served, Dr Malvado asked, 'So, has anyone discovered anything significant today?'

'Did you know,' Alistair said, 'cyanide can be given in small doses and it disappears from the system after a day or two? Aunt Francesca's body wasn't found for two days, and you were conveniently away. Uncle. I think you'd been poisoning her for months.'

Malvado's voice rose. 'That's a ridiculous idea. If I was the murderer, I'd hardly—'

Cordelia interrupted. 'No, it wasn't Malvado. I've read the cards. It was a woman from Francesca's past. You knew her the longest. You killed Francesca.' She turned accusing eyes on Lavender.

Lavender's face coloured. 'You charlatan! You were worried Francesca would reveal you as a fraud. There's some merit in Alistair's theory of poison. Perhaps that's why this sugar cube seemed so important to me.' She took the cube from her pocket and put it on the table. 'Subconsciously, it triggered my memory about poisons. How easy cyanide would be to administer over time. No wonder Francesca was feeling poorly. Cordelia was poisoning her!'

Cordelia rose from her chair in fury, when Sam said, 'Be quiet, all of you. Look what Chewbacca and I found hidden in the garden shed this morning.' He took out the small revolver and laid it on the table. 'I believe this belongs to you, Lavender.'

Lavender looked at it in shock.

'Explain,' Dr Malvado said, his black eyes narrowing.

'I wondered where she hid it. I couldn't find it in her room today, so I thought she'd got rid of it. Yes, it was mine. I lent it to her for safety. She told me six months ago she was worried about being on her own because you travelled a lot. And, in case you forgot, she wasn't shot. Besides, why would I want her dead? She was my best friend.'

'Because she might reveal your little secret in her book,' Sam said.

'What secret?' Lavender grew pale.

'You worked for ASIO.'

'How would you know that?'

'Easy, Francesca told him.' Alistair said, 'Sam was having a secret affair with her. I came upon them once. Why do you think she kept giving me money?'

'You lowlife,' Malvado shouted, raising his fist at Sam.

'We were just friends.' Sam took a backwards step.

Cordelia turned to Alistair and raised an accusing finger. 'Maybe you poisoned her when she stopped giving you money.'

'You're a fake and a liar,' Alistair shouted.

The voices rose until a crash came from the kitchen. Lettica came running into the dining room. 'That damn *sobaka* has run off with the rest of the roast. Someone get him!'

Lavender straightened. 'I know who did it!'

The urgency of her voice caused everyone to look at her.

'Lettica, I remember you now. I know where I've seen you before. You were one of the Russian agents who worked as a translator in London. One of my contacts pointed you out as someone to watch. Your English is very good, but you tripped yourself up, didn't you?'

'You're crazy,' Lettica said

'You said the Russian word for dog, *sobaka*. It slipped out because you were excited.'

'No, I said Chewbacca. You are making this up.'

'Lavender is right. You said *sobaka*,' Sam said.

'And what would a Russian agent want with Francesca,' Lettica said with scorn.

'Her book was going to reveal many things, perhaps some of them about Russian operatives and what they are up to here in Australia. Your government wanted to get rid of her before anything damaging got out. Isn't that right, Svetlana?'

The housekeeper's face turned white.

'Every time I visited you would bring us tea and my aunt would put sugar in it,' Alistair said.

'Exactly. She put the poison in the cubes. One wouldn't kill, but over time ...' Lavender added.

Lettica looked from side to side, then made a dash for the door. She was too quick for them, but as she ran down the hall, there was a bark by the front door. Chewbacca hadn't gone far with his prize roast. There was a thump and a cry. Sam raced out of the room. 'Good boy, Chewbacca, you've got her.'

'Game over,' said Malvado, taking out his phone and stopping the timer.

'Obviously, I won,' Lavender said.

'My idea was cyanide, so really, I won too,' Alistair said.

'What about me?' Cordelia piped up. 'I said it was a woman from the past. I did well on the seance too, didn't I? Should get extra points for that.'

Sam and Lettica came in through the door, followed by the dog. 'Chewbacca caught the thief, so he should get a share, which comes to me.'

'I'm sick of being the villain,' Lettica complained, sitting down.

Francesca entered and sat down next to her. 'It's better than being the murder victim. I'm not even in this game, except for a few moans and wails in the seance.'

Malvado looked at his phone. 'Took you twenty-four hours and thirty-five minutes to solve this one. You've done better. I think this time the credit goes to the four of you, equal points. Who wants to be game master next?'

THE NEMESIS

robin adolphs

The feeling's back. The one that makes me shake all over like a half-drowned dog. And it's all the fault of that egotistical Duvall. That fancy-named, can't-do-wrong, Duvall. How I hate him.

Ever since we'd been hired, yes, on the same day, by Stephens and Son Solicitors, he'd been the pin-up boy. Everyone was taken in by Duvall's supercilious smile, permanently glued to his tanned 'aren't I gorgeous' face. His *modus operandi* was smiling into women's eyes until they were under his spell.

Nobody took any notice of me, Invisible Ivan. It was as though I didn't exist. How could I compete with a handsome, manipulative Adonis? Behind that sugar-coated exterior I could tell he was pure slime.

It came to a head when the boss told the whole 'Team', meaning all the executives and solicitors, we were going on a Workplace Team Building weekend. The intention was to get to know each other better, build mutual trust and learn how to 'read' people. And do it all by playing games. Great. We were really going to a school camp. An idea started to germinate in my mind.

The day came. We set off in a bus of all things. How chummy. It just gave Duvall more of a chance to weave his spells along the way. After four bumpy hours, we arrived at an old mansion, recently converted into a Convention Centre. This did not look like any school camp I'd ever been on. No tents in the bush or paint peeling wooden huts.

From the moment I walked through the groaning, wooden front door, my heart started thumping. This was my kind of place. The corridors were dark and gloomy with gaslights shedding puddles of light along the high-ceilinged corridors. Imagine my horror when I learned Duvall and I were sharing a room for the weekend. But seeing as how I was the only one who wasn't fooled by Debonair Duvall, maybe it was a good idea. Alone with me, he didn't have a gallery of adoring fans.

At breakfast, we were handed our itinerary. I slid my eyes down the day's activities. Not too bad. Should be fun, as long as Duvall didn't get in my way.

In the morning, we played trust-building exercises outside. We fell backwards off a low wall and our Team caught us. Then we led each other around blindfolded. I was so glad I didn't have to lead Duvall around. I would have let him trip or smash into a tree.

The rest of the day we spent mingling and getting to know each other. That really meant digging up dirt on each other, forming malicious alliances, spreading rumours and backstabbing. Amazing what people will tell you when they trust you.

Then we played 'Hot Seat' where, using our newly acquired knowledge, we pretended to be someone we'd just 'interviewed'. Everyone tried to guess who we were. There were no other rules except anyone could question the person on the hot seat. I actually laughed when someone pretended to be Duvall. Had him down pat. Gestures and all.

It took me longer than usual to get dressed for the party. Duvall kept hogging the mirror, but finally I was ready. Actually, I looked pretty good in my penguin suit.

When I finally made it down the stairs, the party was in full swing. Long distorted shadows loomed and contorted on the walls, creating the ambiance for a perfect Agatha Christie murder scene.

My colleagues were giving each other the third degree over cocktails. Some people were even taking notes. Talk about competitive. We'd been told never to judge a person by their looks. If we wanted to be really good at our jobs, we had to know how to assess a person's character.

Then the organiser announced the game for the evening was 'Pick the Murderer'. She gave everyone a 'secret' card with the role we would play at the party. One was the murderer card with the motive on it. I caught a glimpse of Duvall's card. He wasn't the murderer. On the contrary, he was a victim.

The idea was, while we sipped away on cocktails, we would mingle *again* and cross-examine, all the time trying to figure out who would most likely be the one to commit murder. At the end of the night, we'd get a chance to speculate who the murderer was and how we reached our verdicts.

I glanced at Duvall. He was grinning and flirting, strutting around like a puffed-up pheasant. The rage built in my chest. As usual, he was the man in the spotlight. And me? Nobody saw me. I was invisible to them while Duvall was around.

Then it hit me. This was the ideal opportunity to solve all my problems and give them more than a game. A *real murder*. But I had to be clever.

All I could think about was how to get away with the *perfect* murder. Nobody must guess it was me. But they wouldn't, I didn't have the *murderer* card. I already had a patsy; the poor sod who'd been given that card. The cocktail party provided the perfect setting.

As for motive, well that was obvious. I couldn't get on with my life while Duvall was around. He'd eaten his way into my mind. He was everything I was not. Maybe with him gone, I could get some attention.

I looked at the buffet. There were charcuterie boards lined up ready for the hungry horde. And on each board was a long-pronged fork. No picking up food with fingers for us.

I sidled over to the buffet and slipped one of the forks inside my jacket. I now had my *perfect* murder weapon. Duvall was in for a sweet, sweet ride into the hereafter. Today will be the last time he ever gets his own way. After tonight, I'd be the one they all wanted to be with. I'd take his place and he wouldn't be able to do a thing about it because he'd be dead.

I straightened my jacket and glued a smile on my face as I made my way back to the party. As usual Duvall was swarmed by adoring women.

'Hey girls,' I said. 'Tear yourselves away from Golden Boy and go and get another cocktail. And get out of my damned way.'

That got their attention. For once, they saw me. Not Duvall. I could tell by their shocked faces. Maybe my language was a bit off. But any attention was better than none. Then the moment was lost as Duvall started with the jokes, and I became invisible again.

As though on cue, the lights went out and the high-pitched screams of the women rose above the rest. The band started playing creepy music and everyone's attention was drawn its way.

'Got a minute, Mate?' I whispered to Duvall.

I walked down the corridor, feeling Duvall's breath. Tasting it. My heart thudding so hard in my chest I thought they could hear it over the music. I'd never felt this excited in my life. I was judge, jury, and executioner. I raised the fork. My mouth slit into a grin, and I heard the shrill sound of my screams join with Duvall's.

As I shoved the fork deeper into my chest, tearing the last breath from my body I became free. Free from that dominating, insufferable Duvall who took over my life.

Then it hit me. I'd never be able to take Duvall's place. Duvall and I were one. He had taken me with him into oblivion.

And peace.

THE DEVIL'S IN THE DETAIL

michaela sanderson

The priest bolted into the woods, hounds in pursuit. Thick fog concealed his path, the ground was icy, and he slipped, the glowing bag slamming into his hip. The baying grew closer. He struggled up. Through the fog emerged a huge dog with snarling jaws and savage teeth. The priest lurched sideways, the ground underneath his feet crumbling, then gone. Bones shattered as he bounced on rocks and slid into the water. The bag broke free from his frozen fingers, floating away down the icy stream.

When the Hunters found him, a few minutes later, he was dead. A quick search found no trace of the bag.

PRESENT DAY

'This looks like where Liam said he found the gold.' Toby strode towards a felled tree and crouched at its roots. Nothing. He worked his way across the cleared land, jumped the muddy stream, then scrambled along a newly felled tree into its lower branches. He slid down and several eggshells drew him towards the roots of another tree. 'What's this?' A large leather bag was tangled in the muddy roots. Toby crawled forward and wrestled it free.

'Hey! Get out of here! This is private property!' A security guard lumbered towards him. Toby darted away. He slid under the fence, dashed into the bush, and when he realised no one was following him, stopped to see what was in the bag. It began to glow.

The woman slipped the glowing bag to the priest. 'You must keep this safe. It cannot fall into the wrong hands. I'm afraid of what would happen if it did.'

The priest took it and fumbled with the knot of leather.

'No. You mustn't!' The woman stilled his hand. 'If you open it, you will begin a game you cannot stop. A game with terrible consequences.'

He stopped. 'What is in it?'

'A haunted chaturanga set. Terrible yet beautiful ... Take it to the Creator. He will know what to do with it. Go now. Do not stop for anything.'

The door flew open, and men swarmed the church. Hunters. The woman loosed an arrow into the first man's chest, then another into a second. She turned to the priest, 'Go!' She felled a third, then went down in a wave of curses, an arrow protruding from her chest.

In his dad's man-cave, Toby struggled with the knot keeping the glowing bag closed. He grabbed his pocketknife, cut it off, and opened the bag. Inside, he saw two small bags, and four pieces of wood. He poured the wooden pieces out onto the table. They were all the same size, about a foot square. Each had two holes on one side and two protruding plugs on another. They were worn and splintering. Toby clipped them together and studied them. The squares were red and white, but he recognised them. 'It's a chess set.' He glanced over to the shelf where his set was sitting beside his chess clock, then reached into the bag again. He took out a smaller bag and fumbled with the ties around it. He looked inside. White figures. He tipped them out.

'Congratulations, Toby, you have begun the game,' a gravelly voice spoke.

The figures spilled across the table as Toby stared at what stood before him, and screamed.

The man in furs dragged his daughter from her bed. 'The Holding will soon be breached, and the Hunters will steal the chaturanga set.' He thrust a bag at her. 'You must take it to the priest. Tell him to take it to the Creator.'

She pulled on her weapons and hurried to her horse. As she mounted, a terrible scream sounded. The horse reared and she saw her father surrounded by Hunters.

'Go!' He gestured as he fell, and she spurred her horse forward.

'Toby ...'

Toby screamed again as shadows swirled around him, all claws and teeth, monsters from his nightmares. He darted towards the door, but something seized his shoulder. 'Let's play.' A demon, with impossibly long teeth, red skin, and fiery eyes held him high.

'Help!' Toby cried.

'It's too late. You set up the board which means you are ready to play. Empty the other bag.'

'No!'

'Do it,' the demon roared, letting him go.

Toby shrieked and emptied the other bag onto the table.

'It will be safe in the Holding.' The man in furs took the glowing bag from the trembling peasant. *'If what you say is true, then the set should be destroyed. However, it is not for me to destroy what is both essentially good and essentially evil. It is best it is hidden and forgotten.'*

The peasant bowed. 'Thank you, my Lord.'

A servant girl listened. A chaturanga set that could heal the sick. Or unleash demons. The Hunters would pay handsomely for this information.

Red figures tumbled across the table and the shed lit up. Toby looked around. The demon leaned towards him. 'The one who activates the game, must play. You must play or forfeit your life.'

Toby backed away. 'I can't—'

'Let's begin.' The demon slammed his hand down, and the pieces flew into place. 'Take the red pieces.'

'I can't play against you. You're too powerful.' His voice trembled.

The demon considered this. It nodded. 'Very well, I will find you a human player.'

There was a flash of black smoke and Toby was momentarily blinded.

The peasant used his teeth to open the first bag the merchant had given him. Figures made of a beautiful red wood scattered across the table. He picked up one piece and studied it. A man with a beard. The peasant felt a warmth in his injured hand. His eyes widened as the wound healed, the flesh regenerated, the skin knitted. 'Oh Lord.' He dropped the carving. He called his wife and his children. His wife picked up a piece, then dropped it. Her skin lesions were gone.

His son, blind since birth, touched a piece. 'Papa, I can see.'

The peasant opened the second bag. White figures tumbled out. Shadows swirled around his family, dark shadows with claws and teeth. The peasant screamed. He shoved the pieces back into the bag, and the shadows disappeared. He had to give this to his Lord. He would know what to do.

When the smoke cleared, a man stood on the other side of the table. His short hair was dark, his nose bent, his eyes cold and uncaring.

Toby yelped, 'He's not much better!'

The man faced the demon, and bowed. 'My Lord.'

211

The demon stared at Toby, 'Allow me to introduce Adrik Vyronov.'

'Who?'

'Adrik Vyronov. The Checksecutioner.' The demon frowned. 'You have never heard of him?'

Toby shook his head.

'Serial killer. Killed sixty-three people.'

Toby shook his head again.

'No? Tonight, he will kill another to make sixty-four. The number of squares on a chessboard'

Toby drew back, but the demon seized him. 'Let's play.'

The merchant woke, screaming of demons and monsters, once again. The carpenter had cursed him with his last bloody breath, and his journey from India had been marred by nightmares. He'd sold the girl, hoping to ease the torment, but the horrors continued. The evil therefore must be coming through the chaturanga set; he had to get rid of it. Hell, the bag had begun to glow after he sold the girl. It had to be evil. He packed his cart and left the camp. Ahead he saw a peasant man with an injured hand. 'Kind sir, can I interest you in a game?'

The demon threw Toby into a chair and gestured to Adrik to sit opposite him. 'Two games. The first a warm-up. Winner of the second game is the winner overall. Understood?'

Adrik nodded. 'You know quickplay, boy?'

'Quickplay?'

'Fast-timed game. You have chess clock?'

Toby nodded and pointed to the shelf with a shaking finger. 'There. It's my father's.' He spun in his chair to look at the demon. 'I can't do this. I'll lose and he'll kill me. Find someone else to play. Please. I don't want to die.'

Adrik leaned over, 'You won't die. I kill you before that.'

Toby stood.

'Sit!' The demon slammed the clock down on the edge of the table. 'You know the rules?'

'My dad taught me ... I ... I know all the rules.'

'You use the red pieces.' The demon fiddled with the clock, then turned it so the players could see. 'Begin.'

The merchant studied the lowly carpenter before him. 'You want food. You must trade something. What do you have?'

The carpenter looked at his pregnant wife and his three children. They had to eat. He grabbed a large brown bag. 'I have this.' He tipped the contents out onto the wagon. There were four squares that locked together to form a board, and two smaller bags. He emptied them out too. Carved figures spilled out. He picked out a small carving and handed it to the merchant. It was a man, in a robe, bearded, with gentle eyes.

'What is this?'

'A chaturanga set. We play in the evenings.'

The merchant looked at the eldest daughter. She was old enough to be a wife. 'I don't want that. I want her.'

'No, you will not have my daughter.'

The merchant slid his sword free from its scabbard. 'I will take her then.'

The battle was short. The merchant, victorious. He bundled the weeping girl into his wagon, and the chaturanga set.

Toby touched the pawn protecting his queen, and gasped. 'It's warm.'

The demon growled, 'Yes. Love, faith, and forgiveness are in the red pieces. Stupid pathetic emotions.'

Toby slid it to d4 and pressed the clock with that hand.

Adrik moved his pawn to e5, and tapped the clock correctly.

Toby captured that pawn, but almost dropped it. 'It's cold.'

'Yes. Pain, grief, and fear are always cold. So too is death.'

Adrik placed his queen on e7 and leered at Toby.

'Knight,' Toby murmured as he lifted the knight to f3.

The game progressed quickly. Both players moved and slapped the clock rhythmically. Adrik brought his knight to c6 to hunt down the pawn. Toby retaliated by dropping his bishop on f4 to protect the pawn. Adrik dragged his queen to b4, and Toby hurried his bishop back to protect his king.

Adrik slid his queen to b2 and took Toby's pawn. He picked it up, then dropped it, 'That burns!' He turned his hand and there were blisters on his fingertips.

Toby dragged his bishop forward one square to attack the queen. Adrik laughed and moved his bishop with his unburnt fingers, pinning Toby's bishop. Toby dropped his queen on d2.

'Idiot boy!' Adrik captured Toby's bishop.

Without thinking, Toby used his queen to take Adrik's bishop.

Adrik leaned over and slammed his queen forward. 'Check!' Moments later, 'Checkmate!'

'I have wood for you, Abram' The farmer gestured to the cart.

'Thank you. I want to carve some figures.' The carpenter walked to the cart. He traced the two pieces of wood with his finger. Both were many cubits long, one slightly bigger than the other. 'The remains of a cross?'

The farmer shrugged. 'Good wood, Abram. Beautiful colours.'

The carpenter nodded, 'You are right. The deep red. Beautiful. It will make a beautiful chaturanga set. I will buy it.'

Toby began to tremble. 'I can't do this.'

The demon slapped the table, 'Let's play.'

'Give me a moment.' Toby studied the board, muttering to himself. He pushed his fear away. This was not the time to be afraid. He had to be smart. He couldn't win against Adrik by playing a fair game, but maybe, just maybe, he could win by foul means. Surely the demon would appreciate that. The first time he made a stupid mistake cost him a game against his father. His father never let him forget what he had done. Maybe Adrik could be tricked into making a mistake. Toby pretended to straighten the board and moved it a little closer to the clock and the edge of the table.

Adrik waited. 'Come, boy. It over soon. I be gentle when I take your life ... I kidding, no I won't.'

Toby ignored him and slid his pawn to e4.

Adrik shifted his own pawn to e5. Toby lifted his knight to f3. Adrik followed again very quickly, moving his knight to c6. The tapping of the chess clock was a continuous backbeat.

215

Toby counteracted with a quick move; bishop to c4, then reached for the clock, but knocked it to the floor. 'Sorry.' He picked it up and placed it on the other side of the board. 'Is it okay on this side? You'll have to reach over the board to tap it.'

'Yes.' Adrik nodded then slid his knight between Toby's bishop and his pawn. He reached over and tapped the clock.

Toby moved his knight to take out Adrik's pawn, then tapped too. 'Failed serial killer hey?'

'What? No.' Adrik brought out his queen, and it sat just across from Toby's knight in g5. He then used his non-playing hand to press the clock.

'Wrong hand. Only warning.' Toby grinned at Adrik.

Adrik growled.

Toby pushed his knight into Adrik's ranks, just in front of his bishop in f7. 'You think you're good, but you're in jail, loser. Couldn't even murder people without getting caught.'

'I'll murder you, boy.' Adrik snarled and slid his queen to g2, taking Toby's pawn.

'You think you're top shit, but you got caught.' Toby shoved his rook beside his king.

The tapping of the clock was almost simultaneous.

'What you know? I killed sixty-three people; you'll make sixty-four.' Adrik's face was red, his eyes narrow and dark. He slammed his queen on e4, taking Toby's pawn.

Toby moved his bishop to e2 to protect his king. 'Even with the help of the demon, you won't get sixty-four. You're a loser!'

'I kill you, little bastard.' He shoved his knight to f3. 'Check.'

Moments later it was done. Adrik leaned over and grabbed Toby by the shirt. 'I going to enjoy this.'

'You didn't touch the clock, you haven't won.'

Adrik roared and let Toby go. He slammed his hand down on the clock, causing it to bounce across the table. 'I won! Now you mine!'

'You used the wrong hand! I won. You're disqualified.' Toby slammed his fists down on the table.

Adrik charged at Toby, eyes flashing, fingers like talons. 'I kill you!'

But the demon pulled Adrik back and held him with blazing hands. 'You lost. You broke the rules.' The screaming killer vanished.

The farmer wandered the hill of Golgotha, looking for anything he could salvage. Several executions a week ago had drawn big crowds. He scoured the site for something he could sell. He led his donkey down the hill, then stopped. At his feet, lay a dismantled cross. There were red stains around the head area. Red stains where the feet and hands were nailed. He loaded it into his cart. The carpenter would pay generously for this.

The demon stalked over to Toby. 'You won.' He gathered up the chess pieces and bundled everything into the bags. 'You get to keep your life.' A flash of smoke, and the demon vanished. But the bag was left on the table.

The day had been a success. Three men dead. Crowds appeased. The crosses were knocked down to allow the retrieval of the bodies. As ordered, with iron scarce, a Roman soldier pulled the nails from the bodies, and tossed the blood-stained wood down the hill.

With hands shaking, Toby opened the bag. The chess set and the pieces were all gone. Toby tipped it out. Thirty gold coins tumbled across the table. Liam was right. There was gold to be found, but the devil was in the detail.

WELCOME TO DOMINIONCORP

dr aletia johnson

You are right and everyone else is wrong:
A Beginner's Guide to World Domination.

Criminal Mastermind, Evil Overlord, Big Bad Ugly. Have these terms haunted you throughout your career? At DominionCorp we do not endorse them. We see *our* clients as 'World Management Engineers'.

Every world is riddled with corruption, pollution, and widespread social and economic disadvantage. Why? Because the people running them aren't *qualified*! Your world needs someone like *you*, someone with *your* specific vision and *your* specific skill set.

You are different to, *and better than*, everybody else. At DominionCorp, we understand this. Democracy is for suckers. Every world deserves a properly qualified, properly organised, and properly *insured* Tyrant, to create stability and maintain world peace. [1]

Are you the only Nineteenth-level sorcerer with a penchant for necromancy in a world full of unexceptional humans? Do you have a genius level intellect combined with what the uneducated would call 'a complete lack of morals'? DominionCorp *won't* judge you for being who you are. Our goal is to help you *fulfil* your rightful destiny, even if other people might not consider that destiny to be very 'nice'.

Whether you wish to overthrow your local monarch for financial gain or petty revenge, or have been chosen by the one True Deity to bring about His/Her/Its return to His/Her/Its rightful place as your world's anointed Lord and Master, talk to us first. We can help you succeed where others have failed, *especially* if you have to cleanse your world of all unbelievers in the process. Perfection takes commitment, after all.

Our executive range of products and services include:

✔ Minion Protection Plans (Health and wellbeing services for your workforce, now incorporating our patented *Respawn*™ and *MiindWipe*™ technology) [2]

✔ Empire Protection: Insurance and strategic Risk Management advice

✔ Minion Procurement and Training (through our subsidiary, The DominionCorp Minions Union (DCMU)) [3]

✔ Prisoner Services: Offsite interrogation and high-risk prisoner storage [4]

✓ Banking, campaign finance and hoard management services

✓ Thaumatological Support, where available [5]

[1] It becomes *very* peaceful when no-one is allowed to complain.

[2] Repairing damaged minions is more cost effective than creating and/or training new ones each time someone asks, 'What does this button do?'

[3] The DCMU promotes minions' rights, specifically their right to experience continued existence and not die horribly because of other people's incompetence.

[4] Flame Demons, princesses, and orphans with mysterious birth marks routinely escape from standard dungeon facilities. A more *personalised* touch is often required.

[5] To qualify for thaumatological support, the existence of Magic must be supported by the laws of Physics in your region.

21 June

Dear Mr Verdant,

On behalf of our Shadowy Board of Directors, I am delighted to officially welcome you to the DominionCorp family, as one of our Independent World Management Engineers.

We admire your decision to make your world a better, more *organised* place by imposing your iron will and complete control upon it. We trust that your eventual success will lead to proper order and lasting stability for those entities under your (mostly) benevolent rule.

Our organisation is dedicated to help you achieve your goals. Part bank, part insurance company, part human and non-human resource management service, we exist specifically to facilitate *your* World Domination needs.

We pride ourselves on our discretion. For as long as you use our products, DominionCorp will never compromise your data, secret identity or doomsday plans to any law enforcement agency, third party or rival consortium, except for marketing and quality control purposes. Please enjoy your enclosed Welcome Pack, which details the many services we offer.

You have purchased basic *Hero Incursion Insurance* (HII) and a *Minion Protection Plan* (MPP). Your MPP now includes our exclusive *Respawn*™ benefit for all Minion and Peon level employees as standard. As a new member, you are also entitled to one free personal *Respawn*™ service for yourself, should the need arise.

A technician will contact you shortly to organise the insertion of your 'boss-level' Respawn™ chip. Please note, this chip is proprietary and remains the property of DominionCorp, even after it is activated. Once installed, it must only be accessed and operated by qualified DominionCorp technicians and must not be removed, altered or tampered with under any circumstances. Catastrophic failure may occur, resulting in serious injury and/ or dismemberment. By accepting your *Respawn*™ chip, you and your Estate release DominionCorp and its subsidiaries from any and all liability for damages sustained due to chip malfunction or misuse.

Sincerely,

Dr Reginald Craven,

Undisputed Ruler of Nebulons 1-8

Ruler for Life (pending final legal challenges) of Nebulon 9

PhD (Morally Ambiguous Economics),

PhD (Persuasive Thaumaturgy)

PhD (World Management Engineering)

18 September

Dear General Verdant,

Congratulations on successfully capturing your first party of invading 'heroes'. They are being held in our secure dungeons whilst awaiting your displeasure.

As you know, many of your workers were horribly mutilated and/or murdered during the incursion. Fortunately we were able to teleport most of them to our medical facility by activating their Respawn™ amulets. We healed and/or resurrected them as required, then promptly returned them to their normal duties so they could continue serving your needs during the battle, instead of becoming tripping hazards and/or ugly stains on your carpet.

Unfortunately, workers who were *not wearing* their Respawn™ amulets were completely unsalvageable and those wearing them *incorrectly* were only able to be *partially* resurrected. After signing binding non-disclosure agreements and swearing blood oaths which preclude them from seeking revenge, their families were offered financial compensation, and our condolences.

Some staff experienced significant Post Traumatic Stress Disorder as a result of their injuries. With their permission (or their next of kin's permission if they remained partially deceased) they underwent our proprietary *MiindWipe*™ procedure. They are much more relaxed now, but we do recommend they refrain from operating machinery, handling sharp objects and making important legal decisions for the next six weeks or until they stop twitching, whichever comes first.

We investigated the security breach that allowed the 'heroes' to invade your facility. Apparently, they assaulted several of your guards, acquiring their uniforms and disguising themselves as Level 1 Goons. Even though the stolen uniforms did *not* fit them correctly, they looked *nothing like* the guards they had assaulted, and *they did not provide any appropriate identification*, the 'heroes' were still somehow permitted entry via the front gate. Since *Acts of Gross Minion Incompetence* and *Lack of Basic Common Sense* are clearly listed as exclusions in your HII policy, DominionCorp does not accept liability for the damage sustained to your Lair. We *do* recommend taking advantage of our free Risk Management Program however, to prevent such incidents from occurring again. Please see our included brochure for details.

Have you been the victim of a 'Heroic' Incursion?

It is normal to feel violated and angry when 'heroes' invade, but while your first instinct may be to cry, 'Fools, I'll destroy them all!' that won't stop it from happening again. At DominionCorp, we believe it is better to *learn* from your mistakes than to repeat them. We therefore encourage all World Management Engineer clients to take advantage of our complimentary Risk Management Program.

Workshops include:

➢ Unlocking your potential: Basic Competency in World Management Engineering.

➢ Encouraging loyalty, ruling with fear: How creating a supportive 'lair culture' prevents betrayal, reduces minion turnover and is more cost-effective than decapitating peons who displease you.

➢ Proper care and remuneration of Mad Scientists: How to keep them happy and squash those unhelpful 'second thoughts'.

➢ Dealing with heroes: Prevention is better than cure.

➢ Making the best of a bad situation: What to do when the peasants revolt.

14 November

Dear Dr Verdant,

Congratulations on completing your World Management Engineering Doctorate. Thesis title: *Should Walkways near Reactor Cores have Safety Railings Installed? A Risk: Benefit Analysis.* It seems they really *do* cause more accidents than they prevent.

Thank you for renewing your MPP with Re*spawn*™ and upgrading your HII policy from Basic to Comprehensive. You are now covered against *Acts of Gross Minion Incompetence* and *Lack of Basic Common Sense*. Given your recent history, we feel this was a wise decision.

Thank you for reporting the fourteen attempted 'heroic' incursions to your lair this month. We investigated the most recent attempt and discovered the following:

Three nights ago, one of your sentries was observed discussing shift change protocols with a comely maiden at a local tavern after work. Their conversation was overheard by a party of mercenaries sitting at a nearby table.

Later that evening, one of these mercenaries enticed a Peon-level scullery maid to join him for a tryst in the root cellar after her shift ended, granting him access to your lair via the kitchens. To her horror, *after completing the tryst* he overpowered her, gagged her, tied her up then locked her in a storage cupboard to prevent her raising an alarm.

Fortunately, this particular scullery maid was a DominionCorp Minions Union (DCMU) member. She had recently completed our *Hero Incursion Training* course and was able to free herself. Furious at his un-gentlemanly behaviour, she then apprehended, disarmed, and incapacitated the mercenary, *all with extreme prejudice*. His screams eventually alerted the night guards, and a full-scale incursion was prevented.

The scullery maid has apologised for both her initial mistake and her subsequent *enthusiasm* in dealing with the mercenary. She has been disciplined, provided with a written warning and agreed to be retrained as a leather-clad Lady Assassin, a career for which she shows great promise.

The mercenary was *MiindWiped*™ for his own good, after only *partially* surviving his interrogation. He will now serve as an unpaid minion in our 'Zombie Hoard' division until he is claimed by a relative or disintegrates, whichever comes first.

The 'comely maiden' turned out to be a princess in disguise, specifically Lady Penelope of Westphalia. She was working *with* the mercenaries and her goal was to infiltrate your lair, destroy your entire enterprise and personally murder you. Apparently she wanted revenge for you decapitating her fiancé and poisoning her father, King Harold when you attempted to conquer *their* kingdom last month.

We have 'dealt with' the remaining mercenaries as you requested, but Lady Penelope remains a guest in our maximum security dungeon. We have belayed your order to have her executed, in case you wish to reconsider. This would be prudent for several reasons:

1.   Lady Penelope has not one, but *three* fairy godmothers. Fairy godmothers are vengeful creatures who become *wicked* when displeased.

2.   The Princess is much beloved by her people. If you execute her, the peasants of Westphalia *will* revolt and attack your stronghold with pitchforks and flaming torches. The smell might be difficult to remove.

3.   Penelope's stepmother, Queen Raven, is a known Black Witch and Dark Sorceress. Unusually for someone in her position, she appears to genuinely *like* her stepdaughter and is concerned for her well-being. She has demanded Penelope's safe return and also requested the fiancé's body to be returned to her for proper burial. In our experience, it is unwise to upset Queen Raven.

She commands high-level eldritch forces and even *our* dungeons cannot withstand a prolonged assault by her. Frankly, we are surprised she has not disintegrated you already.

4. You do not hold Insurance against any of the following:

Incursion by a Neighbouring Kingdom
Revolting Peasants (Domestic and International)
Thaumatological Incursion
Malicious Acts of Fae

As you know, King Harold remains unwell and Penelope is his sole heir. Instead of *executing* Lady Penelope, we recommend forcing her to marry you. A wedding would unite your two kingdoms and *probably* be cheaper than a full military campaign. If you apologise for decapitating her fiancé and agree to return his remains as an engagement present, Penelope might even do it *willingly*. If you are *very* lucky, she might even convince Queen Raven to not turn you into a pile of amorphous goo.

1 February
Dear Lord Verdant,

Congratulations on your upcoming Nuptials and Coronation. We understand Lady Penelope finally agreed to marry you, in exchange for your freeing her ex-fiancé's soul from its demonic prison, returning her father to good health, and agreeing to stop 'ruining her life'. We wish you both every success and happiness together.

1 February

Dear Lady Penelope,

Congratulations on your upcoming Nuptials and Coronation. We hear Lord Verdant is recovering from his severe case of Fairy Pox and is now able to eat solid food again, albeit only with a spoon, and we are glad your father is also recovering from his alleged poisoning. It is very lucky Lord Verdant had a vial of the only known antidote.

We applaud Queen Raven's ingenuity in brokering peace between your two nations, particularly in her creative use of incendiary dragon excrement. Do you think she would consider working for us?

4 February

Dear King Verdant,

We offer our sincerest condolences for the dissolution of your marriage to Queen Penelope. We understand she stabbed you repeatedly in the chest on your wedding night, screaming, 'This is for you, Ferdinand!'

Fortunately, your Re*spawn*™ chip was activated, and we expect you will make a full recovery. Unfortunately, we are unable to comply with your request to 'deal with' Queen Penelope on your behalf. We did *warn* you that princesses frequently escape from regular, run-of-the-mill dungeons.

Inspired by your forward thinking, King Harold and Queen Raven have joined the DominionCorp family. They now hold *Comprehensive Hero Incursion, Military Incursion by a Neighbouring*

Kingdom, and *Heir Protection* insurance. Kidnapping Penelope violates our 'neutrality against a rival consortium' policy.

Would you be amenable to marriage counselling instead?

7 February

Dear King Verdant,

We received your letter dated 5 February. The things you suggested we do to ourselves were not anatomically possible, but since you are still recovering from your recent *Respawn*™ and post-traumatic *MiindWipe*™ you will not be punished for your insolence, *this* time.

We know your finances are somewhat limited after the wedding, but we strongly recommend reactivating your 'boss-level' Respawn™ chip. You cannot put a price on safety. Might we suggest accepting a mortgage on your Lair? Our Stronghold Refinancing rates are highly competitive.

11 April

Dear King Verdant,

We accept your apology regarding the contents of your previous letter. Once again, we urge you to *reconsider* cancelling your *Personal Respawn*™ Insurance. Although more expensive, 'boss level' Respawn™ chips are far safer and more reliable than *Respawn*™ amulets, which we typically only provide for Minion and Peon level workers. Amulets may be easily removed or lost, particularly in the case of accidental decapitation.

Please note, your *Hero Incursion Insurance* policy is also due. We await payment at your earliest convenience.

14 May

Dear King Verdant,

We acknowledge the cancellation of the following Insurance Policies:

Comprehensive Hero Incursion

Incursion by a Neighbouring Kingdom

Revolting Peasants (Domestic and International)

Personal Respawn™

As requested, your *Minion Protection Plan* remains in place.

We understand you and Queen Penelope have reconciled. We wish you many happy years together.

23 May

Dear Queen Penelope,

Please accept our condolences on the passing of your husband, the late King Verdant. He recently deactivated his personal *Respawn*™ chip, so we were unable to resurrect him when he fell into the palace's Thaumatological Reactor core and was partially decapitated. Witnesses confirmed he was wearing his *Respawn*™ amulet, but since there was no safety railing installed on the walkway, there was nothing to stop him tumbling over the edge and splattering onto the concrete seventeen stories below.

The amulet came off during the fall, but there might still have been some hope, had he not been immediately set upon by a flock of ravenous night birds when he landed. One of them ate his now inactive *Respawn*™ chip and it was not able to be recovered.

As you requested, we will perform compulsory partial *MiindWipes™* on all of your Minions, Peons, Upper and Lower Management Hench-staff, Hired Goons, and anyone else who may have witnessed your husband's untimely demise, for their own mental health and well-being of course.

King Harold swears that both you and Queen Raven were with him at the time of Verdant's 'mishap' and although we do not know what caused him to fall in the first place, his death has been ruled a tragic accident. We hope the Life insurance policy you purchased last week provides some comfort in your time of grief.

29 July

Dear Queen Penelope,

Thank you for the kind invitation to your upcoming wedding to Ferdinand. Upon examining his remains, we were delighted to discover that he is actually Queen Raven's long-lost son! This has been confirmed with both genetic and thaumatological testing, and by matching the unusual mole on his left shoulder against our database of known prophetic birthmarks.

When Ferdinand was born, the then-Lady Raven had him fitted with a *Respawn™* chip before surrendering him to the Sisters of Ultimate Irony. Thanks to her foresight, our expert necromancers were able to reattach his head and revive him with minimal damage to his central nervous system, even after he had been dead for several weeks! He should suffer no long-term ill effects from his recent traumatic experience, thanks to a partial *MiindWipe™*, but please do let us know if he begins acting strangely or suddenly craves human flesh.

Now that your father has recovered enough to rule Westphalia without her help, Queen Raven wants to focus on her own career again. She will be joining our 'Thaumaturgic Persuasion' division, on a part time basis.

As Raven's step-daughter, you qualify for a 'friends and family discount' on all DominionCorp products. Now that you rule your own kingdom, we have a range of additional products you might like to consider. May we contact you to discuss your options? As you know, you cannot put a price on safety.

Sincerely,

Dr Reginald Craven,

Undisputed Ruler, Nebulons 1- 9

PhD (Morally Ambiguous Economics),

PhD (Persuasive Thaumaturgy),

PhD (World Management Engineering)

THE CHALLENGE

robert walmsley-evans

This is a difficult puzzle indeed.

David laced his fingers and squinted at the board in front of him. He saw only draws and stalemates as he focused on each quadrant of the board. He remembered the words of his chess coach, *When presented with a problem, shut everything out of your mind. Focus on the pieces that will help you.*

He breathed deeply. His 'Between a Rook and a Hard Place' t-shirt tightened across his chest. He closed his eyes. So simple, why didn't he see the answer before? A smile widened across his face. David placed his fingers on the queen's crown and slid it across the board, took the bishop, knocked over the king, and in an understated manner announced, 'Checkmate.'

David held out his hand, and his opponent took it.

'Good game Megan.'

'As always.' She smiled.

'Want a break?' He grabbed his black denim jacket from the back of the chair.

She nodded, grasped her water bottle and followed him. They entered the area earmarked for after-game drinks, uplifted bottles of iced tea, and sat beside each other on a couch. David cast his eyes across the playing area.

'Quite a club we've got here,' Megan said.

Back when David first started in this club, he was already proficient at the game, but there was something about being in an informal club which appealed to him. It was on the basement level, down a staircase from the street. The previous owner of the club, Harrison, a large man, with a full beard, and a scruffy haircut, advised everyone on technique, style and execution. 'The quickest and easiest way is usually best,' Harrison used to say.

David rose through the club-level ranking system quickly. Harrison pulled him aside one day. He ran his fingers through his unruly locks and sighed. 'I have taught my last lesson. You've proven yourself worthy to take the reins.' He handed over the keys. 'Now you can teach them. It's my time to retire.'

A fresh-faced freckled boy in large spectacles, fidgeting with his notebook, cleared his throat.

'Tim. How are you?'

'Well, thank you sir. You don't know how much this means to me being your assistant. This holiday job is most appreciated!'

'You can stop thanking me now. What's happening?'

'There's a man here to see you sir.'

'Bring him into the gaming area in five minutes please Tim.'

David turned to Megan. 'He's young and timid now, but I do believe he will outgrow this club and make Grandmaster one day.'

'You can really see who each of them are can't you? You see their true potential.'

'I know what most of these players will do, and who they will become.'

Megan glanced at David. Her long, chestnut hair framed her trusting blue eyes and strawberry lips. Her eyelashes fluttered.

'Even me?'

'Yes, even you.' He kissed her cheek tenderly. 'I believe how you play chess shows what kind of person you are.' David stood offering his hand. 'Another round?' She took his hand, smiled and they proceeded back to the gaming area.

Tim entered the room, dwarfed by an individual in a fine, pink three-piece suit.

'What brings you to my club?' David asked.

'My name is Damian Nichols. I own this building.'

David found his hand enveloped by long, manicured fingers as the man shook his hand and smiled, revealing creased laugh lines at the corners of his eyes.

David's eyebrows rose. He had a bad feeling about this.

'You've been going through my estate agent to lease this place, but I find it more appropriate to tell you in person that I am turning this building into a block of flats.'

There was a gentle communal gasp.

'You can't do that!' Megan said.

'Legally, I can my dear!'

David looked at the distraught faces around him. 'These members are dedicated to this place,' David stared into Damian's wide eyes and said, 'They won't leave without a fight.'

'I'll tell you what ... David is it? Let me play you for it.' He walked towards the nearest vacant chess table. 'I love a good game of chess,' he said over his shoulder. 'If you win, I will make sure these rooms stay structurally sound. If I win, all of you will be leaving. Best of three wins.'

David sat with a thud on a nearby chair. He was struggling to get a good read on this guy. The old air-con unit hummed in the background and ruffled his black, wavy hair. He gazed around the room at the exposed brick and threadbare carpet, trying to gather his thoughts. 'Why?'

'That's my business.' Damian sat down at the opposite side of the chess board. David hesitated. 'Well, what's your answer?' Damian insisted.

David took a drink, licked his lips, and said 'It's a deal.'

Tim pulled David aside and whispered into his ear, 'There is something you should know. When we came through the gaming area, Damian looked at each game our club members were playing. He predicted in advance their moves, down to checkmate, and was correct every time! This man knows more than he's letting on.'

They returned to the table. 'Tim, will you arbiter this game?' David asked. Tim nodded.

Damian waved his hand. 'Don't you trust me?'

'Well … no, these are high stakes. You are seated in front of the white pieces, proceed.' Damian moved his king's pawn.

They played that first game late into the afternoon. It was an even match right up until the last moment, though David felt set up from the beginning. As his king fell, David's eyebrows rose, his mouth hung open. He lifted his eyes from the board to meet Damian's. 'How did you do that?'

'Practice makes perfect my boy.' Damian stood and held out his hand. David shook it. His gaze followed his opponent as Damian left.

'Tim, would you get my tablet? I'd like to check on my worthy adversary. I fear he might be hustling me.'

Megan looked down at David. 'What do you mean?'

'I remember a great player who matches Damian's appearance and demeanour.'

Tim handed David the tablet and he searched Damian's full name in a chess players database. He found an article from years ago about a low-ranking chess player who won the national championship. The journalist stated the victory was a come-from-behind win and yet celebrations were sedate.

'Is there anything more about him?' Megan asked, leaning over David's shoulder, her hair brushing across his face.

'No nothing. He should have gone to the world championship. Maybe he didn't find it to be a challenge anymore. At any rate, I agreed to the stakes. I'll need to train hard for the next game.'

Megan placed her hand on his shoulder. 'That's one of the many things I like about you. You never shy away from a challenge.'

David looked at his watch. 'Everyone, its closing time. Leave your games as they are until tomorrow!' Quietly he said to Megan, 'Would you like to come to my place for dinner?'

At a small table in David's studio flat, he asked Megan, 'What did you think of my game today?'

'You did well. I saw nothing wrong with your game, only he was one step ahead of you the whole time.'

David netted his fingers. 'Everything will work out in the end. You'll see.'

As David rested his fork on the plate, he grinned and Megan asked, 'What are you smiling at?'

'Oh, just reminiscing.'

At their graduation dance the previous year, their true attraction blossomed, though they remained friends. A few weeks ago, David had worked up the courage and asked Megan out. They had shared interests, movies, TV shows, books, but chess was their greatest passion.

After dinner Megan faced the black pieces on the board.

'You don't want the white pieces?' David asked as he turned on some low-fi music.

'I think you'll need to practice both sides, won't you?'

'That's true.' He examined the board. 'I'll try something I haven't done before.' David moved his king side knight. The game ran like an ordinary friendly game of chess.

240

David examined each move in detail, to find the weaknesses in his strategy. He and Megan finished their game in a stalemate. Mentally exhausted, they reset the board, and crossed to his couch. David picked up his tablet and opened his favourite chess site. He examined each move of the greats of his generation. Megan laid her head on his shoulder as David played footage of Damian versus another player of greater rank to study his style.

After David finished his analysis of Damian's game, they ascended the stairs to the bedroom. As he watched her undress, Megan said 'I have faith in you, David. Some of the players in our club are skilled and will one day be County Masters, becoming National and even International Masters. They have faith in you too.'

Wrapped in each other's arms, they whispered chess notations into the night.

Morning light streamed through the glass doors warming the kitchen. David sat at the breakfast table. He read intently and focused on each word from a tatty book, with frayed edges. Footsteps caught his attention. He glanced up and found Megan wrapped in his white bathrobe.

'What are you reading?' she asked.

'An old chess manual my father gave me.' He sighed and placed it face-down on the table. 'I might learn something new from it that I haven't seen before.'

'It's great you're so focused on preserving the club, but it's our first year out of high school. We've got to choose what to do next. We both qualify for university and there's an excellent one nearby. You may need to give up running the club.'

'I can't do that.'

'You don't earn anything from it. It's a non-profit. We need more than that. It's something to think about. That's all.'

David rubbed his eyes. 'It's the last thing Harrison asked of me before he vanished.'

Megan chewed her lip and reached into the folds of the robe. 'Then, I have something that might help. Something Harrison gave me for you, when I thought you needed it. I've been thinking today could be that day.'

She retrieved a small wooden box. 'This was given to him when he went to India. He said it's ancient.'

David opened the box and found a small ivory knight. He turned it over in his hands. It was weighted perfectly, and exquisitely sculpted. There was a note folded in the base of the box. He placed the knight on the table and read the note out loud.

'This knight has provided me with good luck. I know you don't believe in superstition, though there is something to be said for good-luck charms. It will serve you well, as it served me. Harrison.' Beside his signature was a rough drawing of a pawn.

David imagined Harrison standing behind Megan, an approving smile on his face.

He clutched the knight.

David sat, flanked by Tim and Megan on either side. He placed Harrison's gift beside the chessboard and braced himself for the game ahead.

Damian reclined on the chair opposite, this time wearing a purple blazer with white pinstripes. David couldn't help but wonder if he was trying to distract him with that jacket, or did he honestly like it?

'Let's play.'

Tim started the clock.

'What happened to you?' David asked.

Damian looked up. 'What?'

'Why didn't you go to the world championships?'

'You're very bold, for a young person.' He slumped back in his chair. 'All right, I'll tell you. Firstly, I knew I could beat anyone. It was almost too easy, and my agent wanted me on the international tournaments. But I was already in two minds about becoming Grandmaster. Finally, just before that last game, I received a call. My father had died suddenly. Most children would have been given time to grieve, but as the eldest, I was to take over the family business immediately, or it would be liquidated. We would lose everything, including our inheritance. I knew I could not do both. Being Grandmaster was the lower priority.' He sat forward in his chair again. 'I accepted my responsibilities, but yesterday's game reminded me how much I loved chess.'

David took note of the emotions playing across Damian's face and moved his first piece.

'This is the most fun I've had in a long time,' Damian said. 'It's the perfect combination of science and art.'

David smiled. 'It's the use of logic, and psychology that I like. Speaking of which, checkmate.' David sat back and folded his arms.

Damian put his face in his hands and laughed. 'Fair win young David. I will beat you next time.'

'Are you sure about that?'

The next day David and Megan sat on a bench outside the club, watching passers-by.

'What's troubling you David?'

'Many things. The game tomorrow. University. You.' David smiled and slid his arm around her waist to pull her close. 'I think I'd like it at university. We could be roommates.' He kissed her hair. 'But I promised Harrison I would keep running the club until I could find a suitable replacement.'

'What about Tim?'

'He's still too young.'

A well-dressed woman approached. 'Are you David?' she asked.

'I am. Who are you?' But he thought he could guess. Her mannerisms reminded him of a younger version of his recent opponent.

'I'm Damian's sister, Piper Nichols.' She held out her hand and David shook it.

'In normal circumstances, I would say nice to meet you, however, your brother is trying to destroy the building where my club resides.'

'That's why I came to talk to you. I'm trying to persuade him not to. Is there some way you could work something out?'

'Your brother seems stubborn,' Megan stated.

It was the final game. The score was one all.

Megan, Tim, and the other members of the club gathered around David. Damian had his sister beside him and various nameless people in suits.

David did a double take. He wasn't sure whether he loved or abhorred the orange and brown checked coat Damian wore.

'These are my conveyancing solicitor, estate agent, and accountant. I will need them here when I win.'

'Begin.' Tim slapped his hand down on the clocks.

David and Damian nodded to each other.

In silence they responded quickly to each other's moves. David took one of Damian's bishops with his knight. In turn Damian took it with a pawn.

'Draw?' said David.

'Why would I accept that?' Damian asked. 'I'm winning.'

'You could follow me around the board and end in a stalemate. Look again, you'll see it.'

Damian took a few moments. 'What are your terms for a draw?'

David met his gaze steadily. 'My terms are for you to run this chess club on my behalf.'

Everyone gasped.

'Let me finish,' David said. 'With Tim at the helm, make this into a profitable club, and associate it with the Federation.'

'What's in it for you?'

'I know my club will be even better than when I took over, and I can go with my girlfriend to university without worrying about

245

the club. Everyone's happy. Oh, and I'd like lifetime membership for Megan and I.'

David glanced behind Damian's shoulder. The effigy of Harrison gave a nod of approval and then vanished.

Damian took his time to answer. His eyes sparkled. 'I accept your draw, and your deal.' David stood, shook his opponent's hand and kissed Megan.

Late that evening, David and Megan snuggled in bed. They looked into each other's eyes.

'I can't help but wonder Megan said, did you know Damian was going to take the deal?'

'In chess you must know what your challenger is going to do ahead of time. Life is chess.'

THE THREE LIVES OF MINI MUNCHMAN

emma rennison

Three Lives

My socked feet whisper as I steal past the kitchen, tiptoe to the top of the stairs and position myself in front of my brother's bedroom door. Closed, as always.

I tilt my head. The clack-clack-clack of the spokey-dokes on his bike signal his departure, but my palms still glisten with sweat as they wrap around the door handle. The cat brushes against my shins on her way towards my parents' room. She slithers through, her body moulding to the crack between their door and the wall.

There is the smallest of squeaks as the handle reaches halfway followed by the soft release as the latch retreats into the door. I ease it open. Push my neck forward to squeeze my face into the gap, my heart thumping in my ears.

My eyes scan the room, searching for treasure, landing on the white chest of drawers lined with Star Wars figures across the top. Darth and Luke in mid-battle, their lightsabres drawn from their fisted hands. Hoth Han Solo. Tiny clear bubbles bursting from the subtle line across his neck where his hooded head was glued back on.

I turn to his bed. The Walkman he got for his birthday sits at an angle on his nightstand. I place the headphones on, the black foam resting at angles against my earlobes. My thumb presses against the tiny triangle of the play button and the cassette spools rotate. A high-pitched synthesizer squeals through the speakers, and I rip the metal loop from the top of my head, click stop, and return it just as I found it.

Perching on the edge of his quilt, aware that even a slight crease will give me away, I pull on the drawer of the small unit. It rolls open to reveal the leather wallet he bought with his pocket money on holiday. A few francs and centimes bang against the sides of a washed-out margarine tub as it jars to a stop. I feed my hand to the back, my fingers tap around as if playing an invisible piano. They rattle a group of biros together. Slide underneath the rough fabric of his bag of marbles, clinking and clattering like a collection of glass eyes. My thumb and forefinger rub against a smooth corner, pinch on the narrow edge and pull. And there it is. Yellow and black. The Mini Munchman.

It sits perfectly in my palm. The digital time, one hour out, at the top of its grey, Panini sticker-sized LCD. Tiny round faces, no bigger than a sesame seed, display the Munchman's ever-changing mood as they blink around the maze.

I press the mode button until the screen fills with cherries, bananas, pineapples, and grapes. My round-faced hero, grinning and ready to play in the bottom corner.

Angling my ear to the door, I listen for any sign of my brother. The kettle clicks off downstairs and Mum's slippers pad across the kitchen tiles. I release my breath and lean back against the bed, my legs dangling off the side and the tips of my toes balanced on the carpet like a ballerina. My chin pushed to my chest as my head rests against the cool wall. I brush my thumb over the start key, its silver arrow compressing into my skin.

The last highest score flashes up with a short and happy electronic tune. Ghosts materialise, static until the music ends. The little face, happy and bright, jumps once, twice, along the maze landing on tiny pieces of fruit. Each movement leaves a clear path in its trail. A ghost flickers towards me. I hide under a bridge. It follows. The tinny sound of death. Two lives left. I press start for my second go, the remaining fruit waiting to be gobbled up.

My chance is taken too fast, and I race through my final life so I can begin again with a full set. I know the route to eat the fruit, avoid the ghosts and make it to level two. He showed me after I shared the last chocolate bar in my selection box with him. I just need to remember it.

I bend my knees, my heels hooked around the edge of the mattress. I clock up five hundred points and gain an extra Munchman.

Another level. Another speed increase. My finger slips, throwing me into the jaws of the ghost. My bonus life gone. But I've got to keep going.

I raise my arms above my face to divert the screen from a new source of light stretching across the display, washing out the game as I take the secret passage. The cat jumps up next to me and steps across my stomach.

Shadows creep back across the room. I keep pressing. Up another level. Bleep bleep bleep. Faster faster faster.

'What are you doing in my room?'

I drop the yellow console and it bounces off my nose. The cat bolts, digging her claws into my thighs as she launches herself into the air.

'Muuuum!' His eyes on me as he calls over his shoulder.

I swallow and stand. He places his hands flat against the doorframe. His legs spread wide in a star. The cat scuttles between his feet. I take a step, ready to find my own way out, and he pushes past me to snatch the game off the bed.

'I'm sorry. I'm sorry,' I say, my hands up and my eyes scanning the room as I try to think of something, anything, to save my life.

His eyes blacken and his lips thin as they clamp together, puckering up towards his nose.

'You beat my high score!'

Two Lives

I take two stairs at a time until I reach the final three, and jump. Bend my knees as my bare feet sink into the marbled grey carpet.

250

Mum trudges through the kitchen towards the back garden, a laundry basket piled high, balanced in her arms. My brother follows her at a steady distance, his whine on repeat.

She turns and reverses into the door, opens the handle with her free elbow and closes it with her backside. He stands and waits, an extended use of 'please' falling from his lips.

I skip outside to eavesdrop, pretending I'm here to put the guinea pigs in their run. Keen to witness another scolding, or maybe to see if he'll do something with me, like he did a few months ago when I agreed to watch his cartoons rather than mine at Grandad's. The sun hits my face, warm today and due to get hotter while we're away. Dad has work meetings in Cornwall tomorrow and the day after and Mum thought *why not*.

'Really?' I turn to my brother's voice, a joyful octave higher than the low whinging we've all tolerated over the last week. 'Do you mean it?'

'Yes.' Mum extends the final sound into a hiss.

'Thanks, Mum! You're amazing!' My brother picks a damp t-shirt from the basket and hangs it on the line. I can't believe it. It's not even his top.

'But if anything happens ...' She dips her chin to glare at him, pointing a peg his way.

'It won't. I promise.' His words rush out in a race as he hangs a pair of odd socks.

'You will have to feed the cat and the guinea pigs while we're away.'

'Yes, yes.'

'And.' She takes a sock down and matches it with another. 'You have to check in twice a day. We've got the car phone now so there's no excuse.'

'I will! I promise, Mum. This is the best day of my life!' He dashes inside, patting the guinea pig in my arms as he goes. 'Want to play Risk?'

'Okay!' I reply, plopping the little creature in her run. I've asked him every day since the holidays began and he's blanked me each time.

I grab us both biscuits and bound up the stairs, trying to stifle my grin. His door is wide open, the world map laid across his carpet. My favourite colour of battalions in a pile on the side opposite him. Along with the yellow and black of the Mini Munchman.

I scoot down on folded knees and pick it up.

'Haven't seen you play this for ages,' I say as I turn it in my hands and then press the buttons in sequence to try and remember the correct path.

'I thought you might like to take it away.' He shrugs as he counts out troops. 'I know how much you like it.'

I want to throw myself over the board and hug him. But I shrug back, slide it into my back pocket for safekeeping and hang my head, my face hurting from the smile stretched up into my cheeks.

'It's only to borrow though.' His head flicks to me, his eyes dark and his brows raised. 'It's still mine.'

Last Life

'Mum? Have you seen the Mini Munchman?' I hold my backpack open with one hand, and dive into the depths with my other. My fingers tangle in a yo-yo string as I shuffle through never-ending hairbands and a split packet of strawberry Chewits. 'I want to try and beat my top score before we leave.'

'No, love.' She takes a tight ball of clothing, shakes it back into a skirt and folds it into the case. 'Have you cleaned your teeth?'

I shake my head, my gaze drawn to the bay window and the *keow-keow-keow* of the gulls as they hover over the sand searching for titbits from yesterday's top of twenty-six. We were there. Stocked up with bright plastics from the seaside shop next door.

'Chop chop! We check out in ten minutes,' Mum says, perching on the floral quilted throw. The handset of the phone in the air. Her finger pointed, ready to dial. I crab-walk past the sink and Dad, his chin covered in white scraps of tissue held on tight by their tiny red centres.

'Hi, love. All okay? How's the cat? Good. We're leaving soon. Yes. That's right.' Mum's telephone voice blares into the bathroom as I scrub my molars.

'About four and a half hours. Five depending on traffic.'

'Dad, have you seen the Mini Munchman?' I ask. His knee on top of the suitcase to squeeze the zips together.

'No! She hasn't lost it. No, it's all fine. It'll be here somewhere. Got to go, love.' Mum glares at me as she replaces the receiver.

'What are you looking for?' Dad asks, leaning his weight onto the case. A zzz rips around each side.

'Okay. I think that's everything.' Mum glances around the room, checks the drawers we never used and the top of the wardrobe in between the hotel's spare itchy blankets. 'Let's go!'

'But Mum! I don't know where the Mini Munchman is!' My voice rises to a whine.

'When was the last time you had it?' Dad asks, ramming the bags into the corridor.

'Yesterday afternoon?' I answer with a question.

'Well, it's probably in the car then,' Mum says, as if this was going to be her response whatever my reply. With a deep intake of breath, she hoists her oversized leather handbag onto her shoulder and strides towards the lift where Dad has already pressed the button.

'It's not! I know it's not! I would remember!' I yell, feeling the wobble in my voice as the sense of time runs away. It's my last chance to find it! He'll kill me if I don't!

I run past the beds back to the window and rest my forehead against the cool glass to peer down into the hotel's miniature front garden. I roll my head right, then left, then right again. Yellow! My heart thumps hard in my chest and my eyes widen. The sharp corner pokes out, fluorescent against the dry soil. It flicks towards the lower leaves, and flutters in the light breeze. Then detaches itself from the spindly branches and whisks up towards me, close enough to touch. Close enough to reach. Close enough to see it's just a ripped open crisp packet.

I shrug into my backpack, the patterned carpet blurring as my eyes fill. He will never forgive me. Never. I wipe the back of my hand across my nose and sniff hard.

'Come on. We've got to go.' Mum claps her hands together.

Dad bumps the cases down the stone steps, past the seaside shop and towards the side road where the car's parked. I follow behind, my head to the ground, images of apologies and forgiveness running through my mind like a flipbook animation.

The distant chime of Greensleeves begins and I pause mid-step, my downturned head and mouth lifting simultaneously. I remember! I *did* leave it in the car. I put it there before we had ice-cream.

A full open-mouthed grin stretches across my face now, and I jog towards Mum, ready to share the good news. Wanting to tell my brother straight away that I didn't lose his Mini Munchman. Desperate to get home, race up to his room and show him my highest score and how fast I can complete a level now.

'What the? When did this happen?' Dad's voice is loud and sharp, and he calls Mum by her actual name.

She skip steps around the corner and I run to keep up. My feet crunch and I glance down. The concrete path sparkles with flecks of shattered glass. My eyes rise to Dad. The cases dropped by his side and his hands linked across the top of his head.

Mum gasps, extending her arm behind her to shuffle me away.

'They took the bloody phone!' Dad says, his arm elevated to the driver's window, smashed and hollow. 'That cost a bomb!'

I crane my neck to the side. There's a gap where the car phone was installed two weeks before the trip.

Mum opens the backdoor, pokes her head in and then rushes around to the boot. Dad raises his arms and drops them against his thighs, shaking his head.

A sharp breath catches between my teeth, and I step towards the open door. My eyes prickle as I squeeze my fingers into the tight back pocket of the driver's seat, gliding my flattened palm side to side and into each corner. My voice, quiet and trembling, catches as the words come out alongside my empty hand.

'My life is over.'

321 TIME'S UP

jenny woolsey

I stood rooted to the spot, hypnotised by the flashing red and blue lights. Brad lay on the drenched pavement, fully covered by the white sheet. My teeth chattered as I pulled the silver space blanket around me.

'Come this way, Molly.'

I nodded as the paramedic guided me to the waiting ambulance.

On the stretcher, I recalled what had just happened and touched the burgeoning lump on my forehead, made when my head hit the curb.

'Molly, Molly,' were the last two words I heard as I slipped away ...

'Oh, crap!' Louise squealed. 'There's a severed finger on the wheelie bin.' She moved her widened eyes to the body stretched out on the floor then abruptly turned to look at Ben who held the laminated card with the mission. She must only come to our murder mystery escape room adventures to be with Ben because she clearly didn't like them. This was our sixth.

I screwed my nose up as cheap aftershave, like Brut, filled my nostrils. 'What do we have to do?' I asked Ben.

The four of us, Brad, Ben, Louise and I, huddled in the darkness under the blue strobes of a spinning police light.

Ben read, 'John Dawson, the mayor, is dead and you're in the alley behind the pub where he was found. You must identify the weapon, the suspect or suspects, and the motive. There are many clues hidden in the room. Once you have solved the murder, you can leave through the FBI door.'

'And we only have an hour, counting down from now,' Brad said, reading the large red numbers on the digital timer. His 6'6" frame rose above the rest of us.

Brad moved over to the face-down body clothed in a navy suit, lighting it up with his phone. 'Who wants to touch him?'

'I will,' Ben said, bending and patting the body down. 'I know you're too gutless to.'

Brad retorted, 'Watch it, mate!'

'I am watching it, mate,' Ben replied. 'Geez, he reeks of bad aftershave. Trying to impress some chick, I reckon. Molly, one of his shoes is missing.'

I was the designated note-taker this time. We always took turns. I jotted the missing shoe and severed finger into my phone.

'Does the finger belong to him?' I asked.

'No,' Brad said. 'Might be a red herring. Time to roll him over.'

Ben put his hands on the cadaver's side and Louise squatted beside him. They pushed the body over to reveal a grey face with staring, blue eyes and a blood-streaked forehead.

Louise screamed.

'Geez, that's realistic. This has been the best room for props,' Brad said, standing up. 'Obviously, he was killed by a gunshot to the forehead so let's search for the weapon.'

I wrote the clues down then shone my light around to see Ben flick the finger off a bin and open it. He pulled scrunched newspaper, empty beer cans and vodka, rum and scotch bottles out of it. Last, he pulled out a folded parcel of butcher's paper which he unwrapped.

'Got it!' he said in a satisfied voice. 'It's a revolver.'

Ben pointed the gun at Brad, 'Want to see if it works?'

Brad smacked it out of his hand and the weapon clattered on the floor.

'Stop joking around, you two,' I said.

Louise picked up a laminated card from the floor amid the rubbish. 'We have a clue.'

I wrote the revolver down and joined the others. It was a news article about the mayor, John Dawson. He was under investigation, suspected of taking donations for his election campaign from a well-known criminal bikie gang, the Bulldogs. There was a Star of David, a motorbike, and a bag of money drawn at the bottom of the article.

'Okay, so I reckon it's something to do with the donations from the Bulldogs,' I said, adding it to my list.

'We must have to figure out those clues at the bottom,' Louise said.

'Yeah, I agree,' Brad said. 'Look for them in the room.'

'I reckon a rival bikie gang shot him,' Ben said, pushing back his mass of black curls off his face.

'I think so too,' Louise said, 'but we need a name.'

Brad bent down and opened John Dawson's suit coat and pulled out a small book from his right inside pocket. He then searched the left one and pulled out a piece of folded paper.

'Give me the book,' Ben said.

Brad flipped through it and a card fell out. Reading the details, he said, 'It's from Steve Baker who is a founding lawyer at Baker and Baker Solicitors. On the back is yesterday's date, so he had an appointment with them.'

'Does that help?' I asked, jotting down the clue.

'Dunno,' Ben said.

'We have forty minutes left,' Brad announced.

I decided to investigate the corner of the room where no one had been. 'There's a box here with a combination padlock on it,' I said, examining it. 'It's a name with five letters.'

'Try Steve or Baker,' Ben said.

'Baker!' I said as I slid the padlock off and opened the box revealing a navy cotton bag and a card.

I gave the bag to Brad who investigated its contents. He pulled out a large wad of cash.

'There's your bag of money,' Louise said.

'We still don't know what it all means,' Ben said.

'There's twenty-eight thousand dollars here,' Brad said, 'so there's money for a payoff.'

Ben briefly pointed his hand at Brad, his thumb up, his index finger straight with his other fingers curled into his palm. Brad didn't see the gesture.

I read the card and said, 'It's another clue.'

Starlight, Starlight.
Two more, shining bright.
First star I will see tonight.
At the club in white,
Ride at midnight.

'Two stars, now. There was that one on the news article,' Louise said. 'Must mean something. Let's look around for another star.'

'And a white club, which sounds like a bikies' clubhouse,' I said, jotting the clues down.

I crept on, searching the concrete floor and the wallpapered wall.

'Eek!' I cried, as a rodent scampered over my foot. 'There's rats!'

'I hate rats!' Louise said, standing on her tiptoes.

I examined each bottle and piece of paper and the cardboard box.

'I've got it!' Brad said.

On the wall in front of Brad, under a Star of David, *Seminals* was scrawled in fluorescent paint.

'The Seminals must be the rival bikie gang,' Ben said.

'We don't know for sure,' Brad said.

'I know,' Ben stated.

'So we have a revolver, possibly the Seminals as the name, and the motive is to do with the mayor taking donations from the Bulldogs and something to do with a clubhouse. Do we need to be more specific?' Louise mused.

I glanced at the timer. 'We only have ten minutes left. We're not going to make it without help. Let's ask.'

'No,' Brad said. 'I can figure this out.'

'No need yet, Molly. We can find the motive in that time, unless Brad—'

'Unless I what?'

'Can't keep it in your pants,' Ben said.

'Stop it, you two,' I snapped. 'We're running out of time.'

'Five minutes!' Louise stated, wrapping her thin arms around herself.

'Maybe we should ask for a hint,' I suggested again.

'Nope,' Brad said.

'Come on, it's here somewhere.' Ben picked up the scrunched pieces of newspaper strewn around the other wheelie bin, examining each one, before turning the empty bin upside down. 'Aha!'

'What is it?' I asked him.

'One minute left,' a voice boomed from a speaker mounted above the entry door.

Brad quick-stepped over to the bin.

'It's a map,' Brad said.

'It's not. It's a building,' Ben corrected him.

'Does it say whose building?' Louise asked.

'It has to be the new clubhouse,' Brad said.

'Looks—' I started.

'3, 2, 1. Time's up,' interrupted me. It was the end of the game. 'Please exit.' The FBI door opened.

'We failed,' Louise said, dropping her arms to her sides.

'No, we didn't!' Brad snapped. 'We worked it out just as the time was up.'

I shook my head. It was obvious we failed as we hadn't exited before zero.

'We should have made it,' Ben said, narrowing his eyes at Brad. 'But big egos put themselves in harm's way.'

As we slunk towards the door, I said, 'I've had enough of this garish aftershave!'

At the desk, the young guy who had given us the initial instructions asked us how we went.

'We needed a couple more minutes,' Louise said.

'We knew the answer.' Brad wagged his index finger. 'Was it the Seminals bikie gang? The revolver was the weapon and the motive was that the Bulldogs were getting a new building or clubhouse from the mayor and that pissed them off?'

'I can't tell you once you're out of the escape room,' the guy said, 'in case another group is about to play or you want to do it again.'

'Right.' Brad pushed his fingers through his perfectly styled, slicked-back hair, a stray strand falling onto his forehead.

The guy grinned.

'Let's go get something to eat,' Louise said.

I pushed open the front door of the Puzzling Escape Rooms revealing a soaked pavement. It must have rained but luckily it was now only spitting as we hadn't brought umbrellas.

'We're going for a drink,' Ben said. 'See ya later.'

'Ah, okay,' I muttered, noticing his quick exit. 'Bye. Bye, Louise.'

Louise waved at me and they strode on ahead, Ben holding Louise's hand. His other hand was in his jacket pocket.

They disappeared around a corner.

'I'll take you home,' Brad told me. 'I've got things to do.'

'What kind of things?'

'Well, I have that meeting tomorrow with Barnes and I haven't finished my proposal.'

I nodded, my lower lip hardening.

As we jaywalked at the next set of street lights, two sounds like firecrackers echoed around us.

I felt Brad stagger, his weight sending me down with him as he collapsed. I hit my forehead on the curb and he crumpled to the ground.

I pushed myself up to sitting and screamed as I looked into the familiar eyes of the killer standing a few metres away.

'What have you done?' I said with disbelief and shock in my voice. I rose to my knees, bent over the body and screamed, 'Brad! Brad!'

Footsteps fleeing and the screech of tyres were Ben's answer.

'Help!' I called as strangers' voices echoed in my brain like muffled poetry.

'He's gone into cardiac arrest,' snapped a man who had crouched down beside me.

I gazed at Brad as the man started CPR.

Two police officers stood beside my hospital bed, their notebooks filling with my recount of the night before.

The phone of one of the officers rang and she left the room to answer it.

The other stood, waiting patiently for me to continue my story.

The officer returned and said, 'Molly, they've located Ben and Louise. They were found deceased in a single vehicle accident.'

I gasped, my eyes wide.

'Oh!' I exclaimed. 'I don't understand any of this. I thought Ben and Louise were our friends.'

'Benjamin O'Connor and Bradley Sutton were both known to the police.'

'What? Bradley Sutton? He told me his surname was Edwards,' I said, my eyes widening and tears forming. 'That's what it said on his licence ... Oh, God. I know nothing of any of this.'

'You'll be required to come down to the station once you've been discharged,' the female police officer said.

I nodded.

Ben had done his job perfectly. Brad was dead—that two-timing bastard. The car accident with Ben and Louise was unfortunate. And yet, it was perfect as I now wouldn't have to pay Ben, my hitman, for taking out Brad. I allowed a self-satisfied smirk.

I carefully crafted my story for the coppers. I knew the questioning would come. There would be no confession. There was no need for a confession. With Ben dead, there was no way of tracing the gun from the escape room back to me.

HOW NOT TO HOST A MURDER PARTY

elizabeth spratt

You are cordially invited to Roley Winery
to take part in a Mystery Party.

Date: Thursday 19 May

Time: 7 pm

All six players sat at a polished mahogany table with an air of
apprehension.

A place card hosting a number perched in front of each guest.
Odd numbers assigned to the males and evens to the females. A
notepad and pen set out for each player.

'Since I'm number one, I'll start. I assume we all got the same text?' Morgan pushed his tortoise shell glasses back up his nose.

'No.' A computer-generated voice boomed from above.

Six heads jerked to the brown coffered ceiling.

Morgan squinted under the blaze of the fifteen globes of the crystal chandelier. 'Lyle? If that's you, then you sound even faker than usual?'

'Well done Morgan, but that was too obvious. No wonder your crime novels get rejected, the reader knows who the murderer is by the end of the first chapter.' The voice continued.

Morgan zipped his green puffer jacket up in a huff. 'We can't all self-publish and buy a chain of bookstores to promote our books.' He prodded the voice.

'Enough of this digression. Tonight, is a chance to have some fun. Daisy, this should excite you.'

Daisy flicked her red hair. 'If that's you Lyle, try and listen for once. I am not interested in becoming your third wife.'

Laughter burst from around the table.

'Daisy you are blushing.'

'I have nothing to blush about. But your current mistress should.'

'Excellent. Motives are starting to appear before the party officially starts.' The voice boomed. 'Welcome Ladies and Gentlemen to a murder mystery at Roley Winery. Each person is now a suspect in this murder mystery.'

'Murder? The text didn't mention that.' A petite lady leapt to her feet. 'It's too soon after Annabel's death.'

'Sit down Katie.' The voice grew louder. 'I'm devastated that none of us realised how troubled Annabel was, but she wouldn't want us to mope around. She'd want us to bond and enjoy ourselves. I need to point out that I can see all of you and, I know all your secrets.'

A gust of wind howled under the door. Katie tightened her lilac scarf, eyes downcast.

Morgan clapped, 'Wow it really is you, Lyle. 'You can steal our secrets for your next book.'

'I will ignore that unnecessary interruption. There is a pack of cards in the centre of the table. These are punishment cards for anyone who fails to follow the game instructions. I have locked the doors to the winery, no one leaves until you reveal the killer.'

Katie plonked into her seat and muttered, 'Some heating would be nice.'

'I will be the narrator' the voice said, 'and will now read the backstory.

Each person in the group picked up a pen and started to write down the clues relayed by the voice.

'Lyle Hanner is a popular local ...'

Morgan lurched forward in his chair, 'Boy you have tickets on yourself.'

'Enough, the next person to disrupt me must take a punishment card.' All eyes in the room turned to Morgan. 'Now where was I? Ah yes, Lyle forty-eight, and Mayor of the Orangegate region, was an Olympic swimmer, he is now a published author, and owner of the local bookstore. He is famous for his parties, and in this scenario he has invited the touch football team he coaches to a local winery for an evening of gourmet food and wine. The guests are enjoying themselves until one of you discovers Lyle, murdered in the cellar.'

Seat three muttered, 'If only this could become a reality.'

'Tsk tsk Pete. I heard that.' The overhead voice said. 'I'm guessing this will be a treat for you, to be in a debt free winery.'

'Bastard. Man up and come and say that to my face.'

'Temper. Temper. Remember those punishment cards. This is your first warning.'

Pete stared at the cards and leant back in his seat.

'Moving on. Grace, do me the honour of going to the side-counter and retrieve the six envelopes with your names, and distribute them. They are your character booklets.'

Grace in a figure hugging hot pink turtleneck sweater retrieved the envelopes and did what the voice had instructed.

'Now the first rule is that you must read the contents word for word. Start in numerical order.'

'CHARACTER ONE: Morgan Godwin, a forty-four-year-old local journalist, or rather ... I'm not reading this crap.' He slammed the paper on the table making Grace squeak.

'You never take instructions well.' The voice exclaimed. 'Take the first punishment card and read it out to the group.'

Morgan snatched the top card. 'For disobeying the voice, you will mow Lyle's, lawns weekly for three months.'

Seat five chuckled.

'Not happening. This is a game and I won't be mowing anything.'

Katie exhaled. 'Just keep reading the card Morgan.'

'Why should I? Why do we always bow to Lyle's demands?'

Katie threw her gloved hands up, 'In case you haven't noticed, we're locked in this room. The only way we get out of here is by solving this mystery.'

'Fine but next time I get a stupid invite like this on my mobile, I'm deleting it. Enough. Stop glaring at me, I'll continue with this rubbish.' Morgan screwed his nose. 'Or rather, this local gossip.' He started reading again. 'He self-published a crime fiction novel that bombed. Lyle and I competed for the final spot on the Olympic swim team years ago, I lost out. I am Daisy's cousin, and Pete's best mate.' Morgan frowned and his jaw clenched. 'Indeed, he is my only friend.'

'Next.' The voice demanded.

'CHARACTER TWO: Katie Doyle, a thirty-two-year-old country jockey who lacks the confidence to mix it with the best in Sydney.' She smacked the card down. 'That's not true.'

'Katie. Katie, Katie. I thought you would be more obedient. You always ride to instructions. Don't you? Select the next punishment card.'

Morgan sniggered and handed Katie a card.

'Don't shake your head, Katie. Unfold your arms, take the card and in a strong voice read your punishment.'

'Your punishment is to be Lyle's personal masseuse for the next month.'

'Ah Daisy, those green eyes of yours are looking decidedly jealous. I was hoping, that card would have been yours. 'The voice said. 'My, my Grace you look disappointed, you shouldn't have let Cameron see that look. Continue reading.'

Katie's nostrils flared. 'Gets along better with horses than she does humans. Went to school with Cameron, who continues to resist all her numerous advances.' She threw the card onto the table.

'Next.'

'CHARACTER THREE: Pete Burke at thirty-eight-years-old has inherited the family wine making business. Cocky and presumptuous that he will return the business to a profit. Wants to be the next local mayor.'

'Bankruptcy will destroy that ambition. Next.' Said the voice.

'CHARACTER FOUR: Daisy Channel, café owner. A bubbly personality, who believes her pastries are the best in town. Cousin to Morgan. At thirty-nine-years old, the biological clock is ticking and ...' her voice faltered.

'Keep going' the voice said, 'No, let me finish it. You are determined to be Lyle's third and final wife. Sorry to shatter your dreams, but children are not part of his plans. Next.'

'CHARACTER FIVE: Cameron Middleton at thirty-three is a hotel manager near the racecourse. Contrary to what Grace believes, he volunteers on a regular basis for the late-night shift. Loves a punt and inside information.'

'Perfect.' Said the voice.

'CHARACTER SIX: Grace Todd at thirty-five-years-old is a primary school teacher. Married to Cameron for seven years, she is desperate to have a baby. Wants everyone to think she has an impeccable marriage.'

'We do.' Cameron said.

'Hmmh. Interesting only, your voice was flat.'

Grace's eyes twitched towards the ceiling. 'I just want to say this is a horrible game. You shouldn't have used real people.'

'Take the next punishment card. Don't look so petrified my dear, you might even have some fun tending to Lyle's needs.'

'For disobeying the rules, you will wash Lyle's car for the next month.'

'A simple task. Ladies and gentlemen, round one has concluded.'

'Not much of a party. Where's the drinks and food?' Pete scowled picking at a loose thread on his jumper.

'Always thinking of wine aren't you. Time for that after the game. Round two will require honesty. That will be difficult for each one of you. Grace since you crave being useful you can keep being my assistant.' The voice instructed. 'Collect the box from the second drawer in the side-counter. These are the secret clues. Hurry up Grace. This will be exciting.

Grace started to stomp towards the counter, she froze and looked at the ceiling.

'My dear that's the most noise you have ever made. Usually, you are silent and compliant.'

Grace tossed the lid off the box and tipped the contents onto the table. A mixture of envelopes and boxes of varied sizes lay there.

'Careful my dear. Anyone would think you are trying to destroy the evidence. Normally in this game you would have a card and need to assign a piece of evidence to a suspect. But that would be boring. We want to be unique. Remember I said this would require honesty. You will pick the evidence that relates to you.'

A collection of gasps and groans erupted from the table.

'First is a final letter for a loan repayment before the bank seizes possession.'

'Mine.' Pete crossed his arms.

'Grace give Pete his evidence. Second is a blackmail letter. Remember honesty.'

Morgan rose from his seat and yanked the envelope close to his chest.

'Very good. The third contains three naked riding photos.'

'Hang on a second what's in the blackmail letter.'

'Good question Daisy, Morgan please explain.'

Morgan shrugged, 'Lyle stole all my ideas for his novel. I deserve the royalties.'

'Four people left. Which one of you will claim the photos?'

Katie lunged forward.

'Are you sure Katie, I didn't say that the person was riding a horse? Anyone else want to claim these. A couple of guilty looking faces here. I'm not sure that everyone is being honest.'

Morgan grabbed the packet from Katie and threw it across the table to Cameron. 'Open it.'

'Look if Katie claimed it then ...'

'Give it to me.' Grace removed the envelope from Cameron's fingertips and pulled out the photos.

'You cheating bastard.' Grace dropped the pictures and hammered her fists into Cameron's shoulders.

'It only happened once.' Cameron grasped Grace's hands.

'Once!' Grace leapt to her feet. 'We were planning a *family*. All those late-night shifts would be finishing when that whore would be going to early morning trackwork. How did I not see this?'

'I had to keep working those shifts, Lyle is my new boss. He bought the pub and threatened to tell you if I didn't work that shift.'

'In order to keep things moving, I will have to ask you both to save the domestic argument until later. Four is a positive pregnancy test.'

Grace turned to Cameron, 'I planned a romantic dinner for tomorrow night to tell you the happy news. You've destroyed our marriage. I want a divorce.'

A vein near Cameron's eye twitched. 'Is there anything here to drink?'

'Not until someone solves the murder. Then you can drink all you want.' The voice said.

Daisy cringed, 'Cameron, how can you be so flippant about this. Grace, I have a spare room.'

Cameron stood eye to eye with Grace and took a calm breath, 'Who's the father?'

Grace slapped his face. 'How dare you. I'm not the one sleeping around.'

'It would take a miracle for me to ever father a child. The doctor told me last month, I'm infertile.'

A cool breeze swept through the room. They turned towards the door that had swung open in silence.

'What are you all doing here?' Lyle said.

'Are you serious?' Morgan shoved his chair back and charged towards Lyle. 'You ...' He waved his arms about the room. '... organised all of this torment.'

Pete pushed his sleeves up.

Lyle raised his hands. 'I don't know what you're talking about. I received a text telling me to be at Roley's Winery at eight. When I got here, I received a six-digit code to open the door.'

'Liar.' Pete snorted.

Lyle backed away, holding his phone out. 'Here, check my mobile.'

'Lyle, please take my seat, position two between Morgan and Pete. 'Katie said. 'I can explain.'

All faces switched to Katie.

'I'm the one who set this whole thing up. James, Lyle's twin is next door controlling the computer voice.' She started to pace. 'Lyle is destroying all of us. I wanted to expose him for the low life he is. I predict, by the end of tonight Lyle will be gone from our lives for good. How that happens will be down to you Lyle. But you will leave here tonight. If you refuse, every single person here has a motive to kill you, and we will, have no doubt about that.'

Lyle squirmed in his seat and taunted, 'You wouldn't dare.'

'That's where you are wrong.' Katie moved to stand behind Morgan. 'Let me start with Morgan who has more than one motive. We all know that Lyle stole his ideas ...'

Lyle sniggered, 'What a load of rot. I crafted the novel, so what if some of my plot came from one or two of his supposed ideas that he burbles to anyone who'll listen.'

Morgan swung towards Lyle. 'The problem is Lyle you rub your victories in everyone's face and belittle them for their own lack of success. Nastiness pours through your veins.'

Katie interjected, 'Lyle was responsible for Morgan missing Olympic selection. That gold medal should have been his.'

Lyle clapped, 'That's a great motive. Are you trying to write your own mystery novel?'

Morgan raised his fist. 'Listen scum, Coach Jones confessed this to me last year on his death bed. I'll never forgive you. Katie, I hope you don't mind but I will help you out with some motives here. What if Lyle is the father of Grace's baby and refused to divorce his current wife?'

Cameron twisted to Grace, 'Of all people to have an affair with you chose that piece of filth?'

Grace cupped her face in her hands, 'Please Cameron try and understand, the school faced closure unless we met the safety requirements. Lyle was our silent investor and saviour. Except, he always wants a reward. He demanded sex, and well you both have blonde hair, blue eyes, and a similar nose. We were trying so hard to have a baby and it just wasn't happening. I thought Lyle was my only solution.'

Katie shifted to stand behind Pete.

'You Lyle are behind all the rumours about the quality of Pete's wines. His business started to decline, and you preyed on his weakness. You encouraged him to punt on the horses. Pete thought if he could win, he could keep the business afloat, shame all your tips lost.'

Lyle placed a hand on his heart, 'My dear, Pete has you to thank for failing to win on those horses. You were riding them.'

Katie shrugged, 'Sorry Pete, I was under instructions.'

'For which you were well rewarded.' Lyle sneered.

Katie tossed her head back. 'Rewarded, is that what you call it. You threatened to show those photos to Grace and report me to the stewards. Anyone else would call it blackmail.'

'Sorry Katie but there are two pieces of evidence that haven't been revealed.'

Katie glanced at the table. 'Thanks Grace. The next one is a recipe book.'

Daisy stretched her hand out, 'Obviously me.'

Katie shuddered, 'No Daisy, this particular recipe book from the garden, belonged to Annabel.'

Daisy withdrew her hand. 'Annabel? But I'm the chef.'

'Lyle asked me to pack up Annabel's sparse possessions so he could rent the house out.'

'A poor red herring, Katie, unless her ghost is coming back to murder me.' Lyle glanced at his watch. 'Is this going to take long?'

Katie opened the book, 'There are some interesting ingredients in here, and what native fruits to avoid eating.'

'Intriguing,' Lyle stood up and yawned. 'But I skipped volunteering at the homeless shelter for this.'

'Sit down Lyle. For once I agree with you. It is intriguing.' Katie started to pace, 'The police suspect that Annabel was poisoned.'

Cameron rubbed his forehead, 'Katie where are you going with this? I don't mean to sound unkind, but none of us were close with Annabel, she'd only been here three months.'

Katie nodded, 'Yes a short time but long enough for her to pose a threat, a massive threat.' She stopped opposite Lyle and pointed a finger, 'To you.'

Lyle pursed his lips. 'You are reading too much into this open verdict of her death.'

'Her real name was Abby Frank and you raped her when she was fourteen.'

Lyle jumped to his feet. 'You lying bitch.'

Katie placed her hands on the table, 'That last envelope contains Annabel's story. You know most of it, except that she searched for over thirty years for the baby she was forced to give up for adoption. That's why she returned home, to where it all happened. And you killed her.'

'I'm leaving. But rest assured. You'll be hearing from my lawyer. I'll sue you for slander.'

'Lyle, I can prove you poisoned her. There is a handwritten note on page thirty of Annabel's receipt book. I found it hidden under a loose floorboard under her bed.' Kate flicked to the page. 'Next to the picture of the strychnine tree. Annabel has written, these are the berries that Lyle has given me to eat. They are not kumquats like he insisted.'

'To be fair, Katie, she would have had to eat a lot to be poisoned.'

'Don't defend him Daisy.' Katie straightened up. 'There was also a notepad next to her mobile. Someone had ripped a page out. Lyle you should have looked closer at the next page. There was a faint imprint, where Annabel had listed out her symptoms.'

Lyle pounded his fist on the tabletop. 'There was also an empty bottle of painkillers found next to Annabel.'

'Not enough in her system to kill her.' Katie retorted. 'Lyle, it's decision time. Are you confessing to the police tonight, or do we have to dispose of you?'

Lyle shook his head. 'Not so quick Katie. Why did you go to such elaborate lengths? You're not ashamed about your affair with Cameron. Sorry Grace it wasn't a one off. So, why do you care about the death of a stranger, Katie?

'Because I never want to see your face again, Dad.'

GAMER GRANDMA

kellie m cox

hat's this?'

'It's a tablet Grandma,' Lisa replies.

'It looks complicated.'

'They run classes in Lisa's store to teach you how to use it.' Catherine smiles.

'You both know I can't do that. I can't go out to town.'

Catherine pushes a small button on the side of the device to turn it on. The screen lights up and is filled with lots of coloured squares. I have no idea how to make heads or tails of any of it.

'We've loaded it up with lots of games for you.'

'Loaded up with games?'

'Yes Grandma, there's even some for brain training.' Lisa points to icons on the screen.

Catherine slaps her sister on the arm. Good on her for standing up for me.

My brain doesn't need training. It's old, that's all.

'Grandma, there are fun role-playing games. You get to choose your character and even chat to other people playing the same game.'

'Why would I want to talk to strangers on a tablet?'

The girls look at each other. I can tell from their silent expressions they are encouraging the other to speak. Lisa appears to be the bravest today. Her face is drawn, the small lines on her brow deepen. I'm not going to like this.

'Grandma, it's just since Grandpa died, you haven't really left the house.'

Catherine joins in. 'You haven't been to see any of your friends.'

'You girls are just too young to understand. It is difficult when you lose your husband. Married for sixty years, you forget how to do things without the other. It takes time to adjust.'

'Grandma, it has been a year already.'

'A year is not a long time when you are my age.' I fight back the tears.

I place the tablet on the coffee table. A well-intended gift, but of little use to an old lady. I prefer my books and knitting to the new machines my granddaughters enjoy.

Today appears to be a well-planned intervention. I watch Lisa pick up the tablet and begin her first lesson.

The words confuse my foggy brain as Lisa explains the meaning behind their generation's new terminologies. I am grateful for the care and attention my favourite granddaughters shower on me, but wish they would understand that my life is different now. I'm at the end of my life not the beginning like them and much too old to be learning new things like games.

The visit complete, I take to my room for a well-earned sleep. Before I do, I remember to put my tablet on charge just as the girls instruct me. I do wonder if I might be able to talk them into getting their money back by taking the machine in for a refund.

The following morning, the tablet taunts me as it lays on the dresser. I don't want to disappoint. On their next visit the girls will want to see how I used their machine. I will try it just a little before the girls return it. I remember to press the little button. The coloured squares all look the same. I touch one with an aeroplane. A picture of a woman appears. Lisa taught me the word. *What was it?* Something new and fandangle. It starts with an A. *Come on old brain, work.* Avatar, that's it. I must make my own avatar.

I want to be young like when I met my darling Harold. Blonde, like Marilyn Monroe. I want to wear something pretty, bright, and cheery, just as I used to when Harold would swing me around the dance floor. I can even choose makeup. I remember taking hours getting ready for a date, making up my face with hues of mauve and red. She looks like an air hostess. No, that's not the right word. They don't call them that anymore. What is it? Flight attendant? Now it is asking me to choose a country to visit. Oh, so many to choose. Fancy that, at my age, unable to move from inside of these four walls, a little cartoon is going to do the travelling I never got to enjoy.

I click on the picture with the Eiffel Tower. Yes, Paris will do nicely. The avatar disappears, and a plane makes its way across the spinning globe to France. I sit upright, shuffling on my comfortable lounge to get a better view of the screen. Feeling somewhat chuffed, I get ready to land at Charles de Gaulle Airport. The girls will be pleased I made the tablet work. *'Bonjour.'* I practice my basic French and chuckle to myself. Imagine me in Paris, eating crepes and shopping on the Champs-Élysées.

The phone rings and for the first time in several hours I force my attention away from the little screen.

'Hello Grandma. I just wanted to check on you. Are you using the tablet?'

'Oh, Lisa, I made it work and I have been to Paris, Rome, Athens, London. I even went to Buckingham Palace. Can you believe that. Me at Buckingham Palace. I never thought I would ever get to visit. Well, not me of course, my dear, my little cartoon, she visited for me.'

'Your avatar, Grandma.'

'Yes dear, that's it.'

'Have you tried any of the games where you talk to other players? It would be good for you to talk to other people Grandma.'

'I am talking to my favourite person right now my dear. What more could I want?'

Lisa takes on the compliment. A dear child. So sweet and giving of her time to her old Grandma.

'Okay, sounds like you're having fun. Try another game Grandma. There are plenty of them and when I come over again, I'll add some more for you. Unless of course, you want to come into the store and join a lesson?'

If only my Harold was still with me, I could visit the store for a lesson. It's just not so easy these days to do such things alone.

Suddenly hungry I head to the kitchen for a little snack. Gone are the days of cooking for two. What a waste it would be to start up the stove and cook for just one. Baking for my family used to be fun. A lot of things used to be enjoyable once upon a time. As I fill the kettle and search for some sweet biscuits to fill me up, I wonder what the little coloured square does, the thing Lisa was saying lets you talk to other people. Balancing my hot brew and packet of shortbreads, I settle back into my lounge and pick up my birthday gift. It will be sad to say goodbye to my little flying avatar, but curiosity now has me interested to learn about the other games on the tablet.

The next little square asks me to choose a character. I can't seem to find the lovely avatar from before. The choices look a little like elves, but stronger and larger than any elf I've ever seen in a Christmas movie. One stares defiantly with the grace of a young Meryl Streep. Yes, this character will do just fine.

A tiny red rectangle flashes in the corner and I am reminded to put the tablet back into the power point. My fingers ache from the repetitive action of touching the hard screen. My eyes are dry and a little tired from overuse.

The phone stirs me and the darkness outside alludes to nightfall. I stretch over and take the phone from its cradle.

'Hello Grandma. How are you today?'

'Oh, just lovely Catherine.

'How is the tablet going? Lisa said you were enjoying it.'

'Today, I became an elf, I think. My person used a sword and fought creatures. So very brave she was. I used my favourite actress as inspiration.'

'You do know Grandma that you are your avatar. You are what makes her brave. And the flight attendant, you are her exploring those cities. Your passion for adventure is what drives the avatar to travel.'

'My adventurous days are long behind me. I'm an old lady now, but I do appreciate your kind words.'

'Not just words Grandma. You have a full life ahead of you.'

'I need to go now my dear. Thank you for the call.'

The girls just don't understand what it means to be suddenly all alone in the world. Without my Harold everything is more difficult. Not driving for so long makes me nervous to get behind the wheel. Harold did all the driving. Staying indoors has become familiar, comfortable. It's different for them. They have grown up independent, going to university, learning to do things for themselves. It just isn't like that for a woman of my age. Women in my day didn't do such things. We got married, had our families, and stayed home to care for them. Lisa and Catherine and their friends have the right idea by enjoying their own study and hobbies.

A new day means a new coloured square to choose. I pick the one with the clothes hanger on it. My new avatar appears and once more I get to choose her hair and skin colour as well as hairstyle. This appears to be a fashion game. Finding clothes to suit a certain location and event. I imagine I am young again and dressing for date night with Harold. I choose a pale pink lipstick and a mid-length red dress. It's unlike me to choose such a bold colour at my age. Maybe the girls are right, maybe I am braver than I think, even if it is just in the make-believe world. Maybe I can be as colourful and adventurous as my avatar.

A sudden burst of inspiration washes over me and before I have time to lose my courage, I pick up the phone and dial Lisa's.

'Grandma is everything okay?' she answers with a panicked tone.

'Fine my dear. Are you at work today in that fancy store?'

'Yes Grandma, so I can't talk long. What's up?'

'Can you book me into one of those lessons?'

'Oh Grandma, yes of course I can. Do you need a lift? I can see if Catherine is free or order you a ride.'

'No dear, I will be fine. If my little avatar can fly around the world, I surely must be able to catch a bus.'

'Oh Grandma, I am so proud of you. You've got this. See you soon.'

'See you soon,' I reply.

I put down the phone and head to the dresser mirror. Finding my pale pink lipstick, unused since the day of Harold's funeral, I apply just a little, put a few things into a handbag and head for the door. It is a brave new world and I have to get back into it. I stand at the bus stop and squeeze my handbag containing the tablet. If my avatar can do it, so can I. Who knows I might even stop at the travel agent, pick up a brochure for Paris. Harold would be so proud of me but more importantly, I am proud of me.

CONTRIBUTORS

CHRIS RADGE, is an Australian novelist based in Brisbane, Queensland where she writes full time and is a part-time stay-at-home NanMa.

Her published works include Anthologies: **'Smithy'** in *Short Stories of Mystery and Murder*, **'Tinsel Fructify'** in *Short Stories of Forests and Fantasy*, **'Ghost Writer'** in *Short Stories of Ghosts and Graves*, **'Frankenstein's Legacy'** in *Short Stories of Science and Space*, **'Rounder'** in *Meanwhile Murder*, and **'Feathered Hooves'** in *From the Edge*, WAG.

She is currently engaged in writing an Octology of YA Urban Fantasy books called *The Elder Scale Series*, and two children's picture books *Sneezes* and *Yarn* to be published in 2023.

She is a member of Queensland Writers Centre, BWG, Booklinks, Australian Fairy Tale Society, and looks forward to the Rainforest Writing Retreat every year.

Chris is co-host of RWR and the editor/organiser/typesetter of this anthology, and always enjoys the journey from beginning to end.

You can find Chris at

www.chrisradge.com

Amazon

CHARMAINE CLANCY is an Australian author and educator.

Her novels for kids and teens include the best-selling **My Zombie Dog**. Charmaine also writes short stories for grown-ups and is published in various anthologies. She's even won awards for some of her stories.

Charmaine is very passionate about helping students who have struggled with literacy and inspires them to create their own stories they can be proud of. As well as teaching at high school, Charmaine presents holiday writing workshops for children of all ages and hosts the annual Rainforest Writing Retreat for grown-up writers.

All her books are written with humour and dogs. Life is better with both.

You can find Charmaine at

charmaineclancy.com
Instagram.com/hotdoggypress/

GINA PINTO is an editor, researcher, and the author of the nonfiction book *Partly Portuguese, Almost Australian* (2006). Since completing the Master of Writing, her short fiction has been published in various Australian anthologies. In 2022, she won the RWR Anthology Editor's Choice Award for her mystery story *Crossings*. She is currently working on a collection of literary short stories.

You can find Gina at

ginapinto.com
partlyportugueseproductions.com

PAMELA JEFFS is a speculative fiction author from Brisbane, Queensland. She has published five short story collections and has 80+ short stories featured in various national and international magazines and anthologies. She has been shortlisted for multiple awards throughout her career including numerous Aurealis and Ditmar Awards and has also been twice noted in the Writers of the Future Competition.

You can find Pamela at

www.pamelajeffs.com

MATILDA CLANCY enjoys stories that explore the quirks of humanity and the dark twists we take. She studies forensics, the perfect cover for researching murder methods, and enjoys the cringy true-crime shows from the eighties. She  also has a weakness for excruciatingly bad movies and, although a true introvert, will happily discuss *Leprechaun 4: In Space*.

Matilda assists with editing RWR anthology stories and is thought to be brutal but honest by her ~~victims~~ clients.

You can find Matilda at

iTeenGeek.com

www.etsy.com/au/shop/MultiverseMayor

LEA SCOTT has published three psychological thrillers, *The Ned Kelly Game* (2009), *Eclipsed* (2010) and *One for All* (2013). She acts as Chair of the Queensland Writers Centre and mentors new writers under their 'Writer's Surgery' program.

She has facilitated writing workshops and seminars and has appeared at writing festivals throughout Australia and overseas. She has acted as associate editor for a Special Issue of *TEXT Journal of Writing*. Lea holds a PhD in Creative Writing and has also published academic research on writing about trauma and the transformative potential of creative writing.

You can find Lea at

www.leascott.com

CHRISTINE BETTS is an award-winning writer, living and working in Bundjalung country (Northern Rivers of New South Wales). She is the Newsletter Editor for the Gold Coast Writers'  Association and co-facilitates the popular Write & Sip fundraising events.

In 2021, her short story, 'Death of a Show Princess', was Shortlisted for the Scarlet Stiletto Awards. Her story, 'Tough Crowd', won the November Right Left Write competition through the Queensland Writers Centre. In April 2022, Christine won The Tasmanian Writers' Prize for her short story, 'How I Got this Tattoo'.

Christine writes a blog, WriterPainter, where she rambles on about Life and Art.

You can find Christine at

www.writerpainter.com

KATE KELSEN has received recognition from literary awards around Australia, including:

- 'Kindred Counsel': Shortlisted for the 2022 SD Harvey Short Crime Story Award
- 'Ten of Swords': Winner of the 2022 GenreCon Short Story Competition
- 'Undetected', co-authored with Christine Betts. Rainforest Writers Retreat Anthology 2021
- Grieve Writing Competition 2014 & 2015, Readers Digest 100 Word Short Story Competition (2015)

At twenty-one, Kate published her debut novel, *The Wilted Rose,* a novel inspired by the true story of a Brisbane family's experience with mental illness in the 1960s.

In 2016, Kate published *The New Neighbors,* and *Paid to Dance: Stripping Past and Present.*

In her writing, Kate takes a particular interest in exploring various human experiences and perspectives. She predominantly writes crime and psychological suspense, often with a sprinkling of the supernatural. Kate lives on the Gold Coast, Queensland.

You can find Kate at

www.katekelsen.com

LR JOHNSON grew up in a rural Queensland town surrounded by heritage and dust. Always with a mind for storytelling, she discovered novels and writing in early adolescence.

Fantastical worlds and far off places penned by the likes of Tolkien, C.S. Lewis and Lovecraft have sculpted her imagination. She enjoys exploring the human condition of the individual, with themes of psychological growth.

She has a Diploma of Visual Arts majoring in Digital Illustration, and Jewellery Making. She also did a year of Graphic Design, but business logos are not her style of storytelling. She is also a painter, and pottery sculptor.

You can find Lucy at

deviantart.com/lrjproductions

SELENA JANE writes in several genres, including teen fiction, fantasy, and women's fiction.

Born in Loughborough, England. Her childhood memories and love of animals colour her books, as does her passion for travelling.

In 2020, she published her debut YA fantasy fiction novel **Search for the Holy Whale**, a coming-of-age story about the importance of our connection to animals and mother earth.

She is the website manager for the Gold Coast Writers' Associations and is a copywriter by day and novelist by night.

Selena is also a mother, business owner, world traveller, animal lover, marathon runner and avid reader.

She appreciates a well-written book, with great characters and a good storyline.

Selena is enjoying the journey from writer to author and is currently working on *Whatever! This is the 90s, Two Wrongs and Luna's Gift.*

You can find Selena at

www.selenajane.com

FRANK PREM has been a storytelling poet for over forty years. He has been published in magazines, e-zines and anthologies, in Australia and in a number of other countries, and has both performed and recorded his work as 'spoken word'.

Frank has now published sixteen collections of free verse poetry, including memoir, true life stories, what he describes as 'picture poetry' and books suitable for young children.

He and his wife live in the beautiful township of Beechworth in northeast Victoria (Australia).

Frank's published collections include *Small Town Kid, The New Asylum,* and *Devil In The Wind.*

His 2022 publications include *A Specialist at The Recycled Heart, Ida: Searching for The Jazz Baby.*

You can find Frank at

FrankPrem.com

YouTube

Amazon

SARAH HEGERTY is a speculative fiction writer, wife, mum, gamer, and adventure seeker who just wants some sleep. Living in sunny Queensland, Australia, she spends her time fantasising about snow-covered mountains in cooler climates.

Her published works include Anthologies, **'Playing the System'** in *Seven Deadly Sins: Avarice*, **'Living Next Door to Amy'** in *Seven Deadly Sins: Lust*, **'The Six'** in *Short Stories of Forest and Fantasy*, **'Ghost Trap'** in *Short Stories of Ghosts and Graves*, and **'Carpe Diem'** in *Short Stories of Science and Space*.

Although she spends a lot of time writing short stories, she does hope to have longer works published one day.

You can find Sarah at

www.sarahhegerty.com

SARAH TEGERDINE is a writer, reviewer, and author for both children and adults. Originally from the UK she lives in Queensland, Australia with her husband and two daughters. She is a member of the Queensland Writers Centre and SCBWI, The Society of Children's Book Writers and Illustrators. So far, her work has been published in various nation-wide anthologies.

She is an avid reader and is passionate about story, a keeper of journals and a dedicated pop culture nerd. When she is not wrangling her young family, she can nearly always be found busily creating stories that inspire and delight.

You can find Sarah at

Facebook/SarahTegerdineAuthor

SAM GALE A misfit in a world that desires recognisable tags, Sam Gale is a puzzle of the first order. A daughter, a wife, a mother, a mentor, a writer, an adventurer, and a business leader, it is no surprise to learn that curiosity is her drug of choice. Inspired by the stories of explorers throughout time, Sam makes careful study of moments in her own life—to see and heed the splendour enmeshed within life's trials.

She has cycled, travelled, and tramped the world since her earliest years. Her writing speaks from landscapes with which she has a deep connection, her observations of the human experience, and our ubiquitous cry for reason.

You can find Sam at

samantha@symplexity.net

DEBBIE KAHL has dreamt of writing fiction since she was a teenager obsessed with the *Sweet Dreams* books that cluttered her bookshelf. Despite an ongoing battle with author imposter syndrome, Debbie has continued to write contemporary

fiction for tweens, teens and adults winning the inaugural Book Links QLD Mentorship and the CYA Conference Unpublished Chapter Book for middle grade readers, along the way.

When she's not writing, you can find Debbie teaching English and Japanese at a high school in Brisbane, where she finds lots of inspirations for her stories. Debbie is also an integral part of the CYA Conference team, which aims to provide professional development opportunities for young adult and children's writers in Australia.

You can find Debbie at

debbiekahl.wordpress.com

LinkedIn

JC LESLEY in between procrastinating over the second draft of her novel about a blind investigator and her police / guide dog Spike, and sitting on health committees as consumer rep, JC Lesley competes nationally in blind archery.

Before she went blind she had an international operatic career with the Australian and Frankfurt Operas. She is a regular conference presenter, had more than one hundred of her arts, disability and health articles published, and won awards and had short stories published in anthologies including, '**Oh nuts**!' in *Short and Twisted* (2016), and '**Ice Queen**' in *Meanwhile Murder* (2022).

JC Lesley runs her own entertainment and production agency, has been the producer of the Brisbane Lord Mayor's City Hall Concerts for over 15 years, has recorded three solo CDs, and before covid, loved to travel overseas at least once a year to perform.

You can find JC Lesley at

(20+) JC Lesley Author | Facebook
Salubrious Productions Artists with ability

DANIELLE HUGHES is a busy mum of four young kids, living in the south east suburbs of Melbourne and loves writing whenever she can. A lover of fantasy, her published books include *The Lost Unicorn*, *The Mystica Trilogy*, and several short stories in various anthologies. She is currently working on an exciting new fantasy series to be published in 2023.

You can find Danielle at

https://linktr.ee/fourmoonspublishing
Danielle.writes17@gmail.com

ROBIN MARTIN THOMAS is an author and teacher, who writes both adult and young adult romance. Originally from Canada, she now lives in Brisbane, Australia.

Her YA sci-fi romance series, *The Alien Chronicles* includes *My Alien*, *The Alien Within*, and *Once an Alien*.

Her adult books in the Short Sweetz series include High Stakes and Bonjour Cherie.

Her recent release is Finding Gilbert, A YA paranormal/ghost novel.

She is a member of Write-Links, for children's and YA writers, she has also attended many RWR workshops over the years. Robin also connects with writers and readers on her author's Facebook page.

You can find Robin at

facebook.com/robinmartinthomas

www.robinmartinthomas.com

ROBIN ADOLPHS is a published author of fourteen children's picture books and director of Butternut Books. In 2019, Robin published her first middle grade fiction, *Princes of Aranmore*. A highlight for Robin was her inclusion in the Australian Publishers Association contingent at the Frankfurt Book Fair in 2019.

Robin's love of picture books comes from her background in Early Childhood Education and she has taught in Victoria, Queensland, and Germany. She is delighted that her short story 'Not Without a Fight' is included in the 2020 RWR Sci-fi anthology.

You can find Robin at

www.robinadolphs.com
www.facebook.com/AuthorRobinAdolphs

MICHAELA SANDERSON has been writing YA fiction for most of her life. She works closely with young adults and is blessed to be able to take inspiration from their antics. She mentors a student writing group, who have just released their first anthology.

Michaela writes short stories and has experienced success in several writing competitions. She is an avid fantasy writer but will venture into other genres with confidence.

She loves a challenge and has 'won' NaNoWriMo for eight consecutive years, producing a new story each year. She is a member of several writing groups, and enjoys the different perspectives other people bring to her writing. Michaela has completed several online writing courses, and regularly attends the Rainforest Writing Retreat, where she is motivated and encouraged to keep on writing.

You can find Michaela at

www.facebook.com/michaela.sanderson.90
theyellowbird@hotmail.com

DR ALETIA JOHNSON is a GP, writer and martial artist. She writes comedic, trope-smashing speculative fiction and horror. She has also written non-fiction editorial content for ABC News Online.

She enjoys ranting on social media at 2am, trying to convince anyone who will listen that it is actually possible for a tiny, unarmed woman to beat up a big, scary gym-bro. She hasn't convinced anyone yet, but she has attracted a few internet trolls. She doesn't mind. They taste like chicken.

Aletia is a member of the QLD Writers Centre and Springfield Writers Group. She attended her first Rainforest Writers Retreat in 2022 and now they can't get rid of her. In 2021, her short story, 'Catfight', was published in *Tribute*, edited by J.A. Henderson. She is currently working on her first novel, *Cassiopeia: Monsters in the Darkness*. It is her first attempt at being a serious person. It might even be literature.

You can find Aletia at

www.aletiajohnson.com

Email her (or argue with her) at
aletiajohnsonthewriter@gmail.com

ROBERT WALMSLEY-EVANS' greatest passion is fantasy and science fiction writing. He is also a photographic artist. Robert has been published in The Rainforest Writing Retreat Anthologies: *Short Stories of Forest and Fantasy,* and *Short Stories of Science and Space.* He is excited to be included in the *Got Game* anthology this year.

Robert draws upon his British heritage, ancient history and philosophy to inspire his writing. He belongs to a book-club, which gives many opportunities to read and discuss books. His world travels through the Mediterranean, the Netherlands, the U.K, France and the U.S.A have had a significant impact on his literary practice.

Robert has been honing his craft at the Rainforest Writing Retreat for the past nine years. He has gained invaluable learnings and support from this vibrant community.

The *Warriors of Lleuad* is his first novel-length publication and was published in May 2022.

You can find Robert at

mysticstonebooks@gmail.com
fb robertwalmsleyevansauthor
Amazon

EMMA RENNISON is a British-Australian author and mother of two children diagnosed with multiple epiphyseal dysplasia and scoliosis. She has one bionic hip and writes about her family's experiences of disability, as well as works of fiction.

Her first published story, 'No Guts, No Glory', won the 2020 Editor's Choice Award in the RWR anthology, *Short Stories of Science and Space*. She was runner-up in The Jennifer Burbidge Prize 2021 and shortlisted for the Newcastle Short Story Award 2021. In 2022, she had a memoir piece published on SBS Voices as part of their Emerging Writers' Competition, and was shortlisted for the City of Melbourne Lord Mayor's Creative Writing Awards. She was also granted a Writers Victoria Writeability Fellowship to support the writing of her first novel.

You can find Emma at

www.emmarennison.com

JENNY WOOLSEY, M.Ed. (Hons), is an author, ceramic artist, speaker and teacher, on the theme Be Weirdly Wonderful! Embrace your disability and differences. She was born with a rare craniofacial syndrome, lives with low vision and uses a long cane. Jenny lives north of Brisbane, with her three children, three crazy cats and adorable dog.

Disability, difference and mental well-being are the focus of Jenny's Middle Grade and Young Adult novels and all-age short stories. Jenny's school visits and speaking engagements bring particular awareness to disabilities, facial differences, bullying and good mental health practices, and she encourages kindness towards others.

You can find Jenny at

www.jennywoolsey.com

Amazon

ELIZABETH SPRATT was born in Sydney and has lived there her entire life. From Monday to Friday she is a professional accountant, longing to find extra hours in the day to devote to her passion for creative writing. From a young age, Elizabeth  was always penning different stories. Over the past few years she decided to take the plunge and write her first novel. She is currently re-editing a second draft of a spy thriller.

Elizabeth loves mystery and crime thrillers. She loves to travel to all parts of the world. With limited travel options over the past year she decided to combine travel and writing together and attended the 2021 Rainforest Writers Retreat. She is thrilled to be part of the RWR anthology.

KELLIE M COX has worked in psychology for decades giving her an insight and fascination for human behaviour that she draws on to create complex characters.

Her novels published with strong female protagonists include, *Murderous Intent, The List, The Reef, Advice for Life,* and *The Last First Kiss.*

Kellie's stories traverse the globe, taking readers to cities they dream to visit from Paris, Rome, Berlin, Bora Bora, and the Mekong Delta. Her own travel stories forming much of the inspiration for the settings and colourful characters readers fall in love with.

Drawing on themes of life, love and death, Kellie writes in the genres of magic realism, romance, and suspense to create stories that stay with you long after you put them down.

When not writing or seeing clients in private practice, Kellie can be found on the beaches of the Gold Coast flooding her social media with photos of her gorgeous dogs.

You can find Kellie at

www.kelliemcox.com

REVIEWS

Your words are as important to an author as an author's words are to you.

goodreads.com

Please leave a review

amazon.com.au

Feed an author, leave a review. It takes five minutes and helps more than you can imagine.

ACKNOWLEDGEMENTS

RWR would like to thank Chris Radge (Christine Titheradge), Charmaine Clancy, Gina Pinto (Frisken), Anthony Puttee, Noel Morado, and Victor Marcos for their hard work in assembling this anthology.

Likewise, thanks are also due to the RWR retreaters/authors, without their work there wouldn't be a book. A big thanks to all the crew at the Self-Publishing Lab for everything you do. You can contact them at selfpublishinglab.com for a website setup and publishing needs.

And the biggest thanks to Charmaine who thought that a writing retreat would be a great idea and has run with it ever since.

'This was a group of writers from across the country, who came together to share ideas and be introduced to new possibilities, and the concepts they developed were wonderful!

Happy reading, and may the dice be ever in your favour.'

—Shaun Sunday, Brainbeast Studios –
Comic writer, illustrator & game designer

SELF-PUBLISHING AND MARKETING YOUR BOOK JUST GOT SIMPLER

Self-publishing Lab
Formerly BookCover

selfpublishinglab.com

 Online **Classroom**

The Lab is packed with in-depth, step-by-step practical video lessons, tools and resources on preparing, producing, publishing and promoting your book. PLUS the 24/7 community and coaching you need to ensure you achieve your full potential and goals.

 Book **Creation**

Let us take care of these one-off tasks, so you can avoid any headaches. Our team is ready when you are. The Lab is an award-winning one-stop shop for creating and publishing a quality book with a team of professionals who care. Oh, and you'll have fun doing it too!

 Book **Marketing & Coaching**

From Amazon Ads, building email lists to selling at tradeshows, the Lab has you covered. With courses, templates and our online community, all your questions can be answered with the support of the Lab team and other like-minded authors achieving their goals, just like you.

About the Self-publishing Lab

The Lab is an award-winning publishing destination helping thousands of writers avoid the traps in publishing and get started on the right foot.

With over 25 years in the publishing industry, Anthony and the team at the Self-publishing Lab continue to help authors become bestsellers, sell thousands of dollars worth of books online, at schools, workshops and to organisations.

Here's what makes the Self-publishing Lab different

 No contracts or exclusive agreements that sell your soul. You'll keep 100% royalties and control without it costing you an arm and a leg to publish your book.

 We show you how to use technology to sell more books while you sleep, even if you're a tech newbie.

 Have your book distributed and available for purchase online around the world, at bookstores and libraries in print and e-book.

Contact Us Today

 w: selfpublishinglab.com
e: support@selfpublishinglab.com

 PO BOX 187
Browns Plains, QLD
Australia, 4118

WANT TO WRITE A NOVEL?
DON'T KNOW WHERE TO START?